ANGEL OF THE SAWTOOTHS

"Meant to be a Cowboy"

Riding up the ridge line
Keeping an eye out for strays
My Appaloosa feels like running
I'm in the saddle for the day

LYRICS BY D. NAGEL

The ANGEL of the SAWTOOTHS

A RIDERS CLUB ADVENTURE

DENNIS NAGEL

Ridgetop
Books

For
Kimberly, Mike, and Sara

CHAPTER ONE

B rett Wyatt scanned the horizon, looking for the flight from San Francisco. He waited alongside his friend and neighbor, Tom Coogan, in the outdoor reception area at the new Valley Airport, which serviced Hailey, Ketchum, Sun Valley, and the greater Wood River Valley. The airport bristled with activity as one flight after another arrived. Private jets were common at the airport, but their volume had multiplied over the last few days. Rows of Gulf Streams waited like rental cars waiting for a new driver. The rich and famous gathered, and their jets overflowed from the private terminal into the public terminal.

Over the next week, the annual Cottonwood Financial Conference will take over the Sun Valley Resort. It draws well-known corporate executives, hedge fund managers, movie producers, sports figures, media stars, and more. The Cottonwood Conference is about wealth, how to preserve it, and how to grow it. Hopefully, since the attendees were visiting one of the most beautiful areas in Idaho, they would set aside enough time to see the sights and have some fun.

Cloudless blue skies and intense sunlight created a Sun Valley moment for the airport's passengers and visitors. The crisp morning environment welcomed them to Idaho's high country.

A United Airlines jet touched down and rolled toward a nearby gate. Tom shook his head and said, "Damn, that one is from Denver. I thought that was it for sure."

Brett looked down and rested his hand on his friend's shoulder. "Her flight isn't due for fifteen minutes."

Tom threw his hands up. "She is flying from California— there's usually a tailwind."

Tom was an optimistic guy with a big smile, but he impatiently tapped his foot this morning. He hadn't seen his daughter in a long time. Brett's gaze left his closest friend, and he watched the passengers exit the Denver flight.

A tall, handsome man with sandy blond hair stepped off the Denver flight and walked toward the reception area. He wore a light tan sport coat, dark slacks, a soft blue crew neck shirt, mid-tan loafers, and no socks. Several of his fellow passengers eagerly shook his hand. He wrapped his arms around a young couple's shoulders and posed for a group photo.

Tom elbowed Brett and pointed. "That's Kelly Hawk, isn't it?"

Brett scrutinized the disembarking group. "Yeah, it sure is."

"I think he is the greatest quarterback in NFL history."

"Could be. He's at least in the conversation."

With his carry-on slung over his shoulder, Kelly Hawk marched through the exit, glanced toward Tom and Brett, grinned, turned, and quickly walked toward them.

"Why is he coming over here?" Tom asked, a little star-struck.

Before Brett could answer, Kelly yelled, "Hey, Brett!"

As the men came together, they shook hands and embraced in a man hug.

Tom stared at the pair, then tossed his hands up. "Of course, you guys played together in Denver. You're teammates."

Kelly was Brett's teammate a long time ago. Since their football careers ended, their lives diverged into two unique tracks. Kelly Hawk, a high-profile quarterback, turned his talent, intelligence, and history into a marketable brand and built an impressive business empire. Brett entered public service to make a difference. Most of Brett's coaches, teammates, and fans believed he retired a few years too early.

Brett was statuesque—an easy six-five, two-forty. As the years passed, he lost most of his athletic edge, but even in middle age, he offered a powerful presence. He worked out regularly to take care of his mind and body. His muscle tone had reduced with age and fewer gym sessions, but he was still strong enough to rip a door out of a wall. His cropped dark hair contrasted with his bright eyes, and his multicultural ethnicity meant his skin tone was flawless. As imposing as his physical presence was, it didn't define him. Instead, his calm demeanor and innate listening ability gave him a near-empathic ability.

Kelly Hawk purchased auto dealerships, while Brett Wyatt enlisted in the Army as a Military Police Officer. He specialized in the criminal investigation division, and after he completed his enlistment, the FBI recruited him. Special Agent Wyatt analyzed complex crime. He loved the FBI, but his analytical skills were put to use at a keyboard. The desk job tied him down too much, so he retired and moved to Boise.

While he caught up with his old teammate, Brett realized he had left his riding buddy out of the conversation. "This is my friend, Tom Coogan," Brett said.

"And you're Kelly Hawk," Tom said, reaching to shake the famed footballer's hand. "I'm a big fan."

"Thanks, Tom, but I'm far from my playing days." Kelly gripped Tom's hand.

"You look great," Brett said. "Are you up here for the conference?"

"Yes, and some related work. I'm a partner in a new company, the conference's security contractor. It's our first major job, but I'm not hands-on. I'm here to watch and learn."

"You're amazing, Hawk. You move from one venture to another, and your empire grows."

Kelly flashed a smile. "Thanks, Brett. I'm glad I ran into you. We need to talk; your law enforcement background could make you a tremendous asset to our firm. At least, I can see you in an advisory role. I would love it if you came on board. What would you say about getting together to discuss it?"

"Sure. For you, I'd be happy to."

Kelly slapped his old friend's back as if Brett had made a decisive tackle on the playing field. "Great. I'll give you a call. What are you guys up to? You here for the conference?" Kelly asked.

"No, we're up here with friends on vacation, and we brought our horses. We'll spend time around the valley, and then we'll ride the Trilogy Lakes Tour," Tom said.

"That sounds like fun. I'm familiar with the Trilogy Lakes. They're up in the Sawtooth Wilderness Area?"

"Yeah, they're deep into the Sawtooths. It's a ride we've wanted to take for a long time." Brett said.

"I read about the Trilogy Lakes in a book by retired US Senator Ed Wilson. He said they are one of the spots on earth you should see before you die."

While the men talked, another flight landed—a private jet, a beautiful state-of-the-art Gulfstream. It taxied past the private terminal, continued rolling to the public terminal and parked. Suddenly, the Gulfstream's arriving passengers began shouting at the airport employees who were trying to help them. Tom, Brett, and Kelly all turned to look.

"Oh, God, it's Bruce Arnold." Kelly almost sighed.

Bruce Arnold was the founder of the internet giant, Yoster. He was one of the wealthiest people in the world, and his negative personal reputation, which he was known for, mirrored his financial success.

Bruce Arnold, his wife, and two personal security guards marched toward the terminal's reception area. "Everybody back off—now! Get out of the way! Make room for a VIP!" the lead security guard from the Arnold group shouted. At least the friends assumed he was security. He wore a dark blazer, white shirt, and tie. His eyes swept from left to right, and his hands were held aloft, ready to fend off unwanted attention. Directly behind him, a casually dressed, thin, middle-aged man escorted an uncomfortable-looking lady. It was Bruce Arnold and his wife. A red-faced Arnold paused before a TSA agent posted at the reception area entrance. He shouted, "You idiots don't know what you're doing! We're not in the private terminal. We're in a public area. We don't belong here!" Arnold threw his hands into the air and stomped into the terminal.

"The private terminal is at capacity, sir." The TSA agent replied.

"This is unacceptable! I need to see the airport manager. Now!"

"You're blocking the exit. You need to clear the area." Another stone-faced TSA agent said.

A second private security guard followed Arnold and his wife and tried to coax them through. "Sir, please, we need to move to our vehicles. This area is too congested," he said.

Tom was transfixed by the scene. He unintentionally blocked the Arnold group's path while he gawked, and he chuckled while the spoiled rich guy's demands fell on indifferent ears.

"Let's get out of the way," Brett said, grabbing Tom's shoulder.

"Give me a minute." Tom pulled away.

Brett and Kelly didn't want to get involved, so they slipped back six feet to the edge of a seating area.

Arnold stopped and scowled at Tom as the unhappy group approached two waiting SUVs. He asked, "Are you stupid? What don't you understand about the words, back off?"

Tom stiffened, stared at the man, and held his ground.

Bruce Arnold's disruptive behavior distracted everyone from a more significant problem. No one in the crowded area noticed another gathering in the parking lot.

Brett spotted six individuals who stepped out of an older model gray cargo van. Faceless and genderless, each was dressed in a camo beanie, camo jumpsuit, camo gloves, and high-top brown hiking boots, armed with waist belts that holstered a nightstick-sized club and a long skinny spray bottle. The camo beanies covered their foreheads and seamlessly met a pair of strapped-on goggles. Camo N95 masks shielded their mouths and noses.

They moved with almost military precision, forming a broad line and marching toward the terminal. The operatives quickly approached the reception area and established a semi-circle that blocked and cornered the Arnold party. The two groups had nearly converged before one of Arnold's security guards finally lifted his eyes.

"Pig, thief! Pig, thief!" The camo group chanted in unison.

Bruce Arnold cowered and slipped behind his two-man security detail, who had thrust themselves into the middle of the opposition, trying to open a corridor toward their awaiting vehicles. The tactic failed as the individuals in the wings closed in, swinging their clubs.

Brett could tell their intentions were not to kill but to injure. They overwhelmed the surprised security men with back and shoulder strikes. One guard collapsed under the attack; the other dropped to a knee, holding his arms above his head and yelling, "Back off!"

In a smooth and well-practiced maneuver, the attackers backed up five yards and formed a new line. The Arnold group scrambled backward. Several wild-eyed and helpless bystanders, including Tom, were caught in the middle.

The attacker's new line filled the width of the walkway and blocked any escape. All six individuals pulled spray bottles from their belts and sprayed pepper spray at the cornered group. Yelps and screams filled the air. Mrs. Arnold fell to the concrete and wept, rubbing her eyes where the liquid must have hit her. A stream of liquid hit Tom in his face and neck. He tried to wipe the substance away, which didn't help. He wheezed and coughed, fighting for breath. A vile odor filled the air.

Satisfied they had done their worst, the attackers slipped the empty bottles back into their belts and retreated from the reception area in another organized formation.

Before the attackers could escape, Brett widened his stance, flexed his knees, and exploded into action. He looped around the panicked bystanders, running low. He threw his body into the line of attackers, shoulder first. Three camouflaged attackers hit the ground, and the remaining camouflaged individuals scrambled but held their ground.

Seconds later, Kelly Hawk stepped behind Brett and shouted, "Everybody freeze!"

The attackers ignored Kelly's orders and carefully stepped back toward the parking lot. A cargo van rolled adjacent to the walkway directly behind the camouflaged attackers.

Just as Brett regained his footing, the van's sliding door opened, and another disguised individual stepped out with a rifle in hand. He aimed it skyward and fired.

The chaos instantly froze, but screams still permeated the air.

"Whoever moves next gets shot!" The rifleman shouted. He

tightened the rifle to his shoulder and carefully panned from left to right.

Brett positioned himself at an angle where he could launch, but there was too much distance between himself and the camouflaged man with the rifle. He held his ground.

Tom squinted and blinked his burning eyes, struggling to take slow, even breaths.

The camouflaged attackers climbed to their feet and scampered into the van. The rifleman stepped in behind them and slid the door closed. The van sped away.

Kelly put his hand on Brett's shoulder. "What the hell was that?"

"It looks like the conference might have a terrorist problem."

CHAPTER TWO

Sage Coogan moved to the San Francisco Bay Area after college, where she landed a job. She missed Idaho, family, and friends, and tried to come home as often as her job and budget allowed. Sage was a tall young woman with long brown hair, intelligent eyes, and a spunky attitude. She could take over a room in seconds with her big smile and grace. She told everyone she was excited about the Sun Valley vacation her parents and friends had planned.

Brett watched as Sage stepped off the flight from San Francisco and sauntered toward the reception area. Brett stood next to Tom, who was sitting in a chair with his head down. Kelly Hawk had left to pick up his rental car and go to a meeting. They planned to get together in Sun Valley later in the week.

Sage entered the waiting area, spotted her dad, and smiled. She turned and walked toward him until the odor hit her. "She wrinkled her nose and asked, "What is that smell?"

Tom coughed twice, then answered, "Pepper spray. There's been an incident."

"Is that why all the police cars are here?"

"Yes. But your dad will be all right. It will take a little time," Brett replied.

"So, please tell me what's going on around here?" Sage asked.

Brett recited the blow-by-blow version of the morning's events while they walked to Tom's truck.

Tom coughed and then added, "This Arnold guy walked in with his wife and a couple of security men. Those masked guys took out the security guards with clubs and showered Arnold and his wife with pepper spray. It could have been a lot worse if they carried guns instead of pepper spray."

"Oh my God," Sage said. "I've never heard of anything like that ever happening here in Idaho."

"It wasn't an Idaho thing; their target was clear. They were after Bruce Arnold," Brett said.

"So, that's who that asshole was; he's the CEO of one of the big tech companies, isn't he?" Tom gasped.

"Why did you call Bruce Arnold an asshole?" Sage wondered.

"Don't listen to me. I'm having a bad day." Tom shook his head, coughing.

"He's the founder of Yoster and one of the richest people in the world," Sage said.

"They didn't kidnap or try to assassinate him," Tom wheezed. "I wonder what their agenda was."

Brett shook his head while Tom struggled with the effects of pepper spray. He wished he could help.

Tom leaned against his truck and took slow, deep breaths. He bent over, coughing, and dropped his hands to his thighs. His bloodshot eyes watered, and he smelled awful. Pepper spray's disgusting odor irritated everyone in proximity to it, including those untouched by the vile substance.

After several controlled breaths, Tom stood up and opened his truck's driver-side door. "It's time to go home," he said.

"Dad, Brett's driving; you're sitting in the back."

"It's my truck! I'm driving—stop telling me what to do. Being doused with that shit is bad enough. I sure as hell don't need to be bossed around."

"Your eyes are red. You can't drive if you can't see."

"You think I can't see? Watch this!" Tom said indignantly.

Tom swept his eyes over the parking lot. A commercial trash can was placed ten yards away. He trudged over to it, lifted it off the asphalt, and slammed it onto its side. The effort was rewarded by another coughing fit. He sat on the curb, put his hand on his chest, and closed his eyes. A moment later, he looked at his shirt sleeve and hands. "Oh shit," he said. "There's something gross in that damned trash can."

"Do you have a towel in your truck?" Brett asked.

Tom stared at the ground. "Yeah, behind the back seat."

Brett grabbed the towel and threw it to Tom. "You need to settle down."

Sage sat down next to Tom. "Dad—would you listen to me? I'll cover the back seat with towels, and we'll drive back with the truck's windows open. You'll need to strip and go straight to the shower when we get to the condo."

"Okay, okay," he mumbled, sounding embarrassed.

"And don't punch anything," she smirked.

Tom frowned at his daughter. "How did you know I was looking for something to punch?"

"I am your daughter."

Sage dropped her bags into the back of her dad's Ford Pickup, and she climbed into the shotgun seat. Brett drove, and her dad sat in the back row. After adjusting the rearview mirror, Brett glanced at Tom, who had lost his typical smile. Tom stared out the window, frowning, angry, and humiliated.

"Hey, Tom," Brett said. I've got a line from *The Code of the West* that might help. You want to hear it?"

"Sure, it couldn't hurt," Tom muttered.

"You're still quoting *The Code of the West*?" Sage asked.

"Haven't stopped and probably never will," Brett said. "So, are you ready?"

"Can't wait," Sage said.

"*Do what has to be done*," Brett quoted.

Wearing a slight frown, Tom said, "What? I don't get it. What do I need to do?"

"You need to take a shower."

Tom looked up, and a slight smile tugged at the corners of his lips. He shook his head.

"There's that smile," Sage said.

Years ago, Wyoming adopted *The Code of the West* as the state's official code of ethics. Wyoming is the only state with one, which impressed Brett, and he adopted the code as his own.

Brett Wyatt, Tom Coogan, and Mark Taggart enjoyed riding horses together, and while riding in the Boise foothills, Mark had dubbed them the Rider's Club. They all got a kick out of the name, and it stuck. Brett was the club's "leader" and often quoted the *code* to his friends when he felt they needed it. It always helped.

"Thanks for picking me up, guys," Sage said after Brett turned north on Highway 75 toward Ketchum.

"I wonder who those guys were," Tom asked aloud.

"I think they were the Ninety-niners," Brett said.

"Ninety-niners? Yeh, I've heard of them," Tom said. "But I'm not sure what their agenda is."

"Who are the Ninety-niners?" Sage asked.

"The Ninety-niners are a quasi-political-terrorist group. Their agenda is usually to demand income equality in America," Brett said.

"But why Ninety-niners?" Sage asked.

"The term Ninety-niners represents the 99 percent of Americans whom the group believes are being drained of their money, which is transferred to the ultra-wealthy one percent. They believe our government is inept and incapable of solving the problem. They have no respect for the police; they believe all law enforcement is a pawn of big business. Ninety-niners usually operate in small, unaffiliated groups that harass and attack while hiding behind their camouflaged outfits. They commonly spray-paint their ninety-nine logo on buildings. Their focus is on the very rich, and Bruce Arnold is one of the richest billionaires in the world. He's a ripe target."

"They have a point. Income inequality is a huge problem. Look at the homeless situation. It has exploded," Tom said.

"I agree, income inequality is a worthy issue," Brett said. "Even the press offers the Ninety-niners a degree of support, but their methods are unacceptable. They harass, and they sometimes beat the hell out of their victims. Today, they had a rifle at the airport. It was evident they didn't want to use it on the people, but their next step could be to carry guns, and if that happens, they will be considered an armed militia."

"That's a scary thought," Tom said. "But hiding behind masks shows they are a bunch of cowards who don't believe in their cause enough to own it. If I meet them again, their masks won't protect them."

Brett sympathized with his friend. Tom didn't like being a victim; it wasn't his *style*. He had a temper; sometimes, he saw red and threw an irrational fit. The year before, his temper almost got him killed. The Rider's Club decided to turn into a vigilante group, and they investigated repeated attacks on his business. It ended up being perpetrated by a group of professional burglars. The investigation led to a risky situation. It shook and scared them all, but through it all, Tom's values and strengths were amplified, not diminished.

Tom's six-foot-tall frame carried a little extra weight. It was too much for a fifty-year-old man by about ten pounds. He'd be okay if he put more effort into taking care of himself. His short blond hair and matching beard were partially graying, probably from stress more than age. He owned three of the popular Teton Outdoors stores in Boise. His son, Nick, helped manage them. Tom's engaging personality, strong work ethic, and charming smile made him popular with his employees and customers. The stress of running his business worked on him for years until he found the outlet that helped defuse it, exploring the great outdoors on horseback.

Their drive to Sun Valley was pleasant despite the cloud of stink that lingered over Tom. They drove through Hailey, a picturesque small town with great restaurants, shopping, and a thriving service industry. As they moved along the Wood River to Ketchum, the valley narrowed, and the mountains rose higher and grew tighter to the highway on the west side. Near Ketchum, they passed Bald Mountain, Sun Valley's signature ski mountain, one of the best in the world. It stood thousands of feet above the valley, adjacent to the west side of Ketchum. At the mountain's top, chair lifts drop off skiers at over 9,000 feet.

The sun illuminated a string of pearls moving through the trees high on the ski hill. The gondola was running, but not for skiers. Mountain bikers, hikers, and diners enjoyed the ride in the summer. The mountain bikers cruised downhill on challenging tracks. The less adventurous stayed mid-mountain, where they dined and enjoyed the view from the historic Round House Lodge.

They drove into Ketchum, Sun Valley's sister city, and at the second light, Brett turned right onto Sun Valley Road and went past a couple of churches, a classic red barn, and a pasture full of horses. Turning right at the Dollar Road intersection, they skirted around the Sun Valley Lodge, skating rink, and amphitheater. They drove across a small dam that held back a reflective lake and turned into an attractive condominium development that would be their base camp for the next week.

Brett, Mark, and Tom had rented three condos next to each other. They were staged to have a good time. They scheduled multiple activities for their vacation: hiking, golfing, concerts, and target shooting, along with an abundance of downtime. They were also ready for their next riding adventure. They had loaded six horses into two trailers and drove them up from Boise.

Mark waited outside the condos when Brett, Sage, and Tom drove up. Brett had already briefed him on Tom's injury, so he stopped Tom and said, "Let me have a quick look." Gripping Tom's chin, he stared at his irritated eyes. "How's your breathing?"

"A lot better."

"After you get cleaned up, I'll bring over some eye drops; they should help soothe your eyes. Take a long shower and wash your hair and face thoroughly. The irritation shouldn't last too long. You'll be fine."

"That's it?" Tom asked.

"I'll pour you a bourbon after dinner."

"You're a great doctor."

Mark grinned. He turned toward Sage, who stood at the ready with a hose, and said, "Go ahead and clean him up."

Sage hosed down her father, which wasn't too harrowing since he wore shorts and a T-shirt. It was an event witnessed and enjoyed by a small crowd, and Tom took the odd attention with a smile.

Tom had mellowed on the ride home but still stewed from the earlier excitement. He stood dripping in the yard, waiting to go in and follow the doctor's orders. "I've been thinking about the Ninety-niners at the airport," Tom said. "They could become a real problem. The Cottonwood Conference is being held right across the street. We need to be careful."

"You're dead right on that," Brett said.

CHAPTER THREE

The Ninety-niners parked their cargo van in a quiet corner of Bald Mountain's main parking lot. The young man in charge slowly scanned the area in front of the vehicle and to its right. "Anything on your side?" he asked.

"It's clear, Rage," the driver said.

Rage turned around to the six individuals sitting on the rear floor. "Just like we thought, no one parks here until ski season. Remember, keep your mind on the mission. We can't relax yet. Just one more step, and we're home. Double-check everything. Don't leave anything in the van. Keep everything in your pack and dump it in the designated dumpsters. Are you guys ready?"

"We're ready," a young woman said.

"Let's go."

The Ninety-niners exited the van, wearing shorts, tennis shoes, short-sleeved shirts, sunglasses, and baseball caps. They walked through a scattering of cottonwoods to a trail that led to the Wood River bike path. When they got to the trailhead's lot, they broke up into three groups and hiked to their parked cars. After they had dumped their gear, they drove toward their well-hidden camp in the trees near Trail Creek.

Rage drove a fifteen-year-old Subaru through Sun Valley and uphill on Trail Creek Road. He passed the Sun Valley Lodge, golf course, gun club, and a popular trail that followed Trail Creek as it weaved through the trees to their right. After they crossed the creek on a cement bridge, Trail Creek Road turned onto a dirt road and continued uphill.

Rage turned his Subaru onto a seldom-used two-track that broke away from the road. He drove up the two-track through terrain covered with brush, deciduous trees, and pines, then turned onto a faint branch and drove through a cluster of aspens into a lightly used but established campsite.

Rage and two of his fellow Ninety-niners stepped out of the Subaru and waited for the rest of their team. Two more cars drove into the campsite within ten minutes, reuniting all eight Ninety-niners. After the three cars were parked, the Ninety-niners greeted each other and quietly celebrated with hugs and handshakes.

"Any trouble on the way back, Bright?" Rage asked.

"Not with us?" A young woman said. "What about you, Torch?" Bright asked the other driver.

"No problem." Torch said as he smiled.

"Great job, everyone. We made a difference today. All of you should be proud. Remember the next step. If anyone comes to this campground, we're on break from college. It's as simple as that. Sit around the fire pit, relax, and drink beer," Rage said.

They had set up the camp the day before. Eight small tents were flanked by a disorganized pile of supplies. The only place to sit was beside an abandoned fire pit surrounded by thick logs. The evening was clear and smelled of pine. The group listened to the distant sounds from Trail Creek. They didn't find much firewood, and what they gathered didn't burn well, so they sat in the dark around a pathetic fire and shivered.

It didn't matter much today—they were an excited bunch.

Two of the young men tried but struggled to build a campfire. After a few minutes, their meager fire burned out.

"Hey, Torch," a young man called out. "Can you help?"

"I'll try." He approached the firepit and appraised the situation. "I think we need to build a larger fire of kindling below the logs before they will burn, and we'll have to collect a lot more firewood."

"Shit," said the young man, who asked for help.

Rage carried a six-pack of beer and passed them out to the crew.

Torch stared at the beer can. "Do you have an IPA?"

"We're poor college students, remember? This is the cheapest beer I could find."

"Any craft beer at all?"

"No, Torch."

"Imported?"

Rage pointed his finger at his friend and smiled. "You got me again."

Torch laughed and took a sip of his beer. "This is good."

The Ninety-niners relaxed and transformed into a band of college kids on an outdoor adventure. They quietly soaked in the thrill of success. They had been roughed up a bit that morning, but they had completed their objectives and escaped. They humiliated the well-known narcissist who oppressed the lower class. He deserved it.

This group of Ninety-niners was an independent unit, one of the smaller cells out of Portland. Rage and Bright led the small complement. Despite the system's effort to document and extort the lower class, the pair had rejected their family names. Bright led with passion and intelligence. Rage led with anger. The two complimented each other, and Rage had to admit Bright helped keep him under control. Rage had a violent history.

Bright's dark skin accentuated her fit physique, which was

better than most of the young men's. Tall and lean, she could have played basketball for Portland State University. Her shoulder-length dreadlocks on the right half of her head contrasted with the shaved left side. Her big brown eyes showed intense intelligence. It would be a mistake to underestimate Bright.

Rage stood a shade less than six feet, had light brown skin, and a shaved bald head. Lean and muscular, he had the build of an athlete. Before he changed his life and joined the Ninety-niners, he spent a stint as a mixed martial arts fighter, where his unrelenting style was aggressive and angry. When someone stared into his brown eyes, they couldn't sense much, which was how Rage wanted it.

The rest of the Ninety-niners was a diverse group of average twenty-something young men, covered in angry tattoos. The tattoos made them appear more urban than outdoor. Baseball caps and long-sleeved sweatshirts helped soften their hardened look.

After a couple of beers, they all planned an extensive search for firewood. Rage planned to sit out; he had a lot on his mind.

Rage considered that their operation would never have worked without their anonymous contact. A month ago, the mystery man came out of nowhere, initiated communication, and offered strategic information. He provided leads, informing them of Bruce Arnold's movements where he was unprotected, a rare occurrence. The Ninety-niners had traveled north to Seattle to check out two of their contact's earlier leads, and both times, the leads turned out to be accurate. It was too easy. Rage, Bright, and the Ninety-niners were hungry for success, and today, they attacked while they used their contact's information.

Bright and Rage shared an ideology that made it hard to trust anyone over twenty-five. Trust was the issue that haunted them. They didn't know their contact's identity; the accuracy of his leads had established his credibility.

Bright and Rage sat together by the parking area on a couple of large rocks.

"I don't trust this guy," Rage said.

"We could never have had today's success without him," Bright said.

"It bugs me that he's anonymous; all he does is give us information. I don't like that he will only talk to you on the phone. If he doesn't get more involved than that, we're better off without him." Rage kicked a pebble.

"I understand. The way things stand right now makes him hard to trust, but his tips have been spot-on. He's supposed to contact us again. Let's see what he says before we get rid of him."

One of the younger guys approached the pair; Digit was their tech manager.

"Memory cards, please," Digit said.

Rage reached into his pocket and pulled out two memory cards from his wearable cameras. "So, you're on the job," Rage said.

"Yes, sir," Digit replied, placing the cards in his pocket.

"When will the world learn about our adventure?" Bright asked.

"I'll upload this to the cloud immediately, and our Portland team will clean it up. It won't take long. Our video feeds will populate the world within a few hours."

"Awesome," Rage said.

"It is, isn't it? After I upload these, I'll bring you back two clean cards."

"Will you use the satellite uplink?" Bright asked.

"No, I'll jump on high-speed internet downtown," Digit replied.

"You should check out the satellite system before we go into the mountains," Rage ordered, standing up and stretching.

"I already have, and it works fine, but it is slow. I want to get this video uploaded right away.

"Makes a lot of sense. I'm glad we have your expertise," Rage said.

Digit collected cards from each cell member. After gathering them all, he sat down, backed them up on a separate device, jumped into his car, and drove to a predetermined high-speed internet source.

Rage was in awe. High-resolution video from twelve angles would hit the internet within a few hours. All hell could break loose.

CHAPTER FOUR

Mark took charge of the horses, which meant he had to deal with Pat, the crusty owner of Victory Stables. Pat was thrilled to have his stables sold out but didn't enjoy dealing with his needy customers. Victory Stables contained twenty horse stalls, ten on each side of a central corridor. Two large pastures and an outdoor arena wrapped around the facility, and an aspen-covered mountain loomed a short mile to the east. It was an ideal setup unless Pat fell into one of his crabby jags; unfortunately, he seemed to be in one.

"Pat, listen for a second," Mark asked. "We've got six horses stabled with you, scattered throughout your complex. We need them stabled together. It makes everything easier for everyone, including you. You've got lots of horses here. If you don't fix the situation, you'll hear more complaints from your other customers."

Pat turned toward his teenage hired hand. "Can't you do anything right?" he yelled. "Now we're stuck with this mess, and there is no way to fix it without moving every horse."

Mark stared at the stable stall map that hung by the entrance. "It's not that bad; we could fix this if we swapped five stalls.

"That can't work," Pat said.

Mark walked him through the plan.

Pat stared at the stall map and turned away. "Why didn't you think of that?" he asked his hired hand.

Mark was excited to vacation with Brett and the Coogan family. He was the Rider's Club's oldest member and might be the smartest. He was quick-minded, reactive, and detail-oriented. Mark, like a lot of brilliant people, often displayed eccentric behavior. He could ask questions too quickly. Sometimes, his thought processes could outdistance his common sense. It sometimes got him into uncomfortable situations or trouble.

Entering his mid-fifties, Mark wanted more out of life than his career, so he practiced medicine less and spent more time on his interests and family. Mark wasn't a large man; he was medium-height, slim, and fit. He was strong. Working with the horses required heavy lifting—hundred-pound bags of oats and high stacks of bailed hay. Depending on how long he procrastinated his barber visits, his hairstyles varied. He wore orange-rimmed glasses that gave him an unusual look—nobody quite understood why.

Mark and his wife owned a small ranchette at the edge of the Boise foothills. Brett and Tom boarded their horses there under a long-term agreement. The main barn on the property was often the focal point of the Rider's Club's time together, and at times, it became the center of their lives. It wasn't a typical barn. The three men designed it to meet and exceed a horse owner's needs; it was an ideal clubhouse for the friends.

Freshly showered and changed into clean clothes, Brett, Sage, and Tom rolled into Victory Stables. Sage wore khaki shorts, a blue feminine-style T-shirt, and trail shoes. Her long brown hair was tied back into a ponytail. The guys were in their usual garb: jeans, cowboy boots, and long-sleeved shirts. Brett gave Pat a high-five on the way in; they had known each other for years. Victory Stables was the best.

"Sage, stop for a second." Brett reached toward her.

"Okay?" Sage and her dad stopped and stood inside the entrance.

"Now, close your eyes and take three deep breaths. Do you smell the odor of horses, hay, and manure? Did you miss it?"

"Yeah, I think I did," Sage grinned.

Mark hugged Sage. It had been a while.

"It's so great to see you guys!" Sage said. "It has been too long. I've missed you."

Like on cue, a familiar whinny came from the stables. Sage's eyes moved up and down the stalls. "Where is he?"

"He heard your voice. He's around the corner," Mark said.

Sage strode past two stalls and around the corner, and there he stood with his long neck extended over the stall's gate—Tonto, a curious brown and white Pinto.

"Oh, my big boy, I've missed you so much," Sage said as she stroked his nose, neck, and ears. "You are such a good boy."

Tonto affectionately nosed her and sniffed her jacket.

"Of course, I brought you a treat." She reached into her pocket and pulled out a long carrot.

Tonto ate it in five seconds. Tonto was a postcard Pinto. He had a reddish-brown coat with a full band of bright white markings running from his shoulders down his front legs, and a similar set ran over his rump and back legs. He was a curious horse, interested in most things, and he loved Sage. Mark owned Tonto, but when Sage was in town, they spent lots of time together. The Taggarts owned more horses than they could ride for one reason. They wanted to share them with their friends. When it came to Tonto, Sage took priority. Mark wouldn't have it any other way.

Last summer, while Sage was home from California, Mark

devised a plan to capture a crime ring that had repeatedly burglarized Tom's stores. Mark's plan sounded good, but, in retrospect, was rushed and misguided. The criminals almost beat Tom to death. Sage was grateful to be home when it happened, and she fell into a protective mode, determined to care for her dad. When the Rider's Club raided the criminal's compound, Sage stepped up and turned the tide of the conflict with one accurate rifle shot. She might have saved their lives. She burned the rest of her vacation time riding Tonto daily.

At Victory Stables, the Rider's Club was in their element as they hung out in the stalls with their horses and each other. A sense of calm and comradery filled their being; they were ready for a new adventure.

"So, guys, what's the plan?" Sage asked.

"First thing in the morning, we'll trailer up and drive to the Cub Lake Trailhead in the Sawtooth National Recreation Area. From there, we'll take a warm-up ride up to Cub Lake. It's about a three-mile ride with maybe three hundred feet of vertical gain. It's a good place to stop for lunch. After that, we'll ride up a rougher trail, another six hundred feet of vertical gain, and two miles to Mica Lake. I plan to catch some fish there. There is talk of large trout." Brett said.

"Then we'll turn and ride the same route back. Hopefully, we'll get home in time for dinner," Tom said.

"Sounds like a good start," Sage said.

"It should be fun," Tom said. "Once we're back, we'll hang out and relax for a few days before we take the big ride."

"Are you excited about the Trilogy Lakes Tour?" Mark asked.

"Yes! I've been reading about it, and I watched a video. This will be the best ride ever!"

"I've ridden it once before—it was a life experience," Mark said. "The Tour connects three of Idaho's most majestic lakes; it's a loop covering miles of mountainous terrain."

"It will be a long ride," Brett added. "We'll camp out for three nights, but we can stay longer and spend extra time along the trail. I'm planning to catch fish at each of the lakes."

"When did you turn into a big fisherman, Brett?" Sage asked.

"I have always fished and have never considered myself avid, but this seems like the perfect time to get serious."

"Okay, sounds good; we might as well take advantage of some of the best fishing in the state. If you can't catch a fish on a wilderness lake, you can't catch a fish anywhere. Right? We should give it a try. Dad, did you bring a fishing pole for me?"

"Absolutely." Tom gave her a thumbs up.

"Good! I'm excited. It sounds fun, and we are not trying to catch any bad guys this time. Right?" Sage winked.

CHAPTER FIVE

The Managing Partner of Rockford Security was Glenn Rockford. He scanned the large group that attended the emergency meeting on the first floor of the Sun Valley Inn. The room barely held the group of corporate managers, security specialists, public relations specialists, and local, state, and national law enforcement officers.

Kelly Hawk was a new partner in Rockford Security. He was out of his comfort zone as he watched the meeting unfold, but he kept that to himself. He sat in the front row, chin up, eyes forward, listened, and learned.

Mr. Rockford, a formidable brown-skinned man with a military bearing, addressed the group with a loud, low voice. "First of all, shut the damn door. This is a private meeting."

A Rockford Security Specialist exited the room, closed the heavy wooden door behind him, and stood guard outside.

"We have a big problem," he continued. "Most of you have heard about the incident at the airport this morning. A group of terrorists attacked one of our attendees, Bruce Arnold, who is the president and CEO of Yoster. There were no serious injuries, but a few people were checked out at the ER and released. There were bumps, bruises, and an incredible amount of irritation and humiliation. That's not all. Less than an hour ago, a video of the incident hit the internet like nothing I have ever seen. We have made national news, and it's not good. We have a feed ready to view—take a look, and we will go from there." Rockford gestured toward the wall-mounted big screen.

A masked individual dressed in camouflaged clothing appeared on the screen and ranted about the evils of capitalism. After a few seconds of silence, his tone changed. "Members of our faithful have traveled to Idaho. We are there to single out the most corrupt of the evil ones. The evil ones have massed to study how they can steal more from us. We know there is never enough for the greedy capitalists, so today, we make a stand."

The speaker's image dissolved into the outdoor reception area at the Valley Airport. The scene at the airport was shown at one angle and then another. The attack was filmed in a stunning, professional display of sight and sound. A man was overwhelmed by a camouflaged and club-wielding masked attacker, driven to the concrete and bloodied. A woman caught a sprayed substance in her eyes and screamed. Multiple individuals shared her experience as they turned away from the attackers, knelt, and hid their eyes. Shock and panic engulfed the bystanders as they all tried to protect themselves.

The view dissolved to the anonymous speaker. "We tire of warning the capitalists. Now we declare war."

The image dissolved into a blood-red cast overlay and a logo, two digits, "99."

Whispers, grumbles, and groans erupted from the audience.

"I've been in the security business most of my life," Rockford shouted. "But I have never seen anything like this. We have issues we need to address. This terrorist group knew precisely where and when Mr. Arnold's party would arrive that morning. I don't see how that can happen without a major security leak. We have moved into an environment of increased risk. The risk could manifest itself here in Sun Valley and throughout the region. Many of the conference's attendees have planned side trips and other activities. Offsite risk, as encountered this morning, is unpredictable and unacceptable. The best practice is avoidance." He took a quick drink of water and shuffled some paper on the table in front of him.

The attendees shifted on their feet and in their seats.

"Points to consider." Rockford slowed his speech, raised his voice, and paused for effect. "How do we deal with the risks at the resort and offsite?" He paused for answers.

No one answered.

"A great deal of unwanted national attention will come." He paused again.

Again, no one made a noise.

"The PR fallout will reflect on us all." Rockford dropped his eyes at his papers as if he considered what to say next, and then he raised his eyes to meet those who looked to him for answers. "Here is my recommendation. Cancel the Cottonwood Financial Conference."

A rumble of voices and muted comments filled the room.

"As you know, Rockford Security is contracted to provide on-site security for the conference. We have already taken steps to bring in a more significant security force. However, there are limits to our responsibilities and our capabilities. We're in charge of security *here* at the conference. As we have seen, that's not enough. I see representatives from over a dozen companies, officers from the local police, State Police, and the FBI. We need a collaborative effort to keep everyone safe."

Just then, a light-complected, expressionless man dressed in a dark suit stood and positioned himself behind Glenn Rockford.

Rockford picked up his papers, tapped them together, and put them into a folio. He closed the folder and said, "I'm turning this meeting over to the gentleman to my left; he is the agent in charge of the FBI's Boise office, Special Agent David Sturm."

Special Agent Sturm nodded at Rockwell and stiffly stepped up to the lectern.

Kelly Hawk took a deep breath.

Sturm began, "First of all, I agree with everything Mr. Rockford said." His speech reflected the points made in Glenn Rockford's assessment. He dove deep into the Sawtooth Financial Conference attendees' need to restrict their exposure to unnecessary high-risk situations. Maybe they shouldn't float the river, fish the stream, or play golf. They could become a target.

Sturm cited communication as the critical element needed for successful public-private teamwork. Every attendee at the meeting was asked to join a new communication network via text, phone, and email to communicate their thoughts, news, and problems. More work was needed, but it was a place to start.

Special Agent Sturm scanned the audience and addressed the source of the threat. "Speaking for the FBI, we have watched the Ninety-niners for a long time but have yet to charge them with any crimes. We have respected their right to free speech, as we should. Recently, threats have been made via social media, and today, the Ninety-niners escalated and violently attacked people at the airport. As you heard, they declared war. With their criminal actions, we have changed their classification. They are officially classified as domestic terrorists. Before you leave, check in with the local and State Police in attendance. Please introduce yourself to each of them. We also have two of our special agents in the room. In the back corner to my left is Special Agent Roger Nelson, and in the other corner is Special Agent DeShawn Terry."

The Q&A post-presentation addressed security at several levels. The consensus was that it was too late to cancel the Cottonwood Financial Conference, which kept the focus on offsite risk. The conference attendees came to Sun Valley not only to learn; they came to play. Planned events included golf, fishing, river rafting, backpacking, and trail rides. The setting around Sun Valley ranged from the well-developed neighborhoods and shopping to the wilderness. It was impossible to securely cover the vast expanse.

After the session, Kelly Hawk roamed around the room and introduced himself. He offered little helpful input but was immersed in a tremendous learning experience.

In the corner of the room, Agent Terry listened to the concerns of two Yoster security specialists. The Yoster specialists were concerned about a planned trail ride with an outfitter out of Stanley. A group sponsored by Bruce Arnold planned to ride the Trilogy Lakes Tour, which entailed four days and three nights in the Sawtooth Wilderness Area. It was a security nightmare. The obvious solution was to cancel the trip, but Bruce Arnold refused.

After their discussion, Kelly Hawk introduced himself to Agent Terry.

"It's a pleasure to meet you," Agent Terry said. "I'm a big fan."

"Thanks, but I've left football behind. I'm determined to learn the security business now, so it's my pleasure to meet you."

"I know of a couple of ex-NFL ballplayers who became great FBI agents. The transition can work."

"I have friends who joined the FBI, and funny you mention it, I talked to one of them this morning. Do you know Brett Wyatt?"

"Yes, Brett is a close friend." Agent Terry said with surprise.

"He's a good friend of mine, too. We were teammates in Denver."

"Oh, I should have known that." Terry smiled.

Kelly reciprocated the smile and said, "I was with him this morning. He was at the airport when the Ninety-niners hit Bruce Arnold. He had a friend with him, Tom. I think that was his name. That poor guy got soaked with pepper spray."

Agent Terry's eyes widened. "Oh my God! Tom has a temper. He could have freaked out."

"I left the airport not long after the attack and watched him kick a trash can around the parking lot as I drove out."

Agent Terry looked down, suppressing a chuckle. "That doesn't surprise me," he said.

DeShawn Terry lived in Boise and had a solid positive history with Brett and the other Rider's Club members. He would be welcome to join the club, but he'd need to get a horse. And deep down, DeShawn would love to have one. Last year, the Riders pulled him into their investigation and the ultimate capture of a regional burglary ring. They had built a strong bond.

Agent Terry was around six feet tall and had a muscular and fit frame for a man in his early forties. His cropped hair kept the focus on his severe brown eyes and his strong jaw. He looked, acted, and performed like the ideal FBI agent. After he enlisted in the Marines, he joined the FBI and climbed the ranks. A family man, he liked his assignment to the Boise office and hoped to stay there for a long time.

"So, did they pick up someone at the airport?" Agent Terry asked.

"Yes, Tom's daughter. They're all here on vacation. They said they brought their horses. They're riding the Trilogy Lakes Tour. It sounds like a wilderness adventure."

"Did you say they're riding through the Trilogy Lakes?" Agent Terry raised his brows.

"Yes?" Kelly was surprised by Agent Terry's befuddled reaction.

"An outfitter out of Stanley will lead Bruce Arnold's group on the Trilogy Lakes ride. Arnold refuses to drop the trip. It's more than risky; they'll be in the middle of nowhere. You can't even take motorized vehicles up there. He won't cancel."

"That's crazy," Kelly said.

"I've got an idea. Brett is such a solid guy; we should get together and ask for his thoughts. I'm sure he has studied the trail. He could bring us up to speed on the trip and might have some ideas that could help."

"Good idea. Will you be around tonight?" Kelly asked.

"Yeah, I'm at the Inn," Terry answered.

"How about the three of us get together for a beer after dinner?"

"I'd like that." Terry looked at his watch to note the time.

"Great, I'll call Brett and set it up." Kelly moved on and introduced himself to a small group near the exit. A slim, middle-aged man dressed in black spotted him from across the room and made eye contact. He quickly advanced toward Kelly.

When he was close enough, the man said, "Excuse me, I overheard you talking to another gentleman, and the name Brett Wyatt was mentioned."

"Yes, Brett and I are old friends." Kelly took a step back.

"Brett and I also have a close association. I wish I had the time to see him." He reached into his pocket, pulled out a business card, and scribbled a small note on its back. "I haven't had any contact with Brett since last summer. If you see him, please give him my card."

Kelly smiled and said, "No problem. I'll make sure he gets it."

CHAPTER SIX

After a light dinner, Brett took a short walk to the Sun Valley Inn to meet with DeShawn Terry and Kelly Hawk. When he left his condo, he looked next door, where Tom Coogan and his family stayed. They were a good-sized, noisy bunch; there was a lot of laughter inside. Next to the Coogans, the Taggert family also enjoyed some multi-generational family time.

Brett was alone and slightly envious. At times like this evening, he reflected on his history. He had worked through three dangerous careers: professional football, the military police, and the FBI. All three demanded his total dedication and his total time. He was successful to a fault. As he approached middle age, he questioned his choices. He had never married. Sure, he had girlfriends, but he never allowed a relationship to stick. He chose to live a dangerous, short-term existence instead of what's essential in life, like love, marriage, and family. It was a huge mistake—one he couldn't shake.

Maybe time with old friends from the NFL and the FBI would lessen the melancholy. Discussions of security and law enforcement would dominate the evening. It would be a bachelor's evening out with the boys. Kelly and DeShawn shared common ground, with different experiences yet similar energies. They had known each other for several hours and were probably already fast friends.

Brett was a good friend to have. His high moral code and his calm authority were welcomed in his relationships. Confident and sincere, he was loyal to almost a fault, and when there was a need, he would step in and help.

Brett's parents had passed away when he was a kid, and his orphanhood was punctuated by a lack of close relatives. He didn't have uncles, aunts, or grandparents. His childhood was spent bouncing into and out of several foster homes, where his hopes for closeness were dashed. Sports were a salvation of sorts; his teammates became his family, and it extended to close relationships in the military and work, but at the end of the day, Brett was alone.

Brett walked down Dollar Road and turned into Sun Valley Village. The sky was deep blue and cloudless. With the sun dropping toward the western horizon, a welcomed high country chill moved in—*perfect*. He walked through the picturesque village that was dressed in a well-crafted collection of shops and restaurants. He spotted DeShawn and Kelly talking and laughing while they waited outside the Sun Valley Inn.

Brett smiled as he approached. "What's the plan, guys?"

"How about we find a quiet table inside in the Ram Bar? They have at least a dozen local beers on tap," Kelly suggested.

"Sounds good," Brett said, looking at DeShawn. "How come I have to come to Sun Valley to see you when we live in the same town?"

"You know, life is too damned busy." DeShawn reached out to shake his hand and slapped him on the shoulder.

"I've got that, but we need to get you down to the barn and out for a ride one of these days." Brett smiled.

"What about me? I like horses, too." Kelly said.

"Anytime, man. Anytime."

Brett ordered a pitcher of Ketchum's favorite IPA, leaned back, relaxed, and smiled. They would have been happy to hang out and drink beer, but the responsible Agent Terry brought up the subject of Bruce Arnold and the Ninety-niners.

"Kelly told me you and Tom were at the airport this morning when the attack happened. It was the Ninety-niners," DeShawn said, taking a sip of his beer.

"Yeah, I figured it was. I've seen a lot in my day, but never anything like that. Those Ninety-niners were methodical; their attack was almost choreographed, but at least the attack wasn't lethal."

"I heard Tom got hit with pepper spray?" DeShawn asked.

"It hit him right in the face and soaked him."

"Holy shit! He's got a temper; how's he doing?" DeShawn knew Tom well.

"It took him about a half-hour to calm down. I think he let it go."

"Good for him—yeah, good for him. Well, the Ninety-niners posted a video of the attack on most of the social media sites out there. It went viral. On top of that, they added a threat. They threatened war."

"That hasn't been their style," Brett said.

"True, but we can't take the threat lightly," DeShawn said, taking another sip of his beer.

"I agree."

"Do you think their threat implies bloodshed?" Kelly asked.

"There is no way to know the answer to that question. We know, historically, they'd humiliate, but one of them carried a rifle this morning. It could signify a change." DeShawn said.

"The terrorist with the rifle used it to prevent an escalation—defensively," Brett added.

DeShawn frowned as he stared at the foam on his beer. "True, and the Ninety-niners are idealists, but still, their methods could be changing. We have to treat this seriously."

Kelly and Brett sadly nodded.

"As I told you on the phone, Bruce Arnold hired an outfitter to take him and a couple of his friends on the Trilogy Lakes Tour. His security team is concerned about his safety, and Bruce won't listen." Kelly got to the point.

"Someone needs to talk Arnold out of this. He shouldn't go," Brett said.

"We agree, but Arnold is determined. He's going on the ride, and no one has been able to change his mind." DeShawn shrugged.

Brett marinated in silence for a few seconds. "There needs to be an intervention of some kind. Kelly, you're a well-known, well-liked, handsome guy. Maybe you could talk to Arnold's wife and explain the risks. He shouldn't go on the trip. He'd be too exposed. It's too dangerous."

DeShawn gritted his teeth and shook his head. "His security team has already sat down with him and his wife. She agrees with us, but Bruce Arnold won't budge."

Kelly sighed and relaxed a little.

"I've read he has an abrasive personality and is hard to deal with. His stubbornness could put him in a life-threatening situation." Brett said.

"Unfortunately, you're right," DeShawn said.

"So, since he's taking the Trilogy Lakes Tour," Brett said. "Give me a little background. Do you know any details about the outfitter and the other customers on the trip?"

"Yes, a company called Starr Outfitters will lead the trip. Everything we've heard about them is good. They're out of Stanley and have led trail rides for years; they have an abundance of five-star reviews. As for other customers, there aren't any.

Arnold purchased every slot on the trip, which was meant for twelve or more. I guess he has enough money to do whatever he wants."

"I like the idea of the small group. I hope Arnold plans to bring two or three of his personal security team, ideally, with a background in horsemanship." Brett picked up his beer and took a drink.

"Arnold and his security team addressed that issue. Arnold knows a man with the needed outdoor skill set. Bruce said he would contact him directly." DeShawn leaned back in his seat.

Brett looked at DeShawn and raised his brows. "One man? I hope he's good."

"Brett, I'd bet you've got the tour mapped out. From a security point of view, what's your impression?" Kelly asked.

Brett took another sip of his beer before he spoke. "From a security point of view, it's interesting. How about I lay out the trip before we focus on the security challenges?"

"Sounds good. There's the old FBI agent—again," DeShawn smiled and slapped his old friend on the back.

Brett looked at DeShawn and grinned. "The Trilogy Lakes Tour is unique. It's known for its three spectacular high mountain lakes. Whether you ride horses or hike, most take the same general route. We plan to break our ride into four days and camp for three nights. The first leg takes us to Sara Lake, the second to Kimberly Lake, and the third to Christine Lake. Then we'll follow the loop back home. The trailhead starts and finishes at Badger Lake. No motor vehicles of any kind are allowed in the Sawtooth Wilderness Area. Of course, terrorists don't care about rules. They might go in on motorcycles, but that would draw attention. There is a trailhead for hikers and another for horses. Typically, there are more hikers than riders on the trail. Even the forest rangers patrol on foot or horseback."

"If we want to set up a headquarters or come in with a group, would we have adequate space at the trailhead?" DeShawn asked.

"Yes, it should work fine. The SNRA has a big parking area for vehicles and trailers. I'd work with the sheriff, the State Police, and the SNRA Forest Rangers. They should check out everyone who enters the trailheads, and the rangers could increase their presence on the trails."

"We've already contacted all three of them. The police will patrol the trailhead, but the forest rangers don't have extra manpower to put on the trail," DeShawn said.

Brett rubbed his temple with his right hand. "Okay, moving on. The ride is comfortable as you enter the trail. There is a station where everyone stops and signs in for a permit. Once you're in the Sawtooth Wilderness Area, the terrain becomes rugged, and you gain altitude from there on. There are multiple streams; some have basic bridges, and most don't. Some are deep, with rushing water, and can be challenging to cross. The country rises, and the footing becomes compromised on several steep climbs. Some rocky sections get technical, especially for backpackers. For that reason, there are some areas where backpackers and horseback riders have separate trails.

"Some hikers turn back; unfortunately, people have accidents and get injured. If you stick with it, you'll reach Sara Lake after a half-day ride and over a fifteen-hundred-foot vertical gain. And this first leg is the easiest of the three."

DeShawn and Kelly exchanged looks that didn't escape Brett's notice.

Brett continued, "The ride is in the middle of the wilderness, but there are more people out there than you would expect, at least in the first section. It's a popular destination, and some hikers and riders go to Sara Lake and return to the trailhead; some make the round trip all in one day."

"A little traffic could slow down the bad guys," Kelly suggested.

"Exactly," DeShawn said.

"We'll camp at Sara Lake and ride to Kimberly Lake the next day. On the second leg, the vertical gain doubles. It's nice to ride horses in this section. Those poor backpackers will have sore legs. And that's why the outfitting business is healthy. The second leg is challenging, and it is incredibly scenic. After a long ride, you'll reach Kimberly Lake. Good campsites are easier to find there. You still see campers near the lake, but fewer people than on the first leg. Kimberly Lake is in the middle of nowhere; it's pretty isolated. On our third day, we'll ride on to Christine Lake. Most people feel that Christine Lake is the most spectacular of the three. It's the largest and the deepest."

For a moment, Brett stared into a void, and a group behind them clinked their glasses and said, "Cheers" in unison, bringing Brett back to the moment.

He continued, "The ride from Kimberly to Christine leads over the highest point on the trip. The climb has a two-thousand-foot gain and takes you over Lookout Ridge, where you can experience an incredible view. All in all, after you pass the two-mile mark on the first leg, the country becomes wild and so vast that it's impossible to patrol effectively. You're on your own out there. If there are terrorists, they will be too." Brett smirked as he took a swig from his beer.

"From a terrorist's point of view, where do you think they would strike?" DeShawn asked.

Brett wiped his lips with the back of his hand. "That is an impossible question to answer, but… if I were a terrorist, I'd attack in the first section, even with the higher traffic. Further into the tour, they will have rougher terrain. Even in the first section, they'd be out in the middle of nowhere. It would be easy to find an isolated spot to attack. There are opportunities to go off trail and disappear. If they travel off the trail and commit a crime, no one will know."

"I question whether the Ninety-niners have the guts to take on the wilderness," DeShawn said, shrugging.

"Good point. Even if you're an experienced outdoorsman, this sounds like it is a strenuous trip, and the Ninety-niners don't have that reputation," Kelly said.

"On the other hand, defensive measures would be difficult. The Sawtooth Wilderness Area is a wild region. It's almost impossible for anyone to come in for a rescue. Everything that makes it tough for the terrorists almost makes it impossible to defend against them." Brett said.

DeShawn frowned at Brett. "We didn't see this one coming. We can't fly a helicopter overhead twenty-four-seven. Our options are limited. If there is a problem, we'll have to react. Until then, we'll need to keep our feelers out, check social media and other sources, and see if there is any buzz about the Ninety-niners either here or on the Trilogy Lakes Tour."

"Question," Brett said, turning his beer with two fingers. "So, other than one man from Yoster, will there be a police or security presence ready to step in if Arnold's group needs backup?"

DeShawn looked at Brett with cold eyes. "No. We don't have enough time or resources to put something like that together."

"That's too bad." DeShawn's answer wasn't what Brett wanted to hear. Brett leaned on his elbows that he placed on the edge of the table. "I do have another thought. The Riders Club is riding to Cub Lake on a warm-up ride tomorrow. We'll discuss it. I'm sure Mark will come up with at least six ideas."

DeShawn chuckled, "That guy's too damn smart. But if he comes up with something you like, let me know."

"I've got an idea that might help," Kelly said.

"What's that?" DeShawn asked.

"Let's get another pitcher." Kelly raised his glass.

They enjoyed another pitcher together, and then they said their goodnights.

Before Kelly left, he said, "Hey, Brett, a guy at this afternoon's meeting asked me to give you his card. I almost forgot."

Brett took the card, examined both sides, and after an uncomfortable pause, asked, "Kelly, what did this man look like?"

"He was middle-aged, average-sized, and slim. He didn't look like your normal corporate guy. He was dressed in black. Why? Is there a problem?"

"No, I think I remember him," Brett said in a faraway voice.

Kelly shrugged and turned away. Brett handed the card to DeShawn.

DeShawn quickly looked at Brett, opening and closing his mouth without allowing sound to escape. Finally, he gathered his thoughts and spoke. "I'll check it out. I'll get back to you right away. Be careful."

"I will."

CHAPTER SEVEN

T he man called Colorado turned off the improved dirt road and drove onto the steep entry of an old two-track. It hadn't rained in a week, and the terrain was dry and solid. His Chevy Blazer dug in, pulled through a dangerous uphill climb, and rolled along an isolated ridge. Breaking away from the two-track, he drove through a small gap in the tree line and across an awkward washout. At best, the Blazer's traction was limited, but the terrain kept Colorado hidden. He was careful to vary his final approach—today, he slalomed downhill through a thin stand of lodgepole pines. When he cleared the trees, he found himself in front of a log cabin. Once again, he had returned to his abode, alive, from his monthly supply run.

He had built his cabin slowly, one log at a time. His building plan was scheduled for five years, which worked for him. When he wasn't working, he could return to his property in the mountains and escape reality.

Until his life changed three years ago when he had to disappear.

When he moved in, his cabin was not inhabitable; the first winter was brutally cold. Since then, he finished the fireplace and installed a small set of solar panels that charged a battery system. The system produced a subsistence level of electricity, enough for limited refrigeration and, if the charge allowed, one to two LED lights in the evening.

Colorado's posture, hair, and physique were that of a seventy-year-old senior citizen. Three months earlier, he turned sixty. He stood over six feet tall but fell short of that with his stooped posture. His bloodshot eyes cleared less often than they used to due to his increased vodka consumption. His beard and hair were grizzled gray. Still, he was more substantial than most men, but his lower back issues slowed him down. He wore blue jeans, a green coat, and hiking boots.

His internal alarm triggered a small warning as he stepped out of the Blazer. He took a deep breath, stood erect, and scanned his property. The cabin was untouched. Every piece of grass, every pile of stones, and every mound of dirt was unchanged. He felt that everything was fine until he spotted a disturbance in the sand below a drain on the left side of his cabin. It wasn't like that four hours ago. A slight chill ran up his back. *Be careful.*

Colorado stepped back a half step and reached into his SUV's driver's side door.

The bullet exploded in the dirt next to his left foot.

A voice rang out. "Stand still and listen! You are surrounded. Put your hands on top of your head."

Colorado pulled away from the Blazer's door and put both hands on his head. "Who are you?" he asked.

"I'm Joe."

That was enough of an answer. Colorado almost smiled. In his experience, every enforcer was named Joe. The common name was the company cover. "Of course you are."

"And you are the infamous Joe Colorado."

"Just Colorado. I'm retired. Why all the talk?" They might as well get it over with if they wanted to kill him.

Joe laughed and said, "You'd be dead if we wanted you dead. But you have a unique skill set. We have a job for you—one that could earn your redemption. Which you don't deserve after the mess you made in Steamboat."

Colorado was forced to retire to save his life. He had a good run while he worked for the company, but it all fell apart three years ago. He had worked his way up in the organization from a security specialist to an enforcer and then a hitman. In the end, he became a disappearance expert. His career fell apart when a high-profile couple was meant to disappear in the mountains near Steamboat Springs. He eliminated the couple, but their death became national news, including graphic photos and accusative headlines. His client wasn't happy. Even though Colorado got the job done, it wasn't the unsolved disappearance the customer paid for. His employer had a zero-tolerance policy, and the mess in Steamboat was no exception.

Now, the hit was on him.

"It wasn't my fault. I walked into a setup and still completed the contract." Colorado's voice dropped in tone, with more than a hint of irritation. "You can tell Levitt—"

"I can tell Levitt what?" Joe asked.

Colorado cast his eyes downward. "You can tell him his interests are secure with me."

A fit, dark-skinned man stepped around a tree to Colorado's right and into the clearance in front of the cabin. His intelligent eyes and powerful physical stature demanded attention. "Good answer," he said. "You can drop your hands."

He didn't need to state the obvious; Colorado was still covered.

Joe tucked a long-barreled rifle under his arm. "This job requires your outdoor skill set and ability to think independently. You are offered this job because you were the best in the wilderness, but it looks like the years haven't been good to you. You look old and soft. I don't know if you can handle it."

Colorado didn't let his slight ruffle him. "I can handle it. I want you to know, and I want Mr. Levitt to know, that I appreciate the opportunity. I won't let you down."

Joe stared at Colorado for ten seconds before he stepped into the open. Joe pulled a large manila envelope from his back and dropped it into the dirt. "Your instructions are inside. This is a time-sensitive operation. Once you get off the mountain, follow protocol and transmit your information. If we don't hear from you within twelve hours, our relationship will be terminated."

Joe clicked his tongue and shook his head as he disappeared into the trees. When Colorado knew he was gone, he opened his Blazer's tailgate and went to work. He had hauled in the third load of supplies when, in the distance, he heard the roar of a helicopter in flight.

A few minutes later, he sat down at his table. He poured himself a glass of cheap vodka with a dash of water. He pondered his last three years of living alone in the mountains. He wasn't meant to be a hermit, but the vodka helped. He refilled his glass and opened the envelope.

CHAPTER EIGHT

I n the mountain air, Bright woke feeling cold and uncomfortable even though she slept in her clothes. She squirmed into a ball and tried to slide deep inside her sleeping bag. Anything to keep warm. The sound of something moving outside her tent had disturbed her fitful rest. She figured it was Rage and one of his buddies attempting to start a campfire.

She hoped so—she was so cold. She closed her eyes and tried to drift away; she was in no hurry to wake, and she was too cold to move. Suddenly, another sound prevented any hope of sleep from happening. It was a vehicle, maybe a truck. The tires crunched the dirt. After she scooted halfway out of her bag, she opened her tent's flap, slid onto her knees, and peeked out.

An older gray SUV was parked outside their camp and remained idling. Rage was out of his tent, and he positioned himself defensively between his companions and the truck.

Bright felt secure knowing whoever was behind the wheel would have to get past him, and if they were looking for trouble, they found it. Rage deserved his name. He would tear them apart.

"Who is that, Eddie?" The young man at the campfire asked.

"Shut up, don't call me by my old name. I'm Rage now—remember."

"Sorry."

The SUV's engine stopped, and a man stepped out of the driver's side door. He casually walked toward them, stopped, and leaned against the front end of his vehicle. With his butt supported by the vehicle's front bumper, his posture was relaxed and non-threatening.

"Good morning," he said in a loud, pleasant voice. "I'm glad I found you guys. I've driven all over these dirt roads."

The man was middle-aged, of average height and weight, and his hair was hidden under a blue baseball cap. He wore hiking boots, blue jeans, and a medium-weight khaki coat. He sported a pair of aviator-style sunglasses even though the sun was low in the sky. He was clean-shaven, with a light complexion that suggested he spent most of his time indoors. His big smile and strong voice were almost obnoxious. The Ninety-niners didn't see him as a threat.

He reminded Bright of a favorite neighbor who used to live across the street. He was a big-time lawyer who liked to fish. This guy looked like a lawyer in Levi's.

"What do you want?" Rage asked.

"First, I'm a friend and want to compliment you on a well-done job. If I'm in the right place, I believe a young woman here knows me." He looked at Bright, who was still half stuck inside her sleeping bag, and extended out the half-zipped door flap of her tent. She cocked her head.

He smiled and asked, "I've talked to you a few times on the phone—do you recognize my voice?"

Bright studied the man and grinned. "Yeah, it's him," she said.

"No, shit?" Rage asked.

"No shit," the man answered.

"Are you the guy who sent us the leads?" one of the other Ninety-niners asked.

"Yes, sir," the older man replied.

"Why?" Rage asked.

"That is a good question I'd like to discuss in-depth. But here's the short version. I can make a more significant difference in the world if I work with you than without you. That is what I believed when I contacted you, and that is what I'm sure of today. You guys did a hell of a job yesterday. I don't know if you realize the impact of your actions. You not only humiliated Bruce Arnold, but you also sent a message. Your video hit the internet with an incredible impact. Congratulations! The Ninety-niners made a statement heard around the world. I'm pleased to meet you. My name is Fred," he said.

Bright understood; they were on a first-name-only basis and probably fictitious ones. One after another, the young Ninety-niners introduced themselves using their code names. If everything fell apart for any reason, their identity would be protected.

"Excuse me for a moment," Fred said, opening the passenger side door of his SUV. He smiled as he carried out a large cardboard box and two large hydro flasks.

"I don't know what you guys like to eat in the morning, so I brought some good stuff for breakfast. I have ham and eggs on a muffin, sausage biscuits, pancakes, various pastries, and a dozen donuts. You can tell I love donuts." He patted his tummy. "There's some hot coffee, hot tea, and orange juice. Are you guys hungry? I know I am."

The Ninety-niners looked at each other, and nobody objected. Everybody was hungry. The Ninety-niners relaxed and surveyed the breakfast buffet.

Bright crawled out of the tent and slipped into a warm hoodie.

Rage grabbed two sausage biscuits and a sixteen-ounce cup of black coffee. He unwrapped the sausage biscuit, took a couple of large bites, and then washed it down with the coffee. He turned toward Bright, smiled, and flashed a thumbs up.

Bright cradled a large cup of hot tea and grabbed a couple of donuts. She felt the warmth from the inside out.

A few minutes later, Fred approached the fire pit, where a young man struggled to start a campfire.

"It's cold out here," Fred said. "Let me help. The wood around here isn't dry; it makes it hard to burn. Did you have much luck with the fire last night?"

"Kind of, but it kept going out."

"It can be difficult. An old friend taught me how to build a campfire years ago. Let me show you his trick."

CHAPTER NINE

F red sat in a collapsible camp chair he had brought with him. The chairs were a big hit with the kids, not as big as the surprise breakfast, but a close second. Good food, comfortable chairs, and hot drinks can win tremendous support on a frigid morning in the mountains. The Ninety-niners were a bunch of city kids who didn't seem comfortable roughing it. After sleeping on the ground last night, they were tired, hungry, and easy to please.

As Fred taught the kids his campfire-building methods, the kids let their guard down. Campfire-building was well-liked, so Fred expanded into other outdoor skills like outdoor cooking, bathing, and even the practice of constructing a campground outhouse. The more the kids listened, the more enthralled they became.

"Always respect nature," Fred said. "Remember to leave no trace when you camp under the western sky. What you carry in— you carry out."

After his lesson, Fred excused himself as the Ninety-niners warmed their hands in front of the blazing campfire. He picked up his chair and sat next to Bright and Rage, who huddled together. "Hi guys, do you have a few minutes?" he asked.

Bright and Rage sat on an eight-foot log at the front of the campsite's small parking area. Bright gestured toward an empty spot in front of them. Fred took it as an invitation, flipped open his chair, set it on the dirt, and half fell into the low-flung apparatus. It was a whole lot more comfortable than the log.

Fred said, "Rage, I'd like to answer your question. It's something I have pondered for a long time. We have different backgrounds, but we still have common goals. As a young man, I entered the corporate world and was successful. As my career progressed, I was exposed to the ugly underbelly of big business, where winning tactics are immoral, above the law, and profits are built on the working class's backs. There is no loyalty to humanity, business partners, or employees. In corporate culture, the elite sell their souls for cash. Lobbyists buy the obedience of government, and politicians demand a large share."

Fred stood up and looked around the campsite. He raised his eyes toward the sky and took a slow, deep breath. As he brought his eyes down, the lawyer in Levi's took on the image of an emotion-filled evangelist. A small tear ran down his cheek. "Change is needed."

Fred fell back into his chair, pulled a handkerchief out of his pocket, and dabbed his eyes. "But you are unique. You make a difference. I wish I did, but I don't. It's too late for me. Fortunately, I found a way to help when I found you. I'm a small part of the effort by supporting you with information."

"Good answer. I like it." Rage's voice trailed off. Then he whispered, "Thanks… I want to continue our relationship." He looked at Bright.

"I agree," she said.

"I watched the video you posted on social media. It was great," Fred said.

"We uploaded the files, and our guys back home took it from there. I'd bet all the sites have deleted or blocked it by now." Rage said.

"No doubt, but it had an impact while it was there," Fred said with emphasis. "It looked like it came from a professional studio."

"No, only a high-powered computer," Bright said.

"Your video had a strong ending—war. It was impressive and impactful."

"We got the idea from you," Bright said, surprised he commented.

"I know, but your execution was better than I imagined."

"If it made an impact, it was worth it. The one percent need to take us seriously," Bright said as she clenched her fist.

"Whether your threat is real or not, it doesn't matter; you will be taken seriously. Your mission at the airport, its national exposure, and the threat of escalation will leave no doubt." Fred looked up at the sky again and took a deep breath. "Now you have a new problem. You'll draw more attention from law enforcement."

Rage stood up and frowned. "I don't give a shit about the cops. They are out to screw us, anyway."

Bright interjected. "Everything we have done is worth it. Human life cannot be taken lightly. I've been unwilling to accept bloodshed, but now, if the cops become violent, it's fair if we respond in kind."

"I think it's more than fair," Fred said. "Rage, how do you feel about it?"

Rage nodded. "I agree with her. If the cops start a fight, I'll be ready to finish it."

"You two are great leaders because you are different, yet you complement each other with your strengths. You make a great team."

"Thanks," Bright said. "But you aren't here this morning to talk about us. Where are we at on our next operation?"

Fred scooted closer to the pair as if someone might hear them. "We are on schedule. Bruce Arnold and two business associates will leave on the trail ride Tuesday morning. I was concerned the trip could be canceled after your action at the airport, but Bruce Arnold is a stubborn man. He refuses to cancel the trip."

"As you expected," Rage said. "You know how Arnold thinks, don't you?"

"Arnold never compromises, and he never changes his mind. He is well known for those qualities. Interestingly, he won't cancel what I would call a *vacation trip*. Bruce works seven days a week and never takes time off. This trail ride is important to him."

"It sounds like nothing has changed," Bright said.

"That's pretty much true. Arnold has bought out the entire trip. It will be Arnold and his two guests, plus the hosts from Starr Outfitters. There has been an effort to convince Bruce Arnold to bring extra security. Time will tell what he decides on that."

"So, how many people?" Bright asked.

"Probably one." Fred held up his index finger.

Bright stared at the burning campfire. After inhaling, she said, "I don't think we should change our plans."

"Are you guys ready?" Fred asked.

"Yes. We've collected enough backpacking gear and dehydrated food to get us in and out." Rage said.

"You'll travel through some rough country. It will be rigorous, especially if you backpack." Fred sounded concerned.

"We're aware of the challenge. Fitness is a concern, so we've been training. We've been lifting weights and running. We run at least five miles a day," Bright said.

"Four of us will be on the mission: Bright, myself, Torch, and Digit." Rage said.

Fred fought back a smile. "Do you have any questions on logistics?" Fred asked.

"We've gone through the map you sent us. We even watched a pretty good video online. The route appears to be marked with adequate signage. Still, it would be easy to get lost," Rage said.

"As long as you stay on the trail, you should be fine," Fred said.

"We may be forced off trail," Bright said.

"I see your concern, but if you carefully note the landmarks, you'll find your way back. Anything else?" Fred asked.

Rage answered Fred with a severe deadpan expression. "Yeah, I have a big concern. I'm concerned about you."

"I'm here, and I'm listening." Fred made strong eye contact.

Rage leaned closer to Fred. "I get it; you have a wife and kids. So, it's too late for you to become one of us. But did you bring your family to Idaho? If you left them behind, why not join us for this mission? We could use your help."

Fred shook his head and took a deep breath. "Rage, you've asked a fair question. And you're right; I'm up here alone—I should go with you. My problem is that I'm older and have a bad knee. I might slow you down. But I have an idea."

"Let's hear it." Rage raised his voice slightly.

"When I was a kid, there was a western on TV where a bunch of cowboys herded cattle over long distances through dangerous conditions. They had an edge because a scout rode ahead and led them through all kinds of trouble. I could be your scout. I could ride ahead of you or swing back and check your rear. I know where to get a good horse, and I'd have great mobility with one. We could stay in touch by radio. I could scout the trail, and we could react if we see a problem."

Rage leaned back and almost fell off the log. Bright looked at Rage and giggled.

Rage righted himself. "You took me by surprise. That is the

last thing I thought you'd say. You have a hell of a good idea—a scout on horseback!"

"I like it too," Bright said. "But we'll need to talk to the rest of our group. We make decisions together, and everyone has an equal voice."

Fred looked at the pair, nodded, and smiled. "Why don't I leave you to care for your own?" Fred said. "You deserve privacy."

"I'd bet everyone will approve of your idea, but we need to be sure," Bright said.

"I'll line up a horse and pick up a two-way radio set. Let's get together here tomorrow morning. I'll bring breakfast."

CHAPTER TEN

The sun peaked over the mountains to the east, the air was crisp and cold, the sky was blue, and it was time to ride. Brett stood outside of the Coogan's condo. He was ready to pound on Tom's door to roust him and his daughter, but after a second thought, he changed his mind. He had just finished his third cup of coffee and had a caffeine buzz. No need to push. They were all on vacation, after all.

Mark walked out of his condo, looked at Brett, and said, "I'm driving, okay?"

"Fine with me; we're pulling your trailer."

Sage and Tom showed up right on time. Tom opened his condo's front door one last time and yelled upstairs. "Nick, are you sure you don't want to come? We have two extra horses."

"No thanks, Dad. We're playing golf."

"Golf?" Tom shook his head and closed the door.

Fifteen minutes later, they pulled up to Victory Stables. Mark's trailer was parked right outside of the main entrance. Mark hitched it to his Ford F250 while Sage and Brett went inside to gather the horses and tack. The horses had been grazing in the main pasture, and knowing the Riders were on their way, Pat returned them to their stalls. They were ready to go.

Victory Stable's young handler led Mark's horse out first. Mark is a man of many horses, and he brought four on this trip. He knew they would need to pack extra gear and supplies when they rode the tour. He smiled as Trixie stepped up the loading ramp. In many ways, Trixie was his favorite.

She was a beautiful, tall Palomino. Her golden coat set off her long, blond mane. Last year, their friend, FBI Agent DeShawn Terry, rode her on a technical climb on a dangerous trail. When they crossed a thin ridge, DeShawn pushed Trixie the wrong way, forcing them both into a precarious position. Trying to coach the pair out of trouble, Mark told DeShawn to let go of the reins, grab the saddle horn, give Trixie a nudge, and let her take charge. She did. Trixie proved herself to be a real mountain horse that day. DeShawn learned to trust her, and now both Mark and DeShawn loved Trixie.

Next, Tom loaded his horse, Buck. Tom had purchased Buck from Mark several years ago. Both Tom and Buck were thrilled with the deal. Now Buck was Tom's horse—loyal and protective. Buck was a big, healthy quarter horse, always eager for a ride. Sometimes, Buck could be a little headstrong, ready to spit out the bit, but he always calmed down after he was on the trail. He was excited to go.

Sage led out Tonto next. Tonto climbed into his slot, but not before pausing to examine a rag someone must have dropped. He turned toward Mark as if to question, "Why is it there?" The Pinto was almost too bright.

Brett brought up the rear with Pepper, a tall gelding. His coat was dark brown, almost black; his hooves were striped, and his mouth and nose were mottled. A white speckled blanket covered his hind and flanks, the markings common to the breed. Pepper's features were indicative of his roots, the legendary

Indian horse, Appaloosa. Lots of lore exists about Appaloosas' courage, durability, and intelligence. In Pepper's case, he was well-trained and easy to ride. Brett sometimes jumped on him bareback, and with only a piece of bailing twine looped around his neck, they would glide around the foothills. Pepper didn't need a bridle; he had never tasted a bit. He was a hackamore horse.

Mark took the wheel and smiled; four horses and four riders were all on board. It was time for the Rider's Club to hit the trail. Mark drove up Highway 75. Even pulling the four-horse trailer, Mark's pickup handled the uphill climb with ease.

Thirty minutes later, Brett stood at the 8,700-foot Galena Summit lookout and scanned the skyline. He inhaled the warm morning light that enhanced every detail. Even though he had been here many times, he had to stop and look. Brett didn't get to see this view often enough. The headwaters of the Salmon River started as a trace and grew as it traveled through the Sawtooth Valley and expanded as it roared through some of the most spectacular landscapes in the West. In the end, it merged with the mighty Snake.

Brett spoke to Sage while they viewed the valley. "The first time I came here was right after I finished my enlistment in the Army. A group of us drove into a campground on Red Fish Lake. It was dark, and I was tired. I crawled out of my tent at sunrise, and as I stood on the lake's shore, I was overcome by its beauty. I didn't realize how majestic Red Fish Lake, the mountains, and the rest of the valley were. That was the day I became connected to Idaho."

Brett pointed. "Look to the right. See where that dirt road leads into the mountains? Look past it until you see another smaller trace running parallel. That's the road that leads to the Cub Lake Trailhead."

A horse whinnied from the trailer parked behind them.

"Settle down! We will be back in a minute." Sage yelled. "That's Tonto; he wants to know what's happening."

"And I thought Pepper was the only one that needed to know."

Brett yelled to the rest of the Rider's Club, "Hey, you guys ready? Tonto is getting impatient. We've got to go."

They drove for another hour and were relieved when they arrived and saddled their horses at the base of the Cub Lake Trailhead.

The Rider's Club wasn't dressed in casual clothes. They were cowboyed out, wearing cowboy boots, cowboy hats, Levis, and medium-weight coats. Sage was dressed similarly except under her jacket; she wore a lady's teal long-sleeved snap-up shirt with pearl snaps.

They packed lunch for themselves, grain for the horses, and spread the extra supplies between them before saddling up. The horses relaxed and surveyed their surroundings, except for Buck. He was nervous, agitated, and ready to go. He spun around and kicked Mark's trailer with both back hooves. Hard. The empty trailer boomed like a bass drum.

Tom grabbed Buck's reins and pulled him away from the trailer. "He's getting impatient," Tom said. "Sorry."

"I think we all are," Mark said. "Let's get going."

As usual, Brett pulled Pepper out into the lead. Mark, riding Trixie, lined up behind Brett, then Sage on Tonto, and Tom brought up the rear, riding Buck. After a quarter-mile, the trail opened, and the Riders rode side by side. It was a good day to ride in the mountains; the morning cool had already begun to burn off; a cloudless day welcomed them. Their pace was comfortable, and they enjoyed riding together.

A creek flowed alongside the trail as the riders slowly gained altitude as they traveled at a relaxed, comfortable pace. They rode past several groups of backpackers, climbed up a few steep sections, and crossed the same stream twice. The terrain varied but wasn't technical, and the horses were rewarded with several ideal drinking spots.

There were some families with kids along the trail; the kids probably didn't appreciate the perfect introduction to hiking. One little girl planted herself in the dirt on the side of the trail. Her arms were wrapped around her knees, which she hugged to her chest. She defiantly stared at her dad and refused to budge.

After narrowing for a mile, the trail opened again, and the riders climbed the last steep stretch to Cub Lake. There were no dramatic cliffs and rock-strewn beaches at Cub Lake. Instead, the grasslands surrounding it were a calming, park-like deep green. There were few beaches. The west side of the lake flattened into a spongy wetland. The other grass-covered shorelines sloped up and away from the water. Aspen trees were interspersed with pines and surrounded the grass. A mile to the east, a mountainous backdrop finished off the picture-perfect scene.

Brett led the riders to a secluded area on the lake's east side, where they dismounted. There were several spots where the horses could graze. Sage and Brett spread a couple of tarps on a flat area while Mark and Tom cared for the horses.

As they set up a lengthy picket line, Tom checked his watch and shook his head. "Hey, Mark. We need to make sure Brett's fishing doesn't screw up this trip."

"I know."

"When did he become a fisherman? The last I heard, he got frustrated and gave up the sport."

"I don't know; suddenly, he wants to fish." Mark shook his head in disbelief. "I'll try to think of something. After we get to Mica Lake, we'll have an hour's break before we ride back. We need to get home for dinner. If Brett goes fishing, we could be there all night."

Brett smirked as his friends talked about him noisily. He

understood his pathetic fishing history. He had proven himself as an athlete, soldier, and scholar, but had never been much of a fisherman. However, this was the perfect vacation to try again. He wouldn't give up.

With the first leg of their ride behind them, they all settled in to have a comfortable lunch. They didn't use any outdoor skills to make it; instead, they had packed deli sandwiches, coleslaw, potato salad, fresh apples, assorted soft drinks, and beer. Brett thought it was a perfect time to discuss the meeting he had the night before.

"I met with DeShawn and Kelly Hawk last night. DeShawn wanted me to say hi. I flipped him a little crap since we hadn't seen him for a while. He was embarrassed. I bet he would like to ride with us sometime." Brett said.

"He's always welcome," Mark said.

"He has his hands full with security issues after the Ninety-niners attack at the airport. One of his big concerns is a scheduled trip with Bruce Arnold and a couple of his associates."

"You mean his friends?" Mark asked.

"I don't think so; no one ever used the term *friends*. When they say *associates*, it must relate to someone with a business relationship or an employee. Mr. Arnold isn't known to have friends." Brett said.

"That sucks," Sage said.

"It might be the high price of being a billionaire," Tom said.

"Anyway, they hired an outfitter out of Stanley, and this Tuesday, they're taking the Trilogy Lakes Tour on horseback."

Everyone stopped eating and looked wide-eyed at Brett.

"That's why DeShawn and Kelly Hawk wanted to get together. When DeShawn learned about our plans, he figured we had spent time studying the tour."

"And we did," Mark said.

"So, what's going on?" Tom asked.

"I walked them through the entire trip and discussed security. It didn't help much; we didn't develop ideas other than the obvious. Bruce Arnold and his associates shouldn't go. It's too risky."

"Let me guess. Arnold wants to go, and no one can talk him out of it," Sage said.

"That's right."

"He has the reputation of being aggressively stubborn," Sage added.

"You'd have a hell of a time talking me out of the tour," Tom said.

"I told them the four of us were riding up here today, and I'd bring you guys up to date. Maybe we can come up with something that could help."

"They should bring a security team with them," Mark said.

"We came to the same conclusion, and Kelly called someone on Arnold's staff about it. After being pressured, Arnold agreed to bring one extra man. Two or three would have been better, but an extra man helped. I hope he can ride a horse."

"No shit," Tom said.

"We could join them and ride together," Mark said.

"I don't like that at all," Tom said. "It could ruin our trip."

"I'd do it to help, but I'd bet Arnold wouldn't like it either. He bought out an outfitter's trip for twelve. He sounds like someone who doesn't want company," Brett said.

"If we're willing to move our ride up one day, we could ride a half day ahead or behind them. If we did that, we could help if they needed support. If there aren't any problems, both parties will stay apart. We'd ride the tour as if they weren't there." Mark suggested.

"Interesting," Brett replied. "We'd need to have radio contact with them. If they had a problem, at least they could let us know. Even if we were half a day away, we'd be their closest support."

"And if there weren't any problems, they wouldn't screw up our vacation," Tom said.

"Any other thoughts?" Brett asked.

No one volunteered anything else, not even Mark.

"Would everyone be okay with riding out on Tuesday?" Brett asked.

"We're fine with it, right, Sage?" Tom said.

"Fine by me," she said.

"I'll call DeShawn tonight and see what he thinks," Brett said.

"I have another thought," Mark said. "If this happens, we'd need to be in radio contact with Arnold's group, the police, and even the FBI. It could be a pain in the ass. We aren't the Rider's Club *babysitters.*"

Brett couldn't believe Mark's snarky remark. Then it hit him. *He's setting us up for another one of his crazy ideas.*

"Your point?" Brett asked.

"If we do this, DeShawn should ride with us. He's the FBI agent. He could manage all the external communication. We're on vacation. He's not. I have a special horse for him, and it would be fun to have him with us. And he's ridden with the Rider's Club before."

"I doubt he would be able to do that. He's busy with his team in Sun Valley."

"His team in Sun Valley won't be worth a damn if we run into armed terrorists, but if an armed FBI agent rode with us, he could be an equalizer.

"Tell him we have one condition. We won't do it unless he rides with us."

CHAPTER ELEVEN

F red turned down the tight dirt road that led to the Ninety-niners' camp. This morning was a little warmer than yesterday, with scattered clouds and almost no wind. The comforting skies lit up the valley and brought with it an uplifting feeling. Hopefully, it was a sign of what the day would bring.

He pulled to the edge of the campsite and grinned. *The young group had made progress.* They had built a fire, a real campfire. The group's eyes turned toward him as he sat behind the wheel. They were all awake and a hive of activity. Just yesterday morning, they were cold and reluctant to leave their tents. They were a quick study, and a comfortable morning probably helped, too.

He reminded himself not to underestimate the young group. He took a deep breath, smiled, and stepped out of his SUV. "I hope I'm not too late with breakfast. I stopped at the Wrap House in Ketchum. They were pretty busy, but they were worth the wait. They're the best."

Smiles erupted from the hungry kids.

He hoisted a large cardboard box, walked to an area outside the fire ring, and spread out the feast. "Okay, this morning's selection of wraps are ham and egg, sausage and egg, bacon and egg, huevos rancheros, and vegetarian. There's a lot of food here. We have bottled water, orange juice, and coffee. And again, for your sweet tooth, donuts. I also have my favorite, maple bars."

Fred grabbed a sausage and egg wrap, poured himself a coffee, and fell into one of the camp chairs. He addressed Bright and Rage and asked, "Do you want to get together now or after breakfast?"

"We're all here, so let's do it," Bright said. She smiled at Rage and winked.

"Attention!" Rage rose to his feet and shouted. "Everyone who wants Fred to be our scout, give a thumbs up."

All eight members stood up and raised their fists with their thumbs up.

Bright smiled at Fred. "That's unanimous. Welcome to the family."

The group enjoyed breakfast for the next half-hour and discussed the mission. Fred thanked everyone for their support and said he would work hard to make their mission safe and successful.

After breakfast, he sat down with Bright, Rage, Torch, and Digit. "Since I'll be on horseback while you guys are on the backpacking trails, I thought we needed to address communications. I purchased a set of two-way radios and a GPS."

He pulled a matched set of two-way radios out of a box. "With these, we can talk, even if we're miles apart." The Ninety-niners passed the radios from one to another.

When Digit got his hands on the radio, he pulled his long black hair into a ponytail and checked the controls. "It's been a while, but I've used these before. Radios like this are old tech, but they will work better in the mountains than cell phones."

"You're in charge of communications," Rage said.

"I'm good with that," Digit replied, flashing his inquisitive eyes and nervous smile.

Fred turned to Digit. "This radio set has a hundred channels and two charged batteries, which should get us through. I have them both set on channel twelve. Let's set up a system to rotate channels after each conversation."

"Good idea," Digit said.

"Here's the GPS. If we need to go off the trail, it will be indispensable."

Digit held the small device and toggled through the modes on its display. "This is great."

"Any questions?" Fred asked.

"No. I got it."

Rage reassured Fred that Digit knew what he was doing. He was a third-year tech student at Oregon State.

Fred shook his head and smiled. He pulled a cell phone from the box and dropped it into Bright's hands. "You mentioned you didn't bring cell phones on this trip."

"That's right," she said. "They're too easy to trace."

"This is a burner phone. It's loaded with twelve hours of service. It has never been used and is unregistered. This phone should stay with your team at the base camp. We can call them for support if we have an emergency on the trail. It's unlikely you'll use it. If you don't, when you finish this trip or are concerned about exposure, destroy it or throw it away."

"I thought cell phones wouldn't work in the wilderness," Bright said.

"This phone will work here, but not in the Sawtooths. My phone will; I brought a satellite phone."

"What do you think, Digit?" Bright asked.

"Mr. Fred here has it nailed," Digit beamed.

Fred smiled again. "I understand your mission's objective is to make a spectacular example out of Bruce Arnold. Am I correct?" Fred asked.

"Yeah, I'd say you're close. We want to make it personal with Mr. Arnold, and we want to show the world." Rage said.

"Are you going to kill him?"

"That will depend on Mr. Arnold. We prefer to video him making amends. He needs to be accountable for his actions. He needs to make reparations."

Fred closed his eyes and looked at his feet. He took a deep breath and exhaled through his nose. He settled, raised his head, and looked at Rage. "Don't forget. Bruce Arnold is an *asshole*. Everything must be done his way, or he'll throw a fit. Will he be accountable for his actions? I doubt it. He'll threaten you instead."

"If we have to get tough, we have a backup plan," Rage said.

"What's that?"

"We'll tie a rope around his neck and throw him off a cliff."

"Really! Would you shoot a video of that?" Fred's eyebrows almost disappeared into his hairline.

"Either way, we'll shoot a video and upload it online," Rage said.

"Are you looking for a dramatic location?" Fred asked.

"An isolated towering tree or a cliff with a dramatic backdrop could be useful. We should be able to find something spectacular."

"I know the perfect spot," Fred said. "Lookout Ridge is famous; it's between Kimberly Lake and Christine Lake. The trail climbs up one side of the ridge and down the other. There is a flat area at the top with a three-hundred-sixty-degree view. The ridgetop sits above eleven thousand feet."

Rage slapped his hands together and said, "Lookout Ridge— sounds perfect."

CHAPTER TWELVE

DeShawn missed two calls from Brett—too many meetings. To make up for it, he made a morning house call. Brett opened his condo door as DeShawn stepped out of the car.

"Hey, you didn't need to come over," Brett said, gripping his friend's hand.

"No problem. I've had a hell of a time getting out of that hotel. I thought this job would be simple and easy when we came here. Now, it's turned into chaos."

"I bet," Brett said.

DeShawn stepped into the front entrance of Brett's condo. "I checked on the business card. I believe it could be Tony Levitt," DeShawn said.

Tony Levitt was an organized crime boss who worked out of Reno. He controlled multiple businesses, including a thriving group of gambling properties, related personal entertainment, and a wholesale network distributing stolen merchandise. His distribution business sold everything from diamonds to illegal drugs. He made a fortune running a zero-tolerance system that kept him distanced from the law until last year when a crime ring backed by Levitt burglarized Tom Coogan's retail stores.

With the support of FBI Agent DeShawn Terry, the Rider's Club ended the burglary ring's operations. Tony Levitt's distribution system was seized and shut down. All the significant players were arrested and prosecuted except Tony Levitt, who was released on bail by a *friendly judge*.

"Is he still out on bail?" Brett asked.

"Yes. Levitt has another hearing in a few weeks, and his attorney is pressing for a dismissal. He argued the prosecution didn't provide enough evidence to tie him to his wholesale network."

"That's ridiculous."

"It appears Tony's influence may go further than we believed."

"Is he attending the conference?"

"He's not registered as an attendee, but he could be here under a corporate name. I'm sure he's wealthy enough to be invited. Since it isn't illegal for him to be here, we can't arrest him."

DeShawn pulled Levitt's business card out of his pocket and read the note. "*'I hope you enjoy the Trilogy Lakes. Be careful out there. See you soon.'* I take that as a veiled threat. Do you?"

"Yes, but he picked his words carefully. There's a message there. Levitt knows we're here to ride the Trilogy Lakes Tour. This may be a threat, or maybe he wants to scare us. Either way, I don't like it—it's pure Tony Levitt."

"Maybe you should call off the ride?"

Brett and DeShawn maintained eye contact for a few seconds.

"The rest of the Rider's Club are having breakfast next door. Let's share this information with them and let them help decide." Brett said.

———

Brett opened the Coogan's front door and marched into the living area. "Look who I found lost in the parking lot."

DeShawn bounced into the room. "Good morning, everybody!"

"DeShawn, it's good to see you. How about a cup of coffee? I just brewed a fresh pot." Tom jumped up and gave DeShawn a handshake and half a hug.

"Hey, buddy, it's been a long time," Mark added.

Mark shook DeShawn's hand and slapped his shoulder.

"I'll take you up on that coffee, and since you're all here, I've got a story to tell you," DeShawn said.

They caught up as they feasted on a pancake and scrambled egg breakfast. Tom and Mark had taken over the cooking duties. Tom scrambled the eggs, and Mark flipped the pancakes. He only burned a few.

Tom, Mark, and DeShawn had built a strong friendship. Tom mildly reprimanded DeShawn for being a stranger. With a large mug of black coffee in hand, in the shade of a large pine tree on the condo's back deck, DeShawn filled in the friends.

"So, tell them your story," Brett opened up the conversation.

"All right." DeShawn's smile disappeared, and he sat forward in his chair. "It appears Tony Levitt may be in Sun Valley, across the street at the conference."

"Is it legal to cross state lines when he's out on bail?" Mark asked.

"Yes, he can be here legally. There are no restrictions on his bail."

"Did you see him?" Mark's posture stiffened.

"No. Brett's friend, Kelly Hawk, saw him at the Inn, and Levitt asked him to give Brett his card. Kelly's description of Levitt was accurate. Levitt wrote a note on the card that said, 'I hope you enjoy the Trilogy Lakes. Be careful out there. See you soon.'"

Brett let the information settle and then said, "I hoped we were done with that asshole. His note is a threat, and I don't like threats."

"Either do I," DeShawn muttered.

Tom stared down his nose and frowned. "Tricky asshole, isn't he?"

"Is there any legal recourse at all? Mark asked.

"No. Levitt used his words too carefully," DeShawn said, putting his coffee mug down on the table. "So, I have a question for you guys. Why don't you hang out in Sun Valley, enjoy your vacation, and call off the Trilogy Lakes Tour?"

"What? No way!" Mark blurted.

"I'm with Mark; we won't call off the trip," Tom said.

"DeShawn, I should have told you. Tony Levitt can't scare the Rider's Club, which I bet is what he wanted to do. Right?" Brett eyed Tom and then Mark.

"Right." Tom and Mark said in unison.

"We'll be at the Sun Valley Gun Club for a little target shooting this afternoon. Now we have an excellent excuse to take our guns on our ride," Tom said.

"I think we've said enough about Levitt," Brett said. "We have an idea to discuss with you." Brett faced DeShawn.

DeShawn said, "Okay."

"While we were up at Cub Lake yesterday, I updated everyone on our Trilogy Lakes discussion, and we did come up with a plan that might help," Brett said.

"It's a simple idea," Mark said.

"So, this is your idea, Mark?" DeShawn raised his eyebrows.

"Well, yeah. The best of several."

DeShawn took a deep breath, smiled, and said, "Okay, let me have it."

Mark started talking fast. "It's an idea that won't solve all your security issues, but it might help. We could move up our ride one day, so we'd travel on the same days as Arnold. Depending on the time they take off, we could be three or four hours ahead or behind them. We could keep our eyes open and stay in radio contact, and if there are any problems, we'd be close enough to help. Remember, we're on horseback. We could close in quickly. And, if the ride is trouble-free, we won't make contact. We'd be invisible."

DeShawn picked his mug back up from the patio table, stared at the black liquid, and after a few seconds, said, "Our boss and our agents spent most of last night on this problem, and we didn't come up with much. Your idea is better than anything our team suggested. I like it. I like it a lot."

"We do have one concern," Brett said. "We're ready to ride, camp, and have fun, but we'll be ineffective if we're not tied in with Arnold's group. Someone needs to take charge of communication. We'd need to be able to check in with law enforcement and Arnold's team. We won't be able to do that while we're fishing. We'd need someone committed to the job."

"I can see your point. Do you want to bring someone else along?"

"Yes," Mark said. "We want to bring you. You're the FBI agent."

"What? I can't go. I already have a job." DeShawn lifted his chin and stiffened his back.

"We're talking about tomorrow. You've worked with us before. No one else will be prepared or qualified." Brett said.

"Oh, no. You guys aren't talking me into this again."

"I questioned Mark's idea when I first heard it. Then it grew on me—it made sense. Brett said. "Just take a breath and consider it."

"I see your point, but no. I'm up here as part of a team. My boss would never allow it."

"He might after he thinks about it. He might want an agent

nearby if there is a major problem. Does he have a better idea on how to protect one of the world's most important billionaires?"

"You don't know my boss. I don't think he'd go for it."

"Okay, DeShawn, here's the kicker. I brought an extra horse. I brought Trixie." Mark said.

DeShawn leaned forward. He stared at the deck floor. "You're kidding. I bet you're riding Rondo, not Trixie. You usually do." His voice wavered a little.

"I'm not bullshitting you, DeShawn. I wouldn't do that," Mark said. "We brought two extra horses; one of them is Trixie."

"Trixie?" DeShawn shook his head and looked back at the floor.

Everyone waited. No one said a word.

Finally, DeShawn's eyes rose, and he squared his shoulders. "No Promises. I'll talk to my boss."

CHAPTER THIRTEEN

A lex Ford drove his twenty-year-old pickup into the large dirt parking area downhill from the Badger Lake Trail Head. He stepped out of his truck and stretched his sore leg. After massaging his right calf, Alex threw on his backpack and marched uphill with a minor limp. Arthritis in his right knee often radiated soreness toward his lower leg muscles whenever he spent more than an hour behind the wheel, but he didn't care. He was excited to ride the Trilogy Lakes Tour for the third time.

Alex turned seventy last March. He wasn't a kid anymore, even though he acted like one sometimes. Alex was tall and rangy; he wore an old pair of Levi's, well-worn roper boots, an insulated tan coat, and a University of Idaho baseball cap. His short hair turned gray a while back, and over the last five years, he added an extra ten pounds around his midsection. His sky-blue eyes, his hook nose, and his rough beard matched his lively disposition. For an older guy, Alex was physically strong and still tough as nails. He grinned with excitement as his limp faded away.

Up the trail, he spotted a couple of early risers hard at work with a string of horses and a pile of gear. It was just past sunrise, and he wasn't the first on-site—*impressive*.

The morning sun lit Badger Lake, the surrounding mountains, and the forest. Summer weather was holding firm, but cold temperatures owned the mornings in the high country, even on days like this. At this altitude, lodgepole Pines and Douglas Fir dominated. A large section the ridge to the east showed wildfire recovery signs. A thick grove of aspens had started to overgrow the decaying remains of charred pines. The contrast and beauty of the old and new, the dead and living, told their own story. The morning light told another tale, creating dramatic reflections on Badger Lake's smooth surface.

Alex suspected he had found the outfitters he had come to meet. They worked in a roadside cutout reserved for outfitters near the trailhead. A youngish woman with blonde hair was busy unpacking a stack of boxes.

"Good morning," Alex shouted as he walked off the trail.

The lady turned and beamed. With her athletic build and feminine physique, she was more than good-looking. She was dressed in full-on cowgirl garb. She wore jeans, a snap-up western shirt, boots, and a straw cowgirl hat. Her skin was perfect and makeup-free, and her ponytail slipped out of her hat and bounced left and right while she worked.

"Good morning to you too, good sir," she said.

"I'm looking for Starr Outfitters."

"Well, you found them, and its boss. I'm Ruby Starr," she said.

Alex offered his hand. "I'm Alex Ford. Were you notified of the change? I replaced a younger buck."

"Yes, sir, I was. I've received several calls from your corporate office in the last few days."

"And you've heard about their concerns?"

"Yes, thoroughly, and I get it. These are weird times."

"Yeah, that's an excellent way to put it. I hope the whole situation is overblown. I doubt we will see any problems out here in the wilderness. It's the wrong place for any political crap. Bruce has been pressured from all sides to call off this trip, but he has studied the Trilogy Lakes Tour for a long time and is excited to go. He's a stressed businessman who needs a break, and I believe this trip will benefit him. He called me and asked me to come. My job is to make sure we're all safe."

"I appreciate that, Mr. Ford, and the help, but—"

"Please call me Alex, and please speak your mind."

"Well, Alex, you aren't quite what I expected. When I picture a big corporation's security officer, I expect someone with a little more—say *military bearing*."

"Yeah, I get it, and *military* describes the individual I replaced. The Seattle office assigned a capable young man, but Bruce was a little shaken after the attack at the airport. He had had enough, so he called me. You see, Bruce and I go way back. We were family friends before he built his empire. I worked as a cop most of my life, and Bruce looked to me when he needed to create a security department. I developed Yoster's security department and trained many excellent young military types. Five years ago, I retired."

"He called you after you retired, and you still came?" Ruby asked.

"Exactly."

"You must be close."

Alex chuckled. "Sometimes I'm treated like an employee and sometimes like an uncle. I'm never sure where I stand, but I don't care. What is important right now is *you*. You need to understand I'm no kid, but I'm good at what I do. That's why Bruce called. He is out of his element, so he needs *me* here."

"Mr. Ford, I get it. I'm convinced. Welcome aboard." Ruby said.

"Ruby, it's Alex, not Mr. Ford."

Ruby smiled and said, "Sorry. So, Alex, what's your plan?"

"The element of risk is low on this trip. The Ninety-niners are out of their element, and we're ready. I've been on this trip twice before, so I know the lay of the land. If we run into problems, we'll take care of them. We have two helicopters on standby, one medical, the other tactical; both are fifteen minutes out. I packed a satellite phone, a radio, a GPS, and the appropriate weapons. We have a backup team on horseback a few hours behind us. Don't worry; you will never know they are there. This is all about an invisible presence at work. It will not affect your tour."

"Let's hope, for their sake, the Ninety-niners don't show. It sounds like they could find themselves in deep shit." Ruby said.

Alex chuckled again. "Are you carrying firearms?"

"Yes, I have a rifle, and so does my nephew, our wrangler. We carry them just in case there's a problem—usually wildlife issues. In five years, we've never pulled a trigger."

"If we have a problem, let me take the lead, okay?"

"Yes, sir, I wouldn't have it any other way. I have a question for you, too. Can you ride a horse?"

"Yes, ma'am. After I retired, my wife and I moved to Cascade. We have a small ranch with four horses. I ride every day. And I checked out your horses. You have some outstanding stock. I apologize. I'm slowing you down this morning. I can see you still have a lot of work. How can I help?" Alex asked.

Ruby grabbed Alex's shoulder and kissed him on the cheek.

"Can you pack a horse?"

———

A few hours later, Ruby stood in front of her customers, ready to get the trip started.

"Please gather around, folks," Ruby yelled. "Thank you for

choosing Starr Outfitters as your guide on this special ride. We operate through the fall season and lead various adventures, but the Trilogy Lakes Tour is our favorite and the best. We enjoy our job and love to ride horseback through Idaho's wilderness."

Alex, Bruce Arnold, and his associates, Luis Perez and Michael Lane, were bunched together while they listened. A young man stood next to Ruby.

"My name is Ruby Starr; I'm in charge of this outfit. This young man is my nephew, Randy."

Ruby put her arm across his shoulders and gave him a small hug. Randy was a fit young man with short blond hair, light green eyes, and a week-old fuzzy beard.

"I'm thrilled to have Randy here. He's on summer break from Idaho State University. Randy will be your wrangler for this trip, and he is also our camp manager.

"I'm your chef. You'll be eating well. I've been cooking over a fire for a long time and have it down pat. After a day in the saddle, we want you to rest, relax, and have fun. We'll take care of the rest."

Ruby was probably used to an excited and smiling audience at this point, but she looked a little disappointed. There was no reaction from the group. Alex smiled, but the other three tech company executives showed little emotion. They looked distant and deadpan.

This was a tough group.

"Typically, we have a dozen guests with us. Today, we have the four of you.

That's fantastic; we'll have more flexibility and creativity with a small group like this. I'm excited." Ruby's voice was bright and clear.

"To give you a little background about yours truly. After college, I worked as a competitive cowgirl on the professional rodeo circuit. I competed as a barrel racer, a sport that requires speed and agility. I did well on the circuit and loved the four years I competed. So, folks, I know a lot about horses and riding, and I plan to turn all of you into better horseback riders. I left the rodeo to start my career. I moved to Montana and went to work for the best outfitter in the state. It was a wonderful experience, and after five years, I moved here and started my own outfit. I learned how to do it right in Montana, and now Starr Outfitters is the best in the Sawtooth Valley."

While Ruby spoke, Randy slipped away from the group.

Ruby continued her pep rally. "If I were to point out one quality where we stand out, I would say it is our horses. All our stock comes from good bloodlines, and they are in their prime. They are trained, gentled, and screened to ensure the qualities needed for a trip like this."

"Excuse me," Alex interrupted, attempting to help her garner some responses. "All you guys know, I own horses. I've checked out Ruby's horses, and I've got to tell you, they are fine stock, as good as I've seen."

"Thanks, Alex," Ruby said. "All our horses on the ride have been through the Trilogy Lakes Tour. They are intelligent animals, and they have the trail down. They know where they are going. You can depend on them. When in doubt, let them lead, and they will find the way. Thanks to all of you for taking our survey. I asked several specific questions about your horsemanship history. I'm pleased to see all of you have ridden before. It is not always the case. Now it's time for a special moment together. The information you provided helped a lot. I want to introduce you to your new partners."

Randy led in the first horse, and the tech executives' deadpan faces slipped away.

"Please give us a little more room," Ruby asked the guests as she turned toward Randy and the horse. "This beautiful gray is a six-year-old gelding named Charlie."

Charlie was a medium-large horse with distinct muscle tone, no doubt a horse that could run. Charlie wore a halter with a single rope attached.

"Charlie, meet Luis," Ruby said.

Randy smiled and handed the rope to Luis, and he said, "Luis, I want you to walk Charlie back to the corral. Don't look him in the eye. Walk next to him, with easy tension on the rope. Charlie is friendly. Talk to him about whatever you want. I want him to hear your voice. Speak in a calm tone. He'll like that. Now is the time for you to bond together. Charlie is a good boy. Tell him that. I'll meet you over at the corral."

Luis froze for a moment, but he relaxed as Charlie's warm breath washed over him. He then led Charlie toward the corral. Thirty seconds later, everyone could hear Luis's calm voice.

Randy grabbed a striking sorrel next.

"This pretty mare is Suzy," Ruby announced. "Suzy, I'd like you to meet Michael."

Michael, the youngest of the guests, smiled as he walked toward her. Randy coached Michael a little differently since every horse is unique. Michael led the mare away.

Randy matched Radar, a tall black gelding, with Alex and a beautiful buckskin mare called Britt with Bruce.

All four men seemed pleased with their new partners.

CHAPTER FOURTEEN

C olorado parked his Chevy Blazer and hiked uphill to the Badger Lake Trailhead. He had prepared well and packed light, even with the weight of his component rifle and ammunition. He didn't bring a large quantity of ammo. Hopefully, he wouldn't have to shoot a single round, but if necessary, one box would be plenty. He rarely needed more than one shot per target and preferred quieter methods to kill.

He planned to camp only a single night. His back wasn't what it used to be, and sleeping on the ground could aggravate his sciatic nerve. The uphill hike could be brutal; he needed to arrive early to get a head start. He drank a few vodkas to help him sleep the night before. Now he hoped to keep his breakfast down.

After hoisting on his backpack, Colorado entered the trail. His early morning start helped him avoid other backpackers. The trail's flat entrance gave way to a constant incline after only fifty feet. After a hundred yards, his thighs burned, but he kept trudging forward until the trail leveled out on a rim well above Badger Lake. A downed pine tree gave him a spot to sit and provided a viewpoint above the trailhead.

He overlooked the lake, several trails, and the staging areas near the trailheads. Comforting clouds slowly entered the blue skies, diffusing the light and keeping the cool, comfortable temperatures where he wanted them, at least for a while.

Colorado pulled out a lightweight pair of binoculars and searched for activity. With a good view of the horseback rider's trailhead, he glassed the area from the trailhead back toward the parking area. He spotted an outfitter prepping for a trip. Their pack horses were loaded, and three individuals were hard at work: a blonde-haired woman, a young man, and an older man. Each one was paired with one of three men and their horses. It could be a pre-trip riding class for the paying customers who appeared to handle their horses well. They all looked comfortable in the saddle. This was a first-class operation with six people, three outfitters, and three customers. Colorado estimated they would start their journey within an hour.

He scanned back to the parking area, where there was activity. Two police SUVs drove in together. The first had the markings of the Blaine County Sheriff, and the second was the Idaho State Police. The officers, in tandem, stepped out of their vehicles and marched toward the outfitter staging areas.

Unfortunately, Colorado's binoculars weren't strong enough to read their badges. Both of the officers' body language were friendly. The state policeman talked with the blonde woman, and she waved at the older gentleman, who approached and offered the police officer his hand. There were positive and negative nods as they engaged with each other. Based on his body language, Colorado didn't see any sign of distress. Their conversation ended as abruptly as it started; they shook hands, and the police officers walked uphill toward the trailheads. Colorado had no idea what was said, but it was clear the local police were on the job.

Colorado then watched a pickup pull a horse trailer into the parking area downhill from the outfitters. Two men exited the pickup and unloaded a sturdy-looking quarter horse. That was it, just one horse. The rig's driver, a young man, carried out a saddle, a good-sized set of saddlebags, and a hard-sided rifle case. With the other man's help, they saddled the horse and tied on its saddlebags. The passenger unlocked the rifle case and pulled out a hunting rifle with an attached optical scope. He slid it into a saddle holster.

The men finished prepping the horse, and Colorado thought about this guy's agenda. Lone riders were uncommon on recreational rides in the backcountry. In the wilderness, dangers existed beyond that of most remote recreational areas. Hikers could become lost and disoriented, injuries could be catastrophic, and wild animals could be hungry. Most adventurers traveled in pairs. A single traveler has greater risks. The pickup and trailer did not have any official markings. This guy wasn't law enforcement. The passenger and the driver shook hands, and before the driver turned back to his truck, the passenger pulled out his wallet and handed the driver cash. The young man stared at the money, raised his head, and smiled. He probably received a large tip.

The new rider stepped into his saddle and guided his horse toward the trailhead.

Colorado pulled his binoculars down from his eyes, dropped them into their case, tightened the settings on his backpack, and marched up the trail. He found a new viewpoint after a quarter-mile of mild switchbacks and a gradual climb. He removed his load, pulled out his binoculars, and glassed the trail below.

The lone rider had gained some ground. He, too, dismounted and sat in a makeshift overlook.

Colorado spotted the rider pull up a pair of binoculars and glass the area downhill. This new rider appeared to be watching the outfitter group approaching the trailhead. Colorado tried to match his view. The six-person group had six mounted riders and three extra horses hauling supplies. They were in good shape for days with the stores they carried. They were still too distant for Colorado to recognize, but he was sure he watched the group with Bruce Arnold and his wealthy friends. He had a pretty good idea who the lone rider was, too. He was trouble. Neither the Arnold group nor the lone rider knew they were being watched by Colorado. Most likely, neither was prepared for a crisis.

Colorado fought the urge to finish part of his job. From his perch, he had a perfect angle. He could take out the lone rider and walk away, but that would be too messy. He wasn't familiar with the trail ahead and couldn't turn back. He'd need a safe escape route, and he didn't have one yet.

With the lone rider's arrival, Colorado had a big job ahead. He'd have to be cautious with these players this close together.

CHAPTER FIFTEEN

R uby Starr led her customers to the first break on their morning ride. They stopped at a wooden sign that designated the Sawtooth Wilderness border. They were required to stop and sign in for their wilderness permits. The procedure was easy; it didn't require forms or fees. They signed and dated a log sheet. The log was kept in a weathered wooden box attached to a decaying pedestal set on the ground. As informal as the procedure was, it was still necessary. They were leaving the Sawtooth National Recreation Area and entering the Sawtooth Wilderness. It was reasonable to have a written record. It was also an ideal place to take a photo documenting the beginning of a once-in-a-lifetime adventure.

This station was typically quiet but was staffed by an armed US Forest Ranger this morning. Ruby greeted the ranger as she dismounted from her horse. She smiled and said, "Good morning, Wayne."

"Good morning, Ruby," the ranger beamed.

Ruby walked up to him and hugged him. "How is that sweet wife of yours?"

"Nancy is fine. Thanks for asking. I understand you have a special group with you today."

"Yes, we sure do. We have a small group taking a special ride." Ruby turned to her party and said, "Folks, this is US Forest Ranger Wayne Brooks."

The assembled riders nodded their heads.

Ranger Brooks nodded back. He was professional and prepared. He wore a flat-brimmed hat, a green uniform with a matching coat, an enforcement officer's badge, and a sidearm. A weathered hitching post was manned by Ranger Brooks's sizable gray horse.

The ranger sized up the guests as they lined up and signed the log. After riding for only forty minutes, the four guests were happy to step out of the saddle. They needed to stretch their legs.

Brooks took advantage of the moment to welcome and educate. "Good morning," he said. "Welcome to the Sawtooth Wilderness. I understand you're riding the Trilogy Lakes Tour. You are on a trip few people worldwide will ever take. This wilderness is beautiful, and its lakes are unique. You should have an experience of a lifetime, but we want you to also have a safe experience. The wilderness is vast and mostly uncharted. Remember, you are in the Idaho high country. Weather systems come and go with impressive speed; when it happens, all hell can break loose. It is easy to become disoriented and get lost. You need to stick to the trails and stay with your guides. You are riding with Starr Outfitters; Ruby and her wrangler are experts. You may have heard folklore stories about incredible rescues. Unfortunately, those stories are only myths. Ultimately, your safety is your responsibility. Please stay safe and respect the wild country. All fishing is open, so have fun, take pictures, and catch some big trout. I guarantee you will catch fish here even if you think you're a poor fisherman. Keep your eyes open and your cameras ready for wildlife. I know you all have heard about the bears, and it is true. This area is bear country, primarily black bears. But, so far this season, bear activity has been light. We have wolf packs in the wilderness. The Midnight Pack has been sighted near the Trilogy Lakes. This pack has been tracked for several years. They are a concern. But wolves stay away from people. We have never had an attack, and I don't think we ever will. They hunt wild game and want no part of us, but if we harass them, they could be a problem."

After ten minutes of tips from the ranger, the Starr group continued up the trail. It was in good shape and wide enough to give them elbow room. A steep hill covered with pines rose on their left. Ruby took the lead. Following her, Luis Perez rode Charlie, Michael Lane rode Suzy, Bruce Arnold rode Britt, and Alex Ford rode Radar. Bringing up the rear, Randy led the pack horses.

Ruby spoke in a firm voice as she pointed out features of interest, including a raging creek, a waterfall, and multiple sightings of wildlife. After riding up a dry trail that wound around a prominent hill, they entered a dangerous stretch traversing a steep rock shelf.

Ruby turned in her saddle and announced, "Folks, this trail is a bit challenging, but it is worth every step we take. Once we ride out the other side, we will enter a beautiful meadow, where we will dismount and take a water break. Our horses have been here many times before. Trust your horse, enjoy the view, and have fun."

After the exciting ride, they dropped into the expansive meadow. A creek snaked through it, creating deep pools as the terrain leveled. It was a perfect spot for the horses to drink and their riders to stretch and loosen up. Ruby timed their breaks to keep a relaxed, comfortable pace.

They followed the creek bank until they found a shallow stretch suitable to cross. With the spring runoff, the creek flowed at a high rate. They rode across it easily. The knee-high water wasn't a challenge for the horses.

The trail split on the other side of the creek. A twenty-year-old sign pointed right to Spirit Lake and left to Sara Lake.

Ruby told her customers, "With our early start, we have plenty of time to see both lakes. Spirit is too special to miss."

The trail gained a couple hundred feet as it followed the creek. After half an hour, they rode near a fifty-foot-high waterfall that brought out the cameras again. They turned north from the creek and followed an established trail through a forest of Douglas fir, Engelman spruce, and pine. Some of the trees were down, probably from a heavy winter. Several lodgepole pines lay across the trail, creating challenging detours. The terrain bothered the riders, but the horses had no trouble walking through it.

An hour later, they rested on the shores of Spirit Lake. It was a classic mountain lake, with pines and meadows lining the east side and a dramatic cliff stretching out of the water on the opposite side.

Randy took charge of the horses as their excited guests walked the lake and photographed the area. On a rough sand beach, Ruby set up a backcountry lunch buffet. Several logs had been set strategically nearby, creating a perfect dining place. In the clean, crisp air and their ideal surroundings, their lunch tasted as good as any meal the guests had ever eaten.

After lunch, Bruce Arnold sat alone in the sand a foot above the lake's water line. He stared at the water with unblinking eyes. He had been quiet through lunch and then walked over to the beach. He grabbed a small rock and threw it into the water. He then threw another. When the third rock skipped, he smiled.

Bruce Arnold was the founder of Yoster and one of the wealthiest people in the world. It was hard to tell if he enjoyed that status. Bruce was medium-height and underweight, with a slight tremor in his right hand. He had short salt-and-pepper hair, close-set dead gray eyes, and he rarely smiled. Bruce was a tactical, technical genius who bought and sold large corporations as if they were used cars. Yoster's business reputation was positive, but Bruce's reputation was negative. He was a hard man to work with or work for. He had a quick temper, and it was killing him. He needed this vacation.

Michael and Luis walked along the shore to the cliff's edge on the west side of the lake. They peered up the cliff face and spotted a few rough trails suitable only for climbers and adventurists. Neither Michael nor Luis could be classified as that.

Luis was a brilliant technology expert who had worked for Yoster and Bruce Arnold in the company's early days. He was in his late fifties, dark-skinned, and healthy. Luis had a quiet way that commanded respect. He was a dedicated tech professional who was now an executive vice president of one of the world's largest software companies. Yoster had become a more substantial firm while Luis worked there; much of their growth could be attributed to him. He was appreciated, and he left on good terms.

Michael was in his mid-thirties, a brilliant chip designer and all other things tech. He also had worked for Yoster and Bruce Arnold but left the company when they rejected his latest design. After leaving Yoster on good terms, he built his own tech company, Lane Technology. His rejected design built the company. Michael had a slim, medium-height frame and short brown hair. He spoke quietly, had introverted tendencies, and a warm heart.

Randy saddled the horses, preparing for the next leg when Michael and Luis waved him to where they had been walking.

Luis excitedly pointed to a heavily tracked spot in a muddy area. "Hi, Randy. Look at these tracks. They are too big to be dog tracks—do you think they're bear tracks?"

Randy frowned, stared at the tracks, and said, "No, those are wolf tracks."

CHAPTER SIXTEEN

A dirty twelve-year-old Subaru Outback pulled off the road about a quarter-mile short of the first parking area at the Badger Lake Trailhead. The Ninety-niners, dressed as backpackers, opened the wagon's rear door and strapped on their backpacks. They had scouted the area well enough to find a trail that skirted around the parking areas and the traffic. After they had hiked to Badger Lake, they continued along the shoreline until they spotted the backpacker's trailhead.

The four mission-focused operatives had filled their packs carefully and as lightly as possible. They packed minimal camping gear, ample dehydrated food, a single cooking set, water filtration pumps, a two-way radio, a single change of clothes, and a small collection of weapons. Rage and Digit wore Boise State baseball caps. Torch wore a University of Utah sweatshirt, and Bright wore a Bronco blue hoody. They tightened their backpack straps and marched uphill toward the trailhead.

When they thought they were hitting their stride, they were startled by a perky deep voice that greeted, "Good morning," from the trees to their right. The hikers were faced with playing their roles to a Blaine County Sheriff who stood on a rocky shelf above them.

Torch smiled and cheerfully replied, "Good morning."

The sheriff, with an appraising gaze, seemed to analyze them closely. "You hiked around the lake. It's a rather odd route to the trailhead. What are you doing down there?"

"Just checking out the lake. It's awesome! Have you been down here?" Torch smiled. Torch probably looked like the cleanest cut of the bunch with his short dark hair.

"The county sheriff smiled and said," Yes, it's incredible."

"And Sara Lake is even better?"

"Yes, it's a lot better." The sheriff seemed to relax a little.

"Wow!"

"So, is that where you're headed?" the sheriff asked.

"Yeah, we plan to camp out tonight and come back tomorrow. We hope to make it there before dark. Is that possible?" Torch tried to sound carefree.

"If you don't make too many stops, it shouldn't be a problem."

"We're going to camp on the east side of the lake. We heard there are a lot of good camping spots there."

"You can't camp on the lake, but there is good access to the lake on the east side. It's a good spot." The sheriff smiled, then his expression changed to a more severe look. "Where are you kids from?"

"Boise."

"And what do you do in Boise?" The county sheriff's voice became more measured.

"We go to Boise State," Torch replied.

"Are you from Boise, or are you from Utah?" The sheriff eyed Torch's sweatshirt.

"Torch glanced at his shirt, then back to the sheriff, smiled, and said, "Oh. I thought about going to school there, but I decided to stay home."

The sheriff didn't sound completely satisfied, and he asked, "So, Boise is home?"

"Yes, I'm a native."

"Boise is a nice town; I have a lot of friends there. Where did you go to high school?"

This time, Torch hesitated for a moment. He didn't know anything about the high schools in Boise, so he faked it. "Washington High," he said.

"That's the school downtown?"

"Yes, sir."

"Well, that's great. Enjoy your hike, be careful, and remember to pick up after yourselves." The sheriff turned and walked away.

Torch let out the breath he had been holding. He looked wide-eyed at Rage, who replied with a nod. The sheriff bought it. Their cover story got the job done, but they didn't pause to enjoy the small victory. They hustled uphill, entered the backpacker's trailhead, and marched out of sight.

The county sheriff walked back to the parking lot. He briefly talked to a married couple about their plans—not likely to be terrorists. After the conversation, the sheriff frowned, walked to a quiet corner of the parking lot, and pulled out his two-way radio. He stared at it for a moment and switched it on. "Base to Ranger Brooks. Over."

After thirty seconds, he got a reply. "Brooks here. Sorry for the slow answer; I'm on horseback. Over."

"Brooks, Sheriff Thomas here. Four young backpackers are headed your way. I had a short conversation with them and thought they checked out. After thinking about one of their comments, I have a bad feeling about them. They said they were Boise State students. It may be worth double-checking. Over."

"No problem, I can follow up. Anything in particular bothering you? Over."

"I'm concerned about the story a young man told me. He said he was a Boise native. Are you originally from Boise? Over."

"Yes, I am. Over."

"I asked him where he went to high school, and he said he went to Washington High, and he said Washington is the high school downtown. Over."

"There isn't a Washington High School in Boise. The downtown high school is Boise High. Over."

"Does that sound like an innocent mix-up? Over."

"No way. Whoever said that *is not* a Boise native. Over."

"Sounds like he lied to me. Over."

"I'll check it out. Over and out."

———

A half-hour later, the Rider's Club rolled into the horseback drop-off area at the Badger Lake Trailhead. Brett drove his pickup, pulling his two-place trailer, and Mark followed, pulling his four-place. Bringing up the rear was Pat from Victory Stables. With DeShawn Terry riding Trixie, they were left one packhorse short. Either they needed to find another horse or only pack one. Pat simplified the situation by loaning out a frisky gelding named Caleb.

Brett carried a load of supplies in his arms when Pat turned toward him, and with a snarky smile, he said, "By the way, if Caleb gets fussy, back off. When he gets irritated, he might bite, and if he doesn't like you, he might kick."

Is Pat trying to pull my leg? Brett wondered. "Well, I hope he likes us."

Sage, Tom, Brett, Mark, and DeShawn were excited to start. As they dropped the trailers' ramps, all seven horses were unloaded and tethered to hitching rails for saddling. The horses, stepping lightly on their feet, showed their excitement, too. When the Palomino, Trixie, was unloaded, she spotted DeShawn and whinnied.

DeShawn melted.

Brett, Tom, and Mark went to work organizing the trip's supplies and gear. They worked together, readying the load for the pack horses. With two pack horses, the weight split up nicely; neither one carried a heavy load. Mark's pack system was easy to attach, incredibly stable, and easy to pack and unpack. After finishing with the pack horses, they saddled the rest, except Pepper.

Brett pulled him aside. He preferred to saddle his horse.

Brett and DeShawn met with an Idaho State Trooper and a Blaine County Sheriff in the back of the parking lot. An SNRA forest ranger was on horseback, patrolling the trail uphill. Both police officers appeared fit and sharp. Still, Brett suspected the seasoned ranger was the most substantial asset.

Agent Sturm, DeShawn's boss, surprised both Brett and DeShawn. Sturm reached out, grabbed Brett's hand, and said, "Thanks for letting Agent Terry ride with you. With him shadowing the Starr Outfitter's group, our communications and overall security increased. I hope it doesn't mess up your trip."

"We're all good with it and happy to have Agent Terry with us. I doubt we will run into any trouble." Brett said.

A few minutes later, Brett and DeShawn returned to the staging area. Brett saddled Pepper, who was tired of waiting. Mark and Tom parked and secured their rigs while Brett and DeShawn loaded a few extra supplies they had set aside.

"Before we leave, I'd like to thank you all for stepping up," DeShawn said. "I shouldn't be surprised you guys changed your plans to help someone you don't know. That's who you are. We need to get going, but I'd like to update you first. Tom, did you guys bring your hands-free radio system?"

"Yes, plus five GPS units."

"Great. I brought a satellite phone; it will keep us connected wherever we are on the ride. I doubt we need them, but I did bring a Kevlar vest for each of us."

The friends glanced at each other, silently sharing the memory of wearing them before.

"We have several points of contact. The Blaine County Sheriff and the Idaho State Police will patrol Highway 75. It puts them in a good position to react if we call. There is a forest ranger on horseback patrolling the SNRA. We should be able to reach him by radio. Plus, with the satellite phone, I can contact my boss. I've also talked with Alex Ford. He's a security officer from Yoster. He'll ride with the Starr Outfit through the tour, and we'll check in with each other daily. Any questions?"

"Yes," Mark said. "We have the state and county police on the highway and the forest rangers patrolling the SNRA. How in the hell does that help when we're *way* up in the wilderness area?"

DeShawn's eyes narrowed into an icy stare. "In the short term, not much. Long term, they can come in with support."

Brett started to speak, but DeShawn held him back. "It's okay. Mark, your problem is that you're too damn smart. You've just defined the problem with our backup. I'm glad you're on our side."

Mark stared at his shoes.

Brett stepped in. "First of all, I don't think we will have any problems. We'll have a great trip. At the most, we'll have a few discussions with law enforcement. So, don't worry about anything. That's DeShawn's job."

Everyone smiled, even DeShawn.

"If we have a confrontation, we won't need outside help. The five of us make a formidable team. We'll deal with it." Brett looked into the eyes of each of his four friends. "Let's ride."

CHAPTER SEVENTEEN

Fred rode uphill on a scenic stretch of the Trilogy Trail. To his left, the mountainous terrain was covered with rock formations and hardy pine trees, and to his right, a cliff kept a high-rushing creek in check. The heavy flow wasn't unusual for June; the spring runoff would ebb within a month, leaving a much drier scene.

He stopped and signed in at the permit station using an alias; there was no need to document his presence. He stepped into the saddle and was ready to ride when he heard another horse walking up the trail behind him. An armed forest ranger rode up to the station's hitching post. The ranger carried a sidearm, and his sizable gray horse carried the ranger and a rifle.

Fred gave the ranger a quick nod as he rode away.

After a half-mile ride, Fred spotted another trail running through the trees above him. That trail was well positioned along the top of the rise. It appeared to offer a great view. If he could find a way up there, the high ground could give him a tactical advantage. He would be able to find viewpoints where he could monitor all the traffic on the Trilogy Trail, coming and going. Right now, he wouldn't see trouble until he rode into it.

He kept his eyes on the forest to his left and quickly realized this mountain section was too steep to hold a connecting trail. He considered riding through the trees, but that could be risky. There had to be an easy way to access the high trail, likely a connecting branch. Logic told him that if he kept going, he should see one. Hopefully, the mountain would be more forgiving upstream.

Fred urged his horse forward, and the horse responded, charging up the mild incline at a full gallop. The trail leveled and then slowly dropped, and the horse accelerated. The horse loved to run, maybe too much. He had stayed at a gallop for over a mile, and Fred hoped he could stop him.

After a long, hard run, Fred spotted a trail coming out of the forest on his left. He carefully pulled on his horse's reins, and the horse abruptly stopped. Fred leaned over and rubbed his horse's neck. "Good job, buddy; I'm impressed."

Fred was happy with the high trail. It was narrow and smooth and offered multiple viewpoints. He could scout from up here, but right now, he was a mile and a half north of the permit station. He needed to ride south to check on the Ninety-niners' progress.

After riding south on the Ridge Trail, Fred pulled up when he found an overlook with a view of the Trilogy Trail below. The permit station and the surrounding area were clear. He pulled up his binoculars and glassed a larger area, spotting movement below and behind him. The ranger rode his big gray at a canter. He rode past the station and onto the backpacker's trail toward Badger Lake. He slowed and pulled up the big gray. The big horse blocked a narrow stretch of the backpacker's trail, approximately a quarter-mile south of the station. The ranger was positioned to stop and confront the Ninety-niners.

"Oh shit," Fred mumbled as he pulled down the binoculars.

He stared at the forested hillside. He needed to ride down to the trail but didn't have time to backtrack. He questioned his earlier decision. *Could I ride through the trees?*

———

The Ninety-niners hustled up the Trilogy Trail. After scurrying past the backpacker's trailhead, they jogged uphill through a series of curves. Rage spotted a cutout on the left side of the trail. "Let's take a quick break. We're winded, and I need to adjust my backpack."

They had moved up the trailhead more quickly than planned, panicking to distance themselves from the inquisitive Blaine County Sheriff. Now, they had time to reorganize and take a water break. The Ninety-niners were more uncomfortable than tired. They felt that adjusting the straps on their backpacks might help.

They were revived when Rage led the group back onto the trail at a steady, relaxed pace. Bright hiked behind Rage, and they walked side by side through the broader sections of the track. Torch followed, and Digit brought up the rear as he struggled with some of the electronics' extra weight. Maybe they could balance out the load after lunch.

The radio squawked. Digit stopped and yelled, "Hey, hold up, you guys! It's the radio."

Digit fought the backpack's harness system, then slipped it off. He had packed the radio near the bottom of his backpack. "Oh shit!" Digit whispered as he unpacked his gear. He grabbed it after about a minute of digging into his pack. Radio in hand, he answered, "Digit here. Digit here."

The other Ninety-niners stood and waited.

"Digit, you need to answer a hell of a lot faster," Fred said. "I need to talk to Bright or Rage."

Rage grabbed the portable radio. "Rage here."

"There is an armed forest ranger on horseback blocking the trail ahead of you."

"Shit! Do you think the ranger is looking for us?"

"That would be my guess," Fred answered.

"Where are you?" Rage asked.

"I'm up on a hill, scouting the area."

"I'll deal with him. I'll have the guys wait while I go up there and see what he wants." Rage said confidently.

"Not a good idea," Fred said.

"I can handle a ranger. If he hassles me, I'll take him down. It's not like he's a cop."

"The rangers have an enforcement division. They are trained police, and it's not that you can't handle him. It's that you shouldn't. This ranger is riding a horse and is well-armed. I'm the scout here. The ranger isn't looking for me. I'll deal with him. You need to stop, get off the trail, and disappear until I get back to you. Do you understand?"

"Okay, I guess that makes sense." Rage scowled.

"This could take a while. Get off the trail and stay out of sight. I'll get back to you as soon as I can. I have some distance to cover. Keep the radio handy. I'll call you."

CHAPTER EIGHTEEN

F red slid his two-way radio into his coat pocket, took a deep breath, and tried to focus. He needed to move the Ninety-niners past the ranger, which could be problematic. If the two sides collided, the entire plan could fall apart, and his ass would be on the line. With the Ninety-niners off the trail, at least they wouldn't hike into trouble. The ranger was the wild card. When it came to the trails, he was the expert. Even with the kids hidden, he might track them down, but Fred could keep the two apart if he could get back down there. He needed to move. First, he needed to get off the ridge.

The high trail was in good shape, but riding back to where he started could take too long. Fred needed a shortcut. He rode down the edge of the tree line and tried to find a trail through the trees. Finding none, he stayed on the trail until the trees filled in on his right and then turned his horse into the trees and traversed the slope.

Fred rode a pretty good horse, a smart one. The horse found its way, almost like he had ridden through the area before. The terrain became rocky and steep, and the horse tried to turn uphill.

Fred pushed him back downhill, and his horse threw his head. Fred tried to calm him with a steady, low voice. It helped a little, but the terrain continued to deteriorate, and then the horse froze.

Fred knew how to handle a nervous horse. He corrected his body language and turned his horse away from their descent. They circled uphill and turned through a gap in the trees. As they moved forward, they cut between two massive boulders and pulled up. Now, they were stuck. They stood on the point of a cliff. In front of them was a sheer drop of at least seventy feet. They couldn't move forward, left, or right. Fred pulled back on the reins and urged the quarter horse to back up. The big gelding stood firm.

Fred gently stroked the horse's neck and dismounted on the left side, where a little room existed. He rubbed the horse's neck again. "It's okay, boy; we're going to back up and get the hell out of here." He grabbed the reins from where they attached to the bridle and carefully pumped them backward. "Back boy, back boy," he whispered as he pumped the reins. The horse slowly moved back from the cliff. Fred stepped back into the saddle and turned the horse uphill.

Enough of this bullshit. They were wasting time. They rode back through the trees toward the high trail.

Fred rode a diagonal route north through, *hopefully*, gentler terrain. It didn't take long to find the high trail. With time slipping away, he gave up riding off the trail. He didn't want to make another mistake. He gritted his teeth and dug his heels into the gelding, bringing him to a full gallop. He decided to run his horse as far and long as he could. Fred grabbed the saddle horn and held on.

The high trail was smooth, and his horse was tough. After a reasonable distance, they slowed some but continued to gallop. They ran around the bend where the trail split. They followed the downhill branch, which led them down one last drop and onto the Trilogy Trail.

Fred pulled up and let his horse breathe. He led him to a creek flowing through the valley floor. His horse drank, but not too much. After the horse caught its wind and calmed down, Fred dug his heels in again and galloped down the Trilogy Trail.

Fred pushed the gelding until he spotted the permit station; it was time to be careful and keep his eyes open. As he rode past the station, there wasn't any activity. He turned down the trail the ranger had taken and spotted a riderless gray horse. The horse was off the trail and deep into the trees. It was the ranger's horse, but it shouldn't be alone. Something was wrong.

Fred turned off the trail and rode toward the big gray. When he looked to his left, he saw the ranger lying motionless in the dirt. Fred reached for his pistol.

"Don't touch your gun if you want to live," a voice from behind ordered.

Fred pulled his hand away from his pistol and twisted in the saddle toward the voice. An older man with a grayish beard and unkempt hair covered him with a Glock. The man looked comfortable with the lightweight pistol in his hand. The ranger's big gray had his nose in the grass.

How did I miss this guy? There were no tracks. "Who the hell are you?" Fred asked as he sneered at the man.

"I'm the man who just did your job. Now, hands in the air."

The man walked around the horse and checked Fred's saddlebags, pack, and holsters. He removed Fred's rifle and pistol, unloaded both, and nodded.

Fred slowly brought his hands down. He looked again at the motionless ranger. "Is he dead?"

"I put him to sleep. Take a good look; he's breathing. He's comfortable and will wake up. The ranger got too close. If he had confronted the Ninety-niners, the entire operation would have been compromised, and it would have been your fault.

"Money is at stake."

Fred was wide-eyed with confusion; he stared at the man with the Glock. He didn't understand what was happening. Neither man said a word for several seconds. It seemed like much longer. "What do you want?" Fred finally asked.

"So, Joe, or whatever alias you use, our employer is concerned you are acting in bad faith. You haven't checked in as agreed. You're ignoring our partnership. You can't cut us out. You need to rectify the situation and find a solution. This must happen immediately, or your agreement will be terminated."

Fred jutted out his jaw and took several deep breaths. "This is bullshit. We're dealing in good faith. What kind of assurances do you want?"

"First, you must provide progress updates for both assignments. Second, lifesaving assurances, and they better be good. Our employer will contact me with an update. I hope you'll never see me again."

Fred watched the man slip on his backpack and disappear through the trees.

————

A couple of miles downhill, the Ninety-niners waited in a comfortable brush-strewn area behind a stand of lodgepole pines. A small creek nearby provided a natural sound barrier. Fred hadn't contacted them for a long time. Digit was worried, and he kept messing with the radio and adjusting his headset.

Rage sat on a log, kept his gaze low, and whittled a dead branch with his knife. The rest of the group leaned back against their packs and relaxed.

After an hour and a half, a sound filled Digit's ears. "Digit, Digit."

"Digit here."

"All clear. You may proceed."

"What happened?"

"We need to keep the radio chatter down. I'm out."

CHAPTER NINETEEN

After signing in and stretching their legs at the permit station, the Rider's Club was ready to hit the Trilogy Trail. Brett led the way, riding Pepper while everyone else followed in single file or pairs, depending on the trail's width. Brett, Tom, and Mark took turns rotating into the lead, but they all preferred to follow rather than lead since it was more fun to sit back, enjoy the sights, and talk. When the trail turned rough, Brett and Pepper always slid back into the lead. No one had a problem with that. Brett was their leader.

It was clear, sunny, and comfortable as they rode into a light breeze—*ideal*. The high mountain air carried the calming scent of pines. A creek on the right ran high into its banks due to spring runoff. The track took them uphill, which would continue for most of the day. As the rate of climb increased, the creek flowed harder, smashing into defiant boulders with a musical rhythm. When they had to cross, they rode along the creek's bank until they found a shallow, calm flow.

The heavily forested ridge to their left became rocky as Tom took the lead. They crossed the creek and entered gentler terrain on its right side. The trail rolled uphill through a thin stand of lodgepole pines. Tom rode easily in the saddle and kept alert as he led the riders through the hilly section.

Suddenly, Tom pulled on Buck's reins and swung his arm into the halt sign. "Hold up," he yelled. He pointed to a wooded area strewn with rocks. "A lone horse is walking through the trees. We might have scared it."

Riding well back in the line, Brett pulled Pepper around the riders and up to the lead. "Where did you see it?"

Tom pointed. "It was a good-sized gray, and it was saddled. It trotted behind those Douglas firs."

"I'll go to the left side; you take the right," Brett said.

The two men rode into the trees. Brett found a lightly used trail, well-marked by horseshoe prints. He pulled his hands up to both sides of his face and yelled, "Hey Tom, I found his trail."

A few minutes later, Tom arrived, and they followed the path until it came around a bend into a rock-strewn area near a small stream.

The big gray stood with his nose just above the ground, and beneath his nose lay a forest ranger face down in the dirt.

The horse carried well-packed saddle bags. A rifle was strapped into a saddle holster. The ranger didn't move as they rode up. Brett stepped out of the saddle and knelt next to him. Blood caked the back of his head, and he wasn't breathing.

Brett asked Tom, "Would you get Mark… and DeShawn, too?"

The trail ride was on hold.

Mark showed up and took charge; Brett hoped he could coax a flicker of life, but he couldn't. The man was dead. The backside of the man's head was crushed. He took a severe blow, cracking his skull and leaving the back of his head a bloody mess. Mark looked at the dirt around the body and shook his head.

"What do you think happened?" Brett asked.

Mark turned to Brett and DeShawn. "Without more time, I'll

have to give you an educated guess. I'd estimate he has been dead for at least an hour. The blow to his skull looks like the cause of his death. My guess. His horse bucked him off, and he landed on the rocks. He could have crawled over here and died."

DeShawn examined the saddlebags and personal effects. The look on his face was somewhere between sad and angry. He said, "I disagree. I don't think this guy was bucked off his horse. This man wore a badge." DeShawn held up an ID. "This is Officer Wayne Brooks. He is a US Forest Ranger. And he is an experienced ranger." DeShawn paused before giving instructions. "Please don't touch or move anything. This area is a potential crime scene. I'm calling this in."

DeShawn whispered to the deceased man. "This isn't over, Officer Brooks; we will find who did this."

Brett turned to face Mark. "Mark. Why did you say he could have crawled to where he is now?"

"Two reasons: he is lying face down, and there isn't much blood around here."

"A head wound like that would bleed heavily, right?" Brett asked.

"Right," Mark replied.

Brett carefully walked an expanding circle around the lifeless ranger, keeping his gaze down. DeShawn walked another search pattern further into the rocks. When their search covered more ground than a dying man could crawl, Mark approached Brett and DeShawn and asked, "Have you seen any blood?"

"No. So, he didn't get bloodied here." Brett said.

"How far are we from the Trilogy Trail?" DeShawn asked.

"Over a quarter-mile. Far enough that we would have never known he was here if it wasn't for his horse." Brett said.

"He was killed somewhere else. Then he was loaded onto his horse and dumped here," DeShawn concluded.

"Officer Brooks owned a fine horse. I bet whoever killed

Brooks probably led the gray away from here, but the horse found his way back. It knows the country around here better than any of us," Mark said.

"So, we agree… this was murder," DeShawn said.

"Murder," Mark said.

"Murder," Brett said.

Brett rode back and filled in Sage and Tom; they cared for the horses while waiting. A small stream flowed into the creek near the trail. Next to it lay a large meadow with grass and shade. They let the horses graze and drink but didn't unsaddle or unpack. Before they did, some decisions needed to be made. While he had the time, Brett rode up the trail to see what they would ride into next. He liked what he found. Over the next half mile, the Trilogy Trail led through a broad, easy-riding landscape.

He was riding back into their temporary camp when DeShawn and Mark arrived.

"I called the Blaine County Sheriff," DeShawn said. "A sheriff and another SNRA ranger will ride up here. Officer Brooks needs to be transferred to the County Coroner's office. Logistics will be a challenge. No one knows of a potential helicopter landing site, and the police aren't ready to search for one. Not today."

"About a quarter-mile upstream, this narrow drainage opens on the west side. There is a meadow wide enough to land a helicopter," Brett said.

"That could make a difference," DeShawn replied.

"DeShawn, are you going to be able to stay with us?" Sage asked.

"I talked to my boss, and he wants me to stick with the plan. I have work to do before I can ride out of here, but yes."

"I have a thought," Mark said. "I need a little more time before I can turn in my findings to the coroner. So, why don't the three of you ride ahead and set up camp at Sara Lake? We'll follow as soon as we can, then we'll get together this evening."

"That's a good idea," Tom said. "But maybe we should stick together for safety."

"I've taken this trip before. I know the trail; we won't get lost, and I'll be with DeShawn. I'll be safe with him, and you'll ride with Brett."

Twenty minutes later, the friends parted, and Brett, Tom, and Sage rode up the Trilogy Trail. They stopped at the meadow Brett had picked for the helicopter landing site. Brett recorded the GPS coordinates and radioed the information to DeShawn.

As the three rode toward Sara Lake, Brett couldn't help but feel unsettled. They were halfway to Sara Lake on just the first day and ran into a murder. *We need to be careful.*

CHAPTER TWENTY

R uby rode into the lead while Randy pulled up, allowing the four guests to ride past. It was a smooth transition without any verbal communication. Ruby and Randy enjoyed sharing the lead; it helped them both get to know their customers.

Their guests were changing. Ruby could see it and feel it. The further they rode into the wilderness, the more relaxed and upbeat they became. The afternoon light filtered through the trees, creating interesting spotlit highlights. They left behind the creeks and flooded meadows and rode past the signpost pointing toward Sara Lake. Randy cared for the horses while Ruby and their guests walked onto a cliffside viewpoint. For the first time, they gazed down at Sara Lake. They were touched by the majesty. A dramatic mountain rose from Sarah Lake's northern shore. A forest wrapped its way around the expansive eastern shore, and the lake's clear water rippled where several pristine streams fed it.

"It is difficult to say something profound as we take this in. Words cannot say enough, and a photograph cannot fully depict the beauty of God's work." Ruby cleared her voice.

Her guests stayed transfixed on the beauty in front of them.

"There are more than two hundred mountain lakes in this wilderness area. Some large and some small, but none more memorable than Sara Lake. She is a glacial lake, so deep, her deepest, coldest water may have come from a thousand-year-old glacial melt. Sara is the third largest lake in the wilderness; many consider her the most spectacular." Ruby smiled and took a deep breath.

She felt it was the right time to continue. "In the late 1800s, a prominent artist, Sara White, lived in the Sawtooth Valley. She created most of her life's work in this region. One of her most important pieces was painted from this exact vantage point. The painting was well-received and became quite famous. In Sara's later years, this lake was named after her. Some of you may have seen a reproduction of her masterpiece. The original is on display at the Idaho Historical Museum in Boise."

Uncharacteristically, Bruce Arnold spoke. "I've had a hundred people demand I cancel this trip. I'm glad I didn't listen to them."

"I agree," Alex said.

Everyone else smiled.

"Let's take a closer look," Ruby said as they returned to their horses.

They rode downhill on a solid trail. Ruby smiled as Luis, Michael, and Bruce rode with confidence. The connection between each rider and their horse had set in; the matches were perfect. Randy, leading the pack horses, turned off on a branch trail toward the campground they always used. The rest of the outfit would catch up with him later, but first, they would take a closer look at Sara Lake.

After Ruby's guests had dismounted and walked to Sara Lake's shoreline, Ruby gathered the horses and brought them to a gentle stream that, in a short distance, became one with the lake. The horses drank and cooled off. They had worked hard. One last quarter-mile stretch would be all Ruby would ask of them today.

The tech guys meandered along the shoreline while they took pictures and checked out one spot after another. When they arrived at the beach, they removed their shoes, rolled up their pants, and waded into the lake. Ruby could hear them talking and laughing. She assumed they probably didn't do that often.

They rode into the campground a couple of hours later, where Randy gathered their horses and led them to a temporary corral. The campground was a pretty good setup, made explicitly for outfitters. While they were at the lake, Randy had been busy. Six tents were furnished with a sleeping bag, pillow, LED lantern, and a cushioned sleep mat. Each customer's duffle bag was placed in front. A good-sized fire pit was already aflame, and several smooth-topped logs circled it.

"All right, guys, dinner will be ready in about an hour and a half. In the meantime, you're on your own. Several trails lead out of here, but the two most important are the trail we rode up and this one to the left." Ruby pointed. "Fifty yards down that trail is our portable outhouse. It has been dug and curtained. It's ready to use. Explore, have fun, and let us know if you have any questions. We have several hours of good light left."

———

Fred found a viewpoint that allowed him to watch the Starr group as they rode down to Sara Lake. From above the campground, he had the best vantage point of the day. He had been with them for most of the afternoon. They didn't look like a group ready to deal with a problem.

Bruce Arnold rode with a rugged-looking older man, no doubt a security specialist. The older guy looked familiar; Fred couldn't put a name to his face. It would come to him. He could have been distracted by the rare sight of Bruce Arnold smiling. Interestingly,

Fred had never seen Bruce smile—he didn't think he had it in him.

After Fred had seen enough, he rode back toward the Trilogy Trail. He was impressed by his mount as he cantered up the uphill path. They had covered a lot of ground, and some of the ride ran through rough terrain. Most horses would be balking by now, but not this gelding. Fred never learned his name, which he regretted. He settled on calling him his horse, but he deserved better.

Fred periodically checked in with the Ninety-niners over the radio, and Digit answered immediately. The Ninety-niners had made consistent progress throughout the day. They took hourly breaks; Fred advised them to try that old military practice, knowing an overtired group could burn out, especially on a long uphill backpacking trip.

When Fred pulled up and dismounted, he tethered his horse to a tall, skinny pine tree after letting him drink from a small creek. He pulled out some oats and gave his horse a well-deserved snack.

Twenty minutes later, the Ninety-niners arrived. Rage led the way and was surprised to see Fred.

"Good afternoon." Fred smiled as the group found a good spot to sit. "You guys are doing well."

"How about we make a trade if we're doing so good? You hike, and I'll ride your horse," Torch said with a smile.

"No way. Remember? I'm an old guy." Fred was surprised at how energetic they were after a day of hiking. Maybe their pre-trip training had paid off.

"Are we close?" Bright asked.

"We are parallel to Sara Lake right now. But the best place to camp will be north of the lake. It will give you an advantage in the morning."

"How far?" Torch asked.

"About half an hour."

Torch turned to his friends. "You guys want to take a break or keep going?"

"We're not due for a break yet. Let's keep going." Bright said.

Everyone else nodded.

Fred untied his horse and stepped into the saddle. He turned in the saddle and said, "I've scouted out a good camp for you. Follow me."

CHAPTER TWENTY-ONE

Fred, Rage, and Bright silently hiked up a faint trail. Fred held his hand back and flashed a halt signal as they neared a clearing. They turned off the path, worked around a thick cluster of bushes, and scooted behind a collapsed four-foot-thick ponderosa pine. Fred had led them to a blind any duck hunter would appreciate. Well hidden, they spoke in hushed voices and observed the activity below.

"You see the blonde woman? She's the outfitter that leads this trip, and the young man carrying the firewood is her wrangler," Fred whispered.

"What's a wrangler?" Bright asked.

"That's an old cowboy term for the man or woman in charge of the horses. He probably takes care of the horses and a lot more in a two-person outfit like this. The two men sitting next to Bruce Arnold are his business associates and the older guy is probably a security specialist."

Rage rolled his eyes, quietly chuckled, and said, "What does he specialize in, being old?"

"I doubt it." Fred shook his head and struggled to hide his

irritation. "That old guy looks familiar. It will come to me; I'd bet he's tougher than he looks."

Forty-five minutes later, they were back at their camp, sitting around a soothing campfire. Digit and Torch joined them.

Fred looked at Bright and Rage. "What are your impressions of Bruce Arnold's group?"

"I guess they're what I expected. I was surprised the group wasn't larger. There were only six of them," Bright said.

Rage stared at the flames. "That will make our job easier. Only two look strong enough to fight: the blonde lady and the fit-looking wrangler. I doubt Arnold or his friends will be a problem."

"I'd put the older guy on your *strong enough* list. As I said, he seems to be someone we should take seriously. It's easy to underestimate someone by their appearance alone. There have been a lot of great athletes who were below average in size, strength, or speed," Fred said.

"Yeah, I guess you're right. I remember an undersized MMA fighter who kicked ass."

Bright jumped in, "All right, appearances can be tricky; let's assume the old guy is tougher than he looks. I still feel pretty good about taking them down. We'll be armed. I didn't see any of them carrying a gun, and their body language looks docile enough."

"They probably feel safe at their camp tonight, but they may be armed tomorrow," Fred warned.

Torch leaned forward and stirred the fire with a long piece of kindling. "So, let's talk about tomorrow."

"Okay, first, we'll get up early and hit the trail. We need to find the right spot to ambush these guys, somewhere between here and Lookout Ridge. We need a location where we can keep out of sight until they walk into our trap. Then we'll take Arnold and leave the rest of them behind. Just in case, we need a good escape route," Bright said.

Rage wrinkled his nose and took a deep breath. "We won't need an escape route if we execute the basics. We need to surprise them, hit them hard, take Bruce Arnold, and get out of there before anyone reacts."

Torch raised his voice. "I think we're ready. The only unknown is the location. We need to find it early enough to get organized."

Rage looked at Torch and shook his head. "You're right." He faced Fred. "Do you have any ideas, Mister Scout?"

Fred smiled. "Yes, I do. One of the reasons I picked this campground is its location. It gives us a tactical advantage.

"Tomorrow, Arnold's group will have a leisurely morning. They will probably have a big breakfast and spend time at Sara Lake. They are on vacation and being pampered. You aren't."

"I wish we were being pampered; I wish someone would make me a big breakfast," Bright said.

"Me too. My legs are tired." Torch smiled.

"Fred, could you go get some more donuts?" Digit asked.

"And some beer," Rage added.

"Fred has some in his saddlebags," Torch said.

"Digit jumped to his feet. "Really?"

"Got you!" Torch innocently looked away.

Fred chuckled. "I guess I should have brought donuts with me. I'll remember next time. You guys are loose after working damn hard today. I'm impressed. Most people would be exhausted."

"We're tired, but we're prepared; besides, we're friends–it makes this almost fun," Bright said.

"I can see that, and I think it's good. It's a sign that you are a team." Fred nodded, and then he said, "Tonight's campsite gives you a tactical advantage because you're a mile ahead of the

Arnold group. When you hike away from here early tomorrow morning, you'll extend your advantage while they're eating breakfast. You should have plenty of time. You won't have to hike to Kimberly Lake or Lookout Ridge to find a good location. There are good choices closer than that. After you hike two miles, the trail runs through a forest where I saw several good spots. Pick one, set your trap, and wait for Arnold to step into it."

CHAPTER TWENTY-TWO

The sun sat atop the mountains to the west. The clear skies would let the temperature drop while the stars came out. It promised to be a good night for stargazing. Constellations would be clear and complete, and the Milky Way would dominate the sky. Somehow, the wilderness brought the sky closer. From the west, a cold wind approached; maybe that was why the wolves howled.

Colorado completed his last mission, a tactical check of the conflicting parties that could collide tomorrow. He finished at the southern end of Sara Lake with the Arnold group, which was well served by its outfitter.

Their campground allowed easy access to Sarah Lake. Arnold and his friends spent most of their time at the lake; one young man even tried fishing—his attempt was awkward but inspired. An older cowboy stuck close to Arnold and his friends; he didn't look like the others; he could be a seasoned security man. Colorado didn't see much preparedness; they were just your typical unsuspecting billionaire tourists.

Colorado hoped he had everything figured out; there were still unanswered questions. He had made the situation clear to the operative who was working with the Ninety-niners. Colorado even did the operative's job when he disabled the forest ranger. Still, he hadn't received any communication from Levitt or his enforcer.

Colorado's job was in support of a complex kidnapping with the involvement of a scapegoat. A hundred-million-dollar ransom was at stake. No wonder the company was concerned.

Colorado was comfortable hiking through the wilderness. It was his natural habitat. He covered a lot of miles, which helped loosen up his back, creating appreciated natural pain relief.

The wolves were active. Their howls surrounded the area. With all their distinct voices, one could surmise a large, healthy pack. It's too bad they didn't have a little rhythm; still, their song was beautiful. Colorado had never dealt with wolves. They didn't scare him, but he didn't come across them at home. Idaho was different. Idaho was wolf country. He wondered how long a wolf would last against him and his knife. If one or two wolves attacked, he could take them, three or more, probably not. With his bare hands, he could put a man to sleep in seconds; taking his life took a little longer. A sleep hold would never work on a wolf. He could snap the animal's neck if he was lucky, but that would be a kill. For killing, his knife was his preferred weapon. Pistols and rifles were too easy until they failed. He'd rely on his knife; it was quiet, never needed reloading, and never jammed. A shooter might leave their target bleeding, possibly alive, to fight another day.

Colorado never slept in a tent by a warm fire. He preferred to find an inconspicuous spot in the woods. A fire could give away a location. Earlier, he saw a good place on a slope. He'd burrow into the ground and stay warm like a wild animal. No tent, no fire, no exposure. He brought a little something to help him sleep. During the last year, he developed several bad habits. One was hard to fight, and as evening came, his willpower caved—vodka in a flexible collapsible flask. Vodka was heavy, and he should have left it behind. A pint weighed a pound. On a lone backpacking trip like this, an extra pound would have been unacceptable in the old days, but not tonight. He'd live with the additional pound. He could drink and relax; sleep would come.

———

Fred backtracked to check on Bruce Arnold's group. He took a quick look with his binoculars. He saw a row of tents facing a good campfire. They were ready to settle in. He pulled down his binoculars and grabbed his horse's reins. Suddenly, he saw a flash of movement at the edge of his vision. He pulled the binoculars back to his eyes and glassed the area again. He watched a man slide from tree to tree, working his way uphill. Fred was lucky to spot him; the sun was low in the sky, and he had already lost light.

He kept his eyes locked on the man moving away from the camp. The man avoided any breaks in the trees, making it difficult for Fred to keep his eyes on him. Finally, Fred had a quick, full view. "Oh, shit!" he whispered to himself. It was Colorado.

Fred kept the binoculars glued to the man, knowing he might lose him if he pulled them down. The man continued to work through the trees as he climbed up a ridge to the north. Then, he slipped behind a tall pine and moved out of sight. Fred scanned back and forth and checked every gap in the pines, to no avail. He was gone.

Fred rode through the trees and searched. He tracked a lot of deer and elk when he was younger. He hadn't done any of that type of big game hunting for a long time, and tonight, he followed a man who wouldn't leave much of a sign. He pushed his horse through the trees until he came upon a trickle of water so small it could hardly be called a creek. He spied a footprint in the moist dirt.

It was time to tie up his horse; a whinny would give away his approach. Fred pulled the saddle and blankets from his horse's back; the gelding deserved a bit of comfort. His horse took a drink and ate a couple of handfuls of oats. Fred attached him to a tie-down, grabbed his rifle and binoculars, and set out on foot.

It was tricky to track in the dark, but the stars illuminated the wilderness; there wasn't any light pollution, and the waning moon helped a little. He had a flashlight, but even a twinkle of light could expose him.

An hour later, as he cleared the summit on the northern ridge, he found another footprint leading downhill on the other side. The downhill terrain had a gentler incline, with flat areas interspersed among the trees. Fred kneeled in some thin scrub brush, pulled out his binoculars, and glassed the hillside. He checked the terrain quadrant by quadrant in a systematic search. A wolf howled, its voice echoing off the mountain, and then more voices joined in. They were hungry.

Fred saw a slight movement below as if an animal rolled in the dirt. He memorized the spot, set aside his binoculars, and pulled out his rifle. He lay prone in a gap in the bushes. With his rifle's scope, he scanned back and forth in the area where he had seen the movement. He repeated the process until he saw motion again. With his rifle well supported, he watched the man roll onto his side. Fred snickered, thinking he looked like a baby in a crib.

Fred slid into a prone shooting position, aligned his dominant eye behind his rifle scope, took a breath, exhaled slowly, aimed, and fired.

There was a definite pain-induced human grunt. Colorado collapsed onto his stomach. Fred was sure he hit him—a body shot.

The wolves stopped howling.

"You son of a bitch!" the man yelled. "Be a man and finish it."

Fred decided not to move closer; it was better to walk away. A dying man could be dangerous. The man would bleed out; joining him made no sense. It might take a minute, or it might take an hour. If it took longer than that, the wolves would finish him.

Fred crawled away from the man's sightline. After he stood up, he shouted. "I know who you are, Colorado. I talked to your boss, that asshole Levitt. He asked me for a favor. To kill you. Goodnight, wolf bait!"

CHAPTER TWENTY-THREE

Torch rubbed his hands together, formed a cocoon shape, and blew in warm air. Gathering firewood on a high mountain morning was a cold job. As Fred taught him, he laid out starter, kindling, and several small pieces of dry wood. The starter and the kindling lit, and the flames grew as he added more fuel. Soon, the fire put out enough heat to warm them all.

Bright stretched her legs after she crawled out of her compact tent. She had slept well, even though the air was cold and the ground was hard. She climbed to her feet, closed her eyes, breathed deeply, and relished the cold, clean, dry air. She swept her eyes across the forest and the mountains. This was nothing like Portland.

After she made her way to a large log bench in front of the campfire, Bright held her hands toward the flames. Once Torch set up a cooking area and had a pot of water boiling, the others joined them. Their hot water pot was collapsible with a metal base, rubber sides, and a metal spout—another lightweight contribution from Fred. The Ninety-niners quietly sat together and drank instant coffee and hot tea.

The sun brought color to the eastern sky but had not yet

climbed above the mountains. The birds started to sing once they felt the dawn.

The young hikers carried their hot drinks while they hiked to a lookout on a hillside to the southwest. Below them, in all of her beauty, rested Sara Lake. The group took in the grandeur in silence.

"Now I get it," Torch said. "People travel from all over the world to see this. Nature makes everything else seem small. I understand why it needs to be protected. I have the feeling everything else is unimportant."

"What in the hell do you mean by that?" Rage asked.

Torch took a deep breath. His lower lip quivered slightly. "Am I the only one who isn't affected by God's creation? It seems almost immoral to come here to kidnap, humiliate, fight, or maybe kill. I'm not religious, but if there is a higher power, I feel it here and now."

"Hey buddy, it's okay. We're all overwhelmed. Relax and enjoy the view," Bright said as she pointed toward Sara Lake. "This is beautiful. I have never seen anything like it, and I am moved, too. The beauty of nature is important, but we are working toward a greater good for all people, and I believe the two align. However, you make a good point. I don't know. Maybe we should rethink our approach."

"How's that?" Torch asked.

"I don't mind if we kidnap or fight for what is morally right, but I don't want to take someone's life," Bright said.

"Even a corrupt billionaire like Arnold?" Rage asked.

"Yes, even a corrupt billionaire," Bright said, looking back at the lake that began to reflect the dawn's oranges and pinks.

"Digit, what do you think?" Torch asked.

Digit raised his chin in irritation. "I don't give a shit what happens to billionaires." He lifted his camping mug to his lips and drained it. "But I'd like some more coffee."

"Okay, get serious," Rage said. "We've come too far to turn back now. Let's compromise. We all agreed to work together and respect each other. I propose we modify our plans. I don't think any of us want to take a life. So, let's take *hanging the man plan* off the table for now. Without it, we can still make our point. We could put a noose around his neck and fade the video to black. We could strip him down and see how well he survives when his corporate staff and money aren't serving him, but we might have to use violence to protect ourselves and our mission. Think about it."

"I'm good with that," Bright said.

"I'm okay with that, too," Torch said.

"Me too," Digit said.

"Let's go back to camp, have a quick breakfast, pack up, and go," Bright said.

A half-hour later, they sat around the campfire, eating dehydrated eggs and burnt toast. They drank more instant coffee and tea. Breakfast wasn't much, but it energized them. They were near their objective, and their time at the Sara Lake overlook helped them crystallize their thoughts and dismiss their doubts.

Torch cleaned up around the fire pit and put out the fire using another one of Fred's methods. He patrolled the area to ensure the camp was in better shape than when they had arrived. He made sure they left no trace.

The campers broke down their tents, repacked their backpacks, and double-checked each other's packs before they strapped on their loads. After one final walk around the campsite, they marched up the trail toward whatever fate awaited them.

An hour later, the Ninety-niners steadily hiked uphill when their two-way radio squawked. With the radio handy, Digit slipped it out of a sleeve on his pack and handed it to Rage.

"Rage here, good morning. Over."

"Good morning. I have a good report; our subjects are taking extra time at the lake. That should relieve some time pressure. How's your progress? Over," Fred asked.

"We're about an hour into our hike, but the trail has been steep and slow. Over."

"You've probably climbed up a thousand feet. You might want to take a break; you've got another steep section ahead of you, a steep set of switchbacks. When you top out, you'll enter a forested area and a valley where the trail smooths out. Once you're there, you will close in on the section of the trail where you should see several good locations. Over."

"Is there any site that stood out to you? Over."

"There are three good choices, each about a mile apart. I liked the third one the best, but look at the others. You have plenty of time to see which site best supports your plan. I'd decide on that basis. Over."

"Will do. Over and out."

The Ninety-niners took a fifteen-minute break, and then they continued to hike up the trail with Rage leading the way. The trail rose in shelves. After a challenging climb, they would be rewarded with a level stretch. The pattern continued for a half-hour until they encountered the steepest terrain they had seen.

Bright momentarily lost her breath as she gazed at the mountain before her. "I can do this. I have to," she said aloud to herself.

The mountain rose at an angle so steep it made any direct approach impossible. The mountain's face was laced with switchbacks, almost too many to count.

Rage moved close to her and quietly said, "Take off your backpack. We'll lighten your load before we take this on."

"No!" You carry your weight, and I'll carry mine. I can do this."

"You sure? We can split up your stuff between the three of us. It won't be a big deal."

"I'm okay. Thanks."

Rage turned to the other Ninety-niners. "Let's take a ten-minute break before we take on this son of a bitch. Once we get going, we'll stop as often as we need to—whatever it takes to get it climbed."

The trail was steep, as Fred predicted. The switchbacks drained away their endurance. Several times, they had to stop and catch their breath. With the constant climb, they all learned a new definition of steep. Their thighs burned, and their backs ached. When they broke over the summit, they hiked a short distance to a lookout, took a break, and gazed at how much space they had covered.

Bright smiled. They all accomplished a physical feat. They were doing well, really well.

Before their break, they hiked past another group of backpackers walking downhill toward Sarah Lake. They were the first people they had seen that day. Some backpackers reversed the route through the Trilogy Lakes. It would still be a good adventure.

The morning started cold and partly cloudy, with streaks of light breaking through with focused beams of light. Cloudy skies had taken over, accompanied by a constant wind. The clouds raced across the sky, but more kept coming. The weather was changing. It would have been nice for the hikers if it warmed up, but the cold weather was also a blessing in its own way; they weren't overheating.

The trail snaked uphill through trees until it leveled, and they came to a narrow, deep stream. Bright stopped and gazed at the cold, deep water. It was too wide to jump over and too deep to wade through.

Rage quickly walked along the creek bank, found a shallower area where the stream widened, picked a spot to cross, and said,

"I guess this is why we brought waterproof sandals. Let's change and help each other across."

After their dip in the water, the path widened a quarter-mile past the stream, and they entered a flat area with a thin tree line on both sides. "Hold up," Rage said. "I'd bet this is the first spot Fred recommended. Let's check it out."

The Ninety-niners surveyed the area and agreed it could work. Ideally, a thicker forest on the uphill side would help them stay hidden until they sprung their trap. They put on their backpacks and continued hiking toward location number two.

Almost an hour later, they hiked into another area that could work. The area was wide enough to give the operation the extra room they'd need. The site also sat in a bowl where a dense forest surrounded the trail's western uphill side. There were several advantages: high ground, camouflage, and control of the trail's entrance and exit.

The area showed promise until Bright spotted a young couple near the north end of the bowl about fifteen yards off the trail. A blonde-haired woman was curled up under a blanket. Her head rested on a backpack. Thirty yards down the track, a long-haired young man scampered from tree to tree. He studied the tree bark and took some scrapings, which he stuffed into a waist pack. With an SLR camera, he took close-up photos. He must have been involved in a science experiment of some kind.

Bright held a single finger to her lips and pointed at the young woman and the young man.

The Ninety-niners didn't break stride as they marched by.

CHAPTER TWENTY-FOUR

Ruby rang the dinner bell and shouted, "Come and get it, boys. Breakfast is ready."

Luis, Michael, Bruce, and Alex sat around the portable, folding campground table and peeked at what Ruby had made for breakfast. After last night's massive dinner, they shouldn't be hungry, but the mountain air, the riding, and the high altitude amplified their appetites.

"Okay, guys, we've got steak and eggs, backcountry fried potatoes, toast, muffins, juice, and hot coffee. Who's hungry?"

Alex, who overindulged more than the rest at dinner, pushed his way to the front of the line. "Move over; I'm going for it."

Luis, Bruce, Michael, and Randy lined up as Ruby stood back and smiled. This wasn't a trip where you counted calories. Even though her guests were on horseback, they'd burn through every calorie they consumed.

As they ate, Luis spoke up. "Bruce, you surprised me with your invitation to join you on this trip. I was familiar with the Sawtooths, but this is more than I imagined."

"I was surprised, too," Michael said.

"I'm glad you guys are here. I invited you because I respect you both, plus you don't work for me anymore. All my travel is usually business-related. So, I decided to take a trip where my work can't find me."

"I think you've been successful. Isolation is an effective buffer. This certainly *is not* a business trip," Luis said.

"It's good for all of you to get away for a change," Alex said.

"We've all learned business and pleasure don't always mix, and I've never been anywhere like this. I appreciate the invite," Michael said.

The men smiled and dove into their breakfast.

Ruby watched as her customers filled their bellies and opened up to the experience. All three seemed introverted. She considered it to be their nature. Their speech was stiff and abrupt, almost detached as if they lived in a bubble they had created. Living like that would make it hard to find friends, romance, or even a smile. She assumed that it was probably both a gift and an affliction. She didn't think it was worth it.

Of the three men, Luis was the most normal. He instigated the conversation this morning and, in his way, helped Bruce feel comfortable enough to talk. When Ruby had read his bio, she learned that Luis was an organizational, financial, and strategic expert. He had a reputation for being a top-level manager who made tough decisions, and he was known for his extensive knowledge of just about everything. Luis's smile came a little more quickly than the others.

Michael was in his mid-thirties, making him one of the youngest CEOs in Silicon Valley. A mathematical genius, chip design came easy. His designs revolutionized the tech industry, and more innovations were always on the horizon since he worked most of his waking hours. He led a solitary life and left most of his company's daily management to others. He was guarded and quiet. Ruby hoped he would enjoy himself.

Bruce's reputation painted him as a quick-tempered tyrant. It was true, and his frustration was killing him; maybe that's why he refused to let this trip go. Ruby felt that he needed to step away from his everyday life, even if it put him at risk.

Ruby knew many of her customers came to Idaho and Starr Outfitters to get away, and the current company was no exception. Her eccentric customers deserved a break. She was determined to help them in any way she could.

Michael approached Ruby while she took in the characters on this ride and asked, "Excuse me. I know we have lots of ground to cover today, but could we stay here a while longer this morning?"

Ruby was a little confused. "Sure, what have you got in mind?"

"We're wondering if we could go fly-fishing?"

Standing a short distance away, Bruce and Luis waited for an answer, like children in line for a carnival ride.

Ruby's eyes lit up. "Sure, we have plenty of fly-fishing gear and lots of time. Let's do it."

"We've all read about fly-fishing but have never tried it. Can one of you give us lessons?"

"Absolutely."

Alex interrupted, "Ruby, I've been a fly fisherman for fifty years and am proud of it. I want in on this one."

"Sure, honey, this will be fun."

Wide-eyed and smiling, Alex turned to Bruce and his associates and said, "I am so proud of you guys. Fly-fishing! Catching a fish with a long pole and an extra line isn't the easiest, but it's the most fun. Fly-fishing isn't just a sport. It's an art."

Ruby smiled as she watched Alex's unbridled enthusiasm.

She looked at her nephew, who was with the horses. "Randy!" She yelled. "Change of plans. Set up these gentlemen with full fly-fishing outfits. We're going to teach them how to fly fish."

CHAPTER TWENTY-FIVE

T he Riders were almost sad to leave their campground. They enjoyed Sara Lake, even though Brett still hadn't caught a fish. But he kept a positive attitude. He had several bites, and that was progress.

The weather had changed; scattered clouds driven by a light wind created photogenic skies that brought an array of colors to the lake. With a new Canon DSLR in hand, Tom took his time and shot a few pictures he hoped were worth framing. He had tried to capture an image of a bald eagle sitting atop a ponderosa pine. But the eagle wasn't cooperating. Not yet, anyway.

Brett and Mark had loaded their tents, supplies, and gear on the pack horses and were ready to saddle up the rest when DeShawn received the call on his radio.

He walked away from the riders and wore a quizzical expression that didn't go unnoticed by the others. DeShawn checked in with Alex, the Yoster security man riding with the Starr Outfit, several times a day. They planned to tighten the two groups together on this leg of the ride. Hopefully, they still could. DeShawn finished his conversation, shut down his radio, and returned to the waiting friends.

"We've got a delay," DeShawn said, rubbing the back of his neck.

"What's up?" Tom asked.

"Bruce Arnold and his friends want to go fishing and have requested fly-fishing lessons."

"Interesting. I guess that's good—maybe those guys are having fun," Tom said, shrugging.

"Fly-fishing is a therapeutic pastime," Brett added.

Tom chuckled. Fishing hadn't been therapeutic for Brett.

Brett ignored him and asked, "Did Alex give you an idea of time?"

"He guessed around three hours, but he said he'd check back with us before then."

Brett wasn't thrilled about a three-hour delay, but he had read about a side trail that was a great ride and wasn't far from where they were. Since they had three extra hours, he could check it out.

"Looks like we all have a few hours of free time. Let's make the most of it. I'm going to saddle Pepper and go for a ride. Does anyone want to join me?" Brett asked.

"I will," Tom said.

"I'll stay here and unload the pack horses," Mark said.

Brett and Tom rode out of their campground and uphill toward Kimberly Lake. "If my trail map is accurate, we should see a side trail on our left," Brett said.

"Where does the trail go?" Tom asked.

"Not sure. Maybe, a high viewpoint."

"Could be interesting."

The side trail was in good shape. It led up a gradual hill thick with lodgepole pines. After a quarter-mile, a patch of ground cover was crushed and wet with drying blood.

"Hold up. Something looks a little off here." Brett dismounted, knelt, and took a quick look. "There's more blood downhill. Tom, hold Pepper's reins. I'll check it out."

"Be careful."

Ten yards downhill, Brett spotted a crumpled bush; directly below it, a man lay face-first in the dirt. Ten yards further, there was a steep drop and the bloody remains of a wolf. Cautiously, Brett approached and leaned over the limp body.

With shocking speed, the bloodied figure swung an eight-inch blade straight toward Brett's midsection. Brett countered with a left-hand slap to the man's grip and disarmed him after a quick wrist twist. The knife fell from his grip and slid downhill a couple of feet. The blade was covered with blood. The angry man growled. He was older, bearded, and covered in dirt, mud, and blood. His bloodshot eyes were full of determination.

"Calm down," Brett ordered. "We're here to help."

The wild-eyed man stared for a few seconds before speaking in a raspy voice. "Sorry. You surprised me; I just reacted."

"I see lots of blood. How are you hurt?"

"Someone shot me in the back. I've been trying to get back to the trailhead." His speech was hard to understand as he gasped.

"The wolf had nothing to do with it?"

"No, he wanted an easy meal."

"I heard a pack howling last night. Was there more than one?"

"There was a bunch of them, but they lost interest after the...." The man bent at the waist and curled toward his knees, coughing and choking. After a minute, he calmed enough to take some labored breaths.

"I'm going to roll you over and take a look," Brett said. He was impressed with the man's ability to stay alive.

The man grimaced as Brett grabbed his shoulders, rolled him, and viewed the bloody mess. A bullet had torn up his ribcage from the backside. "Does it hurt to breathe?" Brett asked.

The man nodded.

"I'll be right back."

Brett climbed uphill to where Tom waited and grabbed the two-way radio from his saddlebag. "Mark, Mark, come in."

"Mark here. What's up?"

"You need to ride up here with your med kit. We've found a gunshot victim who is in bad shape. We're on a side trail, so Tom will meet you on the Trilogy Trail and lead you up here. Do you understand?"

"Understood. I'll saddle up and be on the trail in five."

Tom turned Buck around and rode away. "I'm on it — we'll be back soon."

Brett stepped back down the slope.

He leaned over the man. "We have a doctor in our group. He should be here soon."

A wave of relief filled the man's eyes.

"What happened?" Brett asked.

"I was camped out, trying to sleep, when someone shot me."

"What? Why?" Brett asked.

"Don't know."

Bullshit! Brett kept quiet for a few seconds before asking, "What's your name?"

The man hesitated and answered, "Colorado."

"Nice to meet you, Colorado. I'm Brett."

"Brett, who?"

"Brett Wyatt."

A glint of recognition crossed the man's face, and his eyes widened. "Like the football player?"

"Yes, exactly."

"I'm a Denver Bronco fan." Colorado coughed.

Brett smiled. "Colorado, we'll talk football later. For now, lie still and relax. Help is on the way."

"Thank you," Colorado gasped.

An hour later, Colorado tried to control his breathing as he lay face down on the campground table. Mark, Tom, and Brett had moved him to a small clearing off the Trilogy Trail. Transporting a gunshot victim off the hill was no small feat, but Colorado was one rugged customer. Colorado had slumped in the saddle but never fell. By the time they reached the clearing, he had lost what little strength, balance, and consciousness he had left.

Mark got ready to examine his latest patient. "All right, Mr. Colorado. I'm—"

"It's just Colorado."

"Okay, Colorado. You can call me Doc. I need to clean you up, and then I'll see how I can help. I know you're uncomfortable, but I'll need to keep you in this position for a while."

"Thanks, Doc," Colorado said before he fell into a coughing fit.

"I know it's hard to breathe, but you need to remain calm. Any allergies?"

"No."

"All right, I have to numb the area around the wound." Mark pulled out a syringe and went to work. "So, who shot you in the back?"

"I don't know, didn't see him. I was asleep."

Brett was confident Mark had everything under control. "Mark, give us a yell if we can help. We'll give you a little space."

Tom and Brett sat next to a dormant fire pit. They would have built a fire to keep warm, but the weather was already turning. The wind slowed down, and sunlight poked through gaps in the cloud cover. The high country's weather was unpredictable and bound to change.

A half-hour later, Sage and DeShawn rode up. They had cleaned up the campground and loaded the horses. Sage led the way, and DeShawn led the pack horses behind him.

"Do you have any information on the gunshot victim?" DeShawn asked.

"He claimed someone shot him while he was trying to sleep. The gunshot wound's location could support that claim." Brett said.

"Really? What else?"

"Not much. He was having difficulty breathing and was a bloody mess. Maybe he can fill us in better after Mark is finished."

"I hope so. I don't think it was as random as he makes it out to be. People don't get shot in their sleep. Something weird is going on up here."

A short time later, Mark yelled out. "Hey, Brett. Grab our biggest camp chair. I need to move Colorado off this table."

The guys helped lift Colorado off the table and, with care, placed him in the chair. Above his beard, his skin had turned pale, probably from blood loss. Mark held a cup of water up to Colorado's lips. He sipped a few ounces.

Mark covered him with a blanket and kneeled in front of him. "Colorado, I'm finished with what care I can give you here and now. I removed the bullet and stitched you up. You are going to have one hell of a scar. The damage to your upper back is superficial. It will be sore but will heal if you take care of it.

"After I cut the coat away from your arm, I found a wolf bite."

"Yeah, he won't do that again."

Mark looked Colorado in the eye and shook his head. "I thought you had a blood loss problem until I realized it wasn't your blood."

Colorado slowly nodded. His eyes closed for a moment.

"You're a tough guy. I took care of the bite—a few more stitches. It shouldn't be a problem. I'll find you a new coat."

"Thanks."

"There is a major problem. A couple of your ribs are shattered. Your lungs may collapse. This could be life-threatening. You need to be flown out of here to the nearest hospital. Right away."

"No," Colorado said.

"I get it," Mark said. "I wouldn't want to be flown out of here either. And I know it's expensive, but I'm telling you as your doctor. This may save your life."

"I said no."

"I'm serious. You need to listen to your doctor."

"No fucking way!" Colorado yelled.

CHAPTER TWENTY-SIX

A lex Ford signed off the radio, sat for a minute, closed his eyes, and nestled his chin into the palm of his right hand. That was one hell of a call. He took a couple of deep breaths and tried to calm himself. Maybe he was too old for this. A younger man would spring to his feet and confront the issue. *The undefined issue.* No, he couldn't think like that. Seventy years old—that's a high number. Get over it. He was older and hopefully wiser. He didn't need to react. He needed to think.

They needed to get their outfit back on the trail. They would be more mobile on horseback if their group were attacked. They could always pull off the trail, hunker down, and take a defensive stand or stay in the saddle and outrun anyone on foot. He needed to be alert and ready to react. He'd double up on his firearms. He'd already carried a pistol as a sidearm. Now, he'd add a holster to his saddle and a rifle to his arsenal. Both guns needed to be loaded and ready.

He pulled Bruce aside and updated him. Bruce seemed unfazed, but he did agree to keep his eyes open and communicate. They also decided on a few emergency commands, like *take cover* or *run*. Overall, Bruce wasn't worried; he had complete faith in Alex.

Alex also needed to bring Ruby up to date. She needed to know what happened, and if he read her right, Ruby would be an asset if trouble came their way. She didn't seem like the type to back down, nor did her nephew. Ruby would more likely take charge and try to protect her customers.

The radio conversation was informative and jarring. Ranger Brooks was killed, probably murdered. A second man was shot and left for dead. Alex had believed the threat to Bruce was an overreaction, but now he was concerned. There didn't seem to be a connection between the murder and the shooting, but there weren't many coincidences on a trail ride through the wilderness. Alex's cop instincts screamed; he needed to be ready.

He stowed his radio and approached Ruby while she readied the horses. "Ruby, do you have a minute?" he asked.

A short time later, Alex rousted Bruce, Luis, and Michael. "Hey guys, you need to help saddle the horses."

The mood of the camp was relaxed. Bruce was transforming; the great outdoors had taken over and helped him develop a new, healthy perspective. The first sign was that he had found his smile. All three men had bonded with their horses, another new unexpected pleasure. They enjoyed their first fly-fishing exposure and embraced the practice of catch and release. For first-time fly fishermen, they were damn good, but they weren't quite the consummate outdoorsmen yet. After only a day in the saddle, they were saddle-sore.

Bruce was surprised by Alex's request to help. "I've never saddled a horse—I'd put more faith in Randy."

"It's not about knowing. It's about learning," Alex offered. "Saddling a horse is a life skill. You should know how to, even if you'll never need to. My father taught me when I was a boy, and since that day, that knowledge has been a part of me. What happens if someday you decide to buy yourself a horse?"

Bruce smiled. "If I buy a horse, I'd want a mare just like Britt."

Ruby spoke up, "She isn't for sale, Bruce."

"That's too bad; I'd buy her right now." Bruce chuckled.

Alex rested his hand on Michael's shoulder. "Michael, I've taught a lot of folks how to fly fish, but I have never seen anyone pick it up as fast as you. You cast toward the fish on every attempt. Incredible accuracy. How did you pull that off?"

Michael faced Alex with a deadpan expression and said, "The stream next to us entered the lake at a constant speed, and there was a crosswind from our left. I could estimate the wind speed accurately, but I needed to consider a variance with the water movement when the two bodies merged. I visualized a grid that replicated both the wind and water intersection and took the last strike into account. After that, I attempted to drop my fly into the quadrant with the highest probability."

Alex rapidly blinked for a silent moment.

"Michael is a mathematical genius. He's full of surprises," Bruce said.

"Maybe you should give me fishing lessons. Could you show me your method?" Alex asked.

"Right now, we're going to learn how to saddle our horses," Bruce interrupted.

Ruby stood next to the horses; she waved Bruce and Michael over. "Let's do it," she said.

Alex usually liked to have the last word. "Michael, I'm serious; let's meet on Kimberly Lake tonight.

"I look forward to it," Michael smiled.

"I do, too."

CHAPTER TWENTY-SEVEN

Brett sat next to DeShawn while he briefed his boss over the radio. They discussed Colorado and speculated about who he was and whether he was a threat. The answer was unknown on both counts. Colorado or Mr. Colorado had no record of any kind—no arrest record—no phone number—no address—nothing. He either lived under a false identity (likely) or lived a very private life. Neither DeShawn nor Brett bought the latter.

The temporary camp was small enough that there wasn't much privacy; everyone could hear Mark and Colorado's conversations. It had been a few hours since Mark had medicated Colorado, and as the medicine wore off, Colorado's pain slowly returned. Even though Mark had addressed his injuries, Colorado would need to follow up with a doctor if he made it back to the Wood River Valley. Since he refused a helicopter ride, Mark talked to him about self-care methods that may help him survive the hike down to the trailhead. Then, for the last time, Mark explained how reckless it would be to try to hike out of there.

Colorado stuck with a single word: "No."

Mark was irritated when Colorado wouldn't listen to his medical advice, and he was personally offended as his field doctor.

Mark yelled for Brett, "Maybe you can talk some sense into him. I need to grab some meds from my saddlebag."

It was time they talked. Colorado still struggled to breathe, but his color was improving. His sickly pale skin tone normalized as he gained strength, and his dull eyes brightened, but he still frequently grunted and groaned in pain. When Brett hauled him off the mountain, he seemed like a man who might not make it. Since he got worked on, he had shown some improvement, but none of the riders believed the tough old man was capable of hiking out of there alone.

Brett stood over Colorado and crossed his arms. "It looks like Mark is doing a good job caring for you. He is a great doctor; you should consider his advice."

"I appreciate everything he has done, but I won't leave in a helicopter." Colorado frowned and stared at the ground.

He is hiding something.

Brett sat next to him and made eye contact. "Too high of a profile?" Brett asked.

Colorado nodded.

"Well, let's try something less public. I'll saddle up an extra horse and lead you to the trailhead. We can take it slow and easy, whatever it takes to get you to safety."

Colorado shifted his eyes with almost a pained expression, coughed, cleared his throat, and took a deep breath. "Brett, your reputation precedes you. You're a good man, and your friends are too, but you need to distance yourself from me. The sooner, the better."

"What do you mean?"

Colorado gritted his teeth.

"I have a hard time accepting the notion that walking away from a severely injured man is a good idea," Brett said.

"Do I have to spell it out? I'm not the only one in danger here. You and your *Rider's Club* friends are in danger, too." Colorado coughed again, shut his eyes, and tried to control his breathing.

Brett's mind raced. He looked Colorado in the eye. "You can't know that unless… you're involved?"

Colorado gave a slight nod and chuckled. "If I was ever involved, which I won't admit, I'm not anymore, especially after I took a bullet in my back.

"Brett, you're a good man, and so is the doc. So, I'm only going to say this once." Colorado coughed and took in a shallow breath. He whispered, "There are three targets. There was a hit on me, and there is a hit on you and your Rider's Club. Remember last year? They also have plans for Arnold and his friends. So, you and your friends will never see me again. I'll either die or disappear. But don't count me out—I've lived in the mountains all my life—I will make it out of here."

Brett closed his eyes and took a deep breath. "If anyone can, it's you. I'll never forget the wolf."

Mark returned, carrying a medical supplies satchel. "Any luck talking sense into him?"

"Not really." Brett leaned toward Colorado and grabbed his hand. "Take care of yourself, my friend." Brett walked past Mark and patted his shoulder.

Mark knelt in front of his patient. "Okay, I wish you would listen to my advice, but since you won't, at least take this medicine." He handed Colorado a container filled with three sets of pills.

Colorado nodded.

"I've written instructions. There are three meds: antibiotics, anti-inflammatories, and pain pills. You need to take the antibiotics and anti-inflammatories twice a day. But be careful with the pain pills. Any questions?"

"I'm not much for pain pills. You wouldn't have any vodka, would you?"

"Sorry, I'm not a vodka guy." Mark shook his head and smiled. "You're tough, but the body is fragile." Mark reached into his pocket and pulled out a business card. He wrote a short note on the back. "If you make it, and I pray you do, stop by Aspen Urgent Care when you get down to the Wood River Valley. They're affiliated with our Boise office and can follow up on my care. A local anesthetic might make you more comfortable, and they can fit you with a rib brace. Tell them to check with me if they ask you questions you don't want to answer."

"Yes, sir. And Doc, thank you."

"You're welcome."

Mark left Colorado and sat down on a log next to Tom.

Tom excused himself, walked to the pack horses, and rummaged through his saddlebags. He strolled behind the horses, circled back, knelt beside Colorado, and showed him two collapsible trekking poles. "We carry these poles at our outdoor store. I brought them along to test them, but I think they may be more useful to you. They are carbon fiber, extremely light, and strong. You can adjust their length to fit. They might help stabilize you, especially on steep and rocky terrain."

Colorado grabbed one of the poles, flipped open one of the adjustment clips, extended it, and flipped the clip closed. "I've seen people use them in the mountains, but it was nothing I cared to try until now. These could help."

Tom leaned close to Colorado and whispered as he pulled a small flask out of his coat. "This isn't vodka, but it's decent bourbon. Sip it slowly and enjoy the bite."

Colorado smiled. "Bourbon works, thank you."

"Take care of yourself," Tom said as he walked away.

Brett walked to a small trailhead at the edge of their temporary camp area and signaled DeShawn to follow. They walked down a narrow trail and stopped when they were in the trees and out of earshot.

"We've got a problem," Brett said.

CHAPTER TWENTY-EIGHT

DeShawn's radio squawked. "Agent Terry, here."

"Deputy Knight with Blaine County here. Agent Sturm has requested that you contact him at H-1. As soon as possible, over."

"Is there any information available related to this request? Over."

"No, sir. Over."

"Thank you. Over and out."

DeShawn closed his eyes, took a deep breath, and calmed himself.

Agent Sturm was either in Sun Valley or the FBI's Boise office. Either way, he was out of the radio's range. It was time for the satellite phone.

"Agent Sturm," he answered clearly.

"Terry here, sir."

"I'm glad you're still in range."

"The reception is still strong, but as we climb higher, it could break up. It depends on the lay of the land."

"I received your report. I must agree with your analysis. Ranger Brook's murder and Mr. Colorado's attack are related."

"Thanks, but I don't see how we can act against Colorado now."

"Agreed, but Agent Terry, he isn't why I asked you to call. We have another problem."

DeShawn Terry took a deep breath and exhaled slowly. "Sir?"

"The Ninety-niners have posted again on multiple social media platforms. Their posts have been taken down, but unfortunately, they pushed their message through. They made a new threat. They claimed to have captured Bruce Arnold and threatened to hang him for his crimes against humanity. They hinted at a location for the execution: a ridge on the top of the world. Pretty theatrical."

"Sir, I just updated Alex Ford on the Ranger Brooks and Colorado situations. Bruce Arnold is safe. He has not been taken. Not yet, anyway."

"That's what I suspected. I know you would have contacted us immediately."

"My concern is that there may be a communication error on their part. The Starr group's trip was delayed a few hours. Arnold and his friends took a side trip to go fishing. Perhaps the Ninety-niners had planned to kidnap Arnold this morning, but the extra fishing trip delayed their attempt. I doubt they have a satellite phone. Maybe the people posting these messages jumped the gun. If that's the case, a kidnapping attempt could be imminent."

"That is a reasonable analysis. If you're right, the Ninety-niners accidentally tipped us off."

"Exactly. We'll need to react immediately. Starr Outfitters hasn't broken camp yet, so we'll try to tighten up and ride closer to them. If needed, we'll join them. We need to be in a position where we can act quickly."

"Contact Alex Ford and bring him up to date. I'm glad Wyatt is with you. His outdoor skills could be a real asset," Sturm said.

"Yes, sir. The Rider's Club and I work well together. We're already a good team."

"Do you need any additional backup?"

"If the Ninety-niners plan to hang Arnold on a ridgetop, I'd bet they mean Lookout Ridge. It's one of the most dramatic viewpoints of the tour. If everything goes to hell and we have a confrontation on Lookout Ridge, we'll need a helicopter with armed backup on standby, one that can react quickly."

"Where does Lookout Ridge fit in your timeline?"

"Tomorrow, midday."

"I'll have a helicopter ready."

DeShawn stowed his satellite phone and picked up his radio.

"Alex, Alex," he said.

"Alex here."

"Terry here; what's your location? Over."

"We're on horseback and are riding toward Kimberly Lake. We have been on the trail for about an hour."

"We'll be on the trail soon and plan to tighten up to less than a mile. The Ninety-niners posted more threats on social media this morning. We need to watch our backs, and you need to be careful. We have lost some time with some other issues. If possible, slow your pace. It could help us catch up."

"Will do. Anything else?"

"Yes. We both need to move up our alert level. Let's check in with each other every thirty minutes."

"Good idea—will do. Over and out."

DeShawn approached Brett and asked, "Do you have a second?"

After a short conversation, Brett took charge. He walked to the horses and barked out some commands, "Attention, everyone. The Starr group is on the trail; we've got to hustle and catch up. One more thing. I want everyone armed." Brett didn't smile. He gritted his teeth and didn't explain. It wasn't a request Brett wanted to give.

"Why's that?" Tom asked.

"I'll explain on the trail."

Their horses were already fed and saddled. Once they finished reloading the pack horses, they hit the trail. It didn't take long. This section of the Trilogy Trail was well-traveled and in good shape. It would narrow and become steep over the next couple of miles.

The riders started at a comfortable pace, giving them time to talk before the trail became challenging.

"First, I want to apologize for involving us in a law enforcement action. It has already affected our trip," Brett said.

DeShawn looked down at the trail with a severe grimace.

Tom locked eyes with Brett. "You didn't. If I remember right, we all agreed to do this. Like we always do."

"That's right," Mark said. "DeShawn, it's not your fault either. We ride as one, remember?"

DeShawn looked up and nodded his head. "Thanks, Mark. That means a lot."

"So, bring us up to date," Tom asked.

"All right. The Ninety-niners have posted a new threat online. Both DeShawn and his boss believe that the Ninety-niners will attempt to kidnap Bruce Arnold today—possibly this morning," Brett said.

"How far ahead of us are they?" Mark asked.

"At least a couple hours," DeShawn said. "We lost time because of Colorado, and he is another issue. I offered to help him down the mountain to the trailhead... he turned me down and claimed we were all in danger. I could have let it go as bullshit, but he called us the Rider's Club. He knows who we are and why we are here."

"Did any of us tell him we're the Rider's Club?" Tom asked.

Everyone said no, and Pepper whinnied.

Brett leaned over and rubbed Pepper's neck. "I told you not to talk to the bad guys anymore.

"Seriously, Colorado didn't want us to call in a helicopter because he didn't want to be exposed," Brett said.

"He must have been scared by something. Scared enough to risk his life," Mark said.

"Good point. "I think he wanted out on his terms."

DeShawn jumped in. "My take on what he said is that there are more parties beyond the Ninety-niners involved in kidnapping or murdering Bruce Arnold. Maybe one of those parties has a reason to go after us."

"The Ninety-niners are a bunch of young adults who want to change the world. They don't have a background in violence. They work alone. Colorado isn't a Ninety-niner, and whoever shot him probably isn't either," Tom said.

"Do you think someone else could step in and kidnap or murder Arnold and let the world believe the Ninety-niners were responsible?" Mark asked.

"The ramifications of that theory are staggering," Brett said.

"How could that make us a target?" Tom asked.

"I have a theory," Mark said.

"Lay it on us," Brett urged.

"Tony Levitt. We know he's in Sun Valley, and he knows we're up here. He could be involved in a big-dollar kidnapping attempt. If Colorado worked with conflicting parties, he could have been shot to get him out of the way. Of course, Levitt has no love for us."

"These are all interesting theories, but they are only that. We need to stay vigilant. Now, you know why I asked you to carry your firearms. We must be careful and remember, only use your firepower as a last resort," Brett said.

"If we need support, my boss agreed to bring in an armed

helicopter," DeShawn jumped in. "If necessary, I'll make the call. He supports and appreciates everything you're doing. If any of you have any other thoughts, let me know. In the meantime, we need to close the gap with Starr Outfitters."

Tom's horse, Buck, threw his head, and Tom tightened the reins.

"Everybody, look at Buck," Brett said. "You can see it in his eyes. He's ready to go. It's time to pick up the pace."

"Hold on a second," Tom said. "Brett, can you quote us a little code?"

"Sure. *When you make a promise, keep it*."

CHAPTER TWENTY-NINE

Colorado sat alone in the camp chair the riders had left behind. He wished he could take it with him on the trek down to the trailhead, but it was too heavy and awkward. Too bad, it was pretty comfortable, especially for a camp chair. He worried about getting onto his feet after he sat or lay down. The trekking poles might help him stand up like a pair of ski poles can help you get back on your skis after a fall.

There was no going back on his decision to refuse a helicopter flight off this mountain. It would have been nice, but Colorado made the right call. This was the only way he had a chance to live.

He ate two granola bars and rehydrated with water and coffee, which calmed his stomach and improved his energy—a little. He swallowed one of Doc's antibiotics, anti-inflammatories, and half a pain pill. Doc never told him what the pain pill was, maybe an aspirin, maybe an opioid. It didn't matter; he was hurting but didn't want to be light-headed. He needed to keep his equilibrium on the downhill hike. Hopefully, half a pill wasn't too much.

With the trekking poles set at half-length, he leaned and transferred his weight forward and pushed up onto his feet. The technique worked—barely. His back, ribs, neck, shoulders, and arms burned. Even his legs ached. Everything was affected.

He discarded most of his supplies, including his backpack. There was no way he could carry it, not with his injuries. His upper body was too tender. Colorado fashioned a waist pack hooked to his belt and put a few essentials into it. He adjusted the length of the trekking poles and tried to keep his balance as he approached the trail. He stopped and steadied himself after a few steps. He'd like to make it to his Chevy Blazer today. Realistically, his best bet was tomorrow at his slow pace. If it took longer, he might not make it at all.

He kept his eye on the trail as he put one foot in front of the other. His back loosened up enough to travel at about half his average hiking speed. Now, he had time to think about more than how to survive.

He was lucky to be alive, thanks to Brett and his friends. Brett was impressed that he had held off a pack of wolves. Only one attacked. To the rest, he was carrion. They smelled death coming —an easy meal. The punk who shot him believed he was at death's door, too. A pack of wolves and a few men might have benefited from his death, but they all made the same mistake. They didn't finish him.

Colorado's biggest fears had manifested themselves. His employer had turned on him. This job was an opportunity to take advantage of his skill set one last time before they eliminated him —bad faith to a terminal degree. The mistake might be theirs if he makes it back.

The people he worked for were never his friends; they were users. Colorado realized the truth now. He had known the Rider's Club for half a day and had more faith in them than anyone else. Brett offered to take him to his Blazer, knowing it would ruin his ride into the wilderness. Brett called him his friend. Character is what they had—all of them.

If he made it down the trail, Colorado could start over. They shot him while he lay on the ground and slept, then left him for dead. Being dead could work to his advantage. Everything in his life could change—his name, where he lived, how he lived, everything. To the world, he was a dead man. He was invisible— *how empowering.*

He considered the potential for payback. His employer held him accountable for a messy disappearance, which wasn't his fault, even though they knew the truth. But their rule was no exception—zero tolerance, even if it meant shooting someone while they slept. If he survived, he could collect a few debts due to him.

Colorado needed to be careful and take care of himself. His back burned, and his ribs felt unnatural—something was wrong. His cough returned, and every time he coughed, he couldn't breathe. His head pounded with pain and dizziness. He had hiked a little over two miles, which left a long distance over the rugged terrain ahead. He had no choice; he was done for the day.

He needed to find a spot to eat, sleep, and recharge. He could take his pills and try Tom's bourbon. A little bourbon sounded like a good idea.

Thankfully, the trail led downhill. If he was stronger tomorrow, he might make it.

CHAPTER THIRTY

E ven though Ruby's group started their morning ride a little later, she couldn't stop smiling. The fly-fishing lessons were a big hit with her guests. She might suggest it to every group they bring up. Michael had tried to fish with a spinning reel and pole without success the previous night—this morning, he was so successful that Alex pressed him for fly-fishing tips.

The ride north from Sara Lake was steep, and, in some spots, it was treacherous. However, Michael, Luis, and Bruce handled it like veterans. They weren't so focused on the trail that they missed the wilderness they rode through. With his compact system camera, Luis took pictures throughout the ride. Ruby looked forward to seeing some of his shots after they made camp.

The goal today was to ride to Kimberly Lake, with enough time left to set up camp, tour the area, hike to the lake, and spend some quality time fly-fishing. Today's main activity was the ride itself; it would lead them higher into the mountains through spectacular terrain and, ultimately, to Kimberly Lake.

Ruby pulled her horse to a halt; they had to deal with the mountain in front of them and the second, most extensive, set of switchbacks on the tour. Alex, Bruce, Michael, and Luis silently stared at the slope and the weave of the trail.

Ruby faced the men. "Time for a break," she said as she smiled, leading them to a comfortable area off the trail, where they dismounted and stretched their legs.

Ruby opened a compartment carried by one of her pack horses. "Okay, guys, I'm going to lay out a few snacks and some drinks, including a thermos full of coffee. Let me know if you'd like anything else."

She set out the folding chairs, but the men preferred standing while they relaxed; they were still tender from the prior day's ride.

Ruby looked up at the steep switchbacks and winced; hiking through them would be tough. Fortunately, the horses handled it better than any man or woman could, but it was a rough climb for the horses, too. On every tour, she took a break at this point. It was necessary to rest the riders and the horses before the most strenuous climb of the day.

Randy fed and watered the horses while the guys ate late-morning snacks. After he finished, he gave Ruby a thumbs up. Fifteen minutes later, the Starr group was back in the saddle, riding toward the switchbacks.

"Gentlemen, don't overthink this ride. Remember, these horses have been here before. They know the trail. Follow my lead, trust your horse, and enjoy the ride. You've got this." Ruby turned her horse uphill and led the way.

The ride up the switchbacks was initially a challenge, but with Ruby's coaching, Luis, Michael, and Bruce adjusted their balance and handled the long climb. The trail was well-used and well-defined. For every ten yards they gained vertically, they rode five to ten times that distance as they looped back and forth. Unfortunately, it was the only way to climb this slope. The horses kept their heads down and kept moving. Ruby led the way, and Randy brought up the rear.

The weather had been inconsistent. It was cold while the boys fished on Sara Lake under scattered clouds. As they rode, dark clouds rolled in with a strong breeze. The overcast sky would have warmed them without the wind. Ruby and the boys turned up their collars and tried to keep warm. Baseball and cowboy hats were worn brim down as they rode. After a quick burst, Alex's cowboy hat flew off, and Randy snared it before it sailed off a nearby cliff to be lost forever. Once it was back on Alex's head, he put more effort into keeping its brim down.

After they topped out on the switchbacks, the trail leveled, and the trees thickened. The lodgepole pines stood straight and tall to their left, right, and ahead of them as the trail disappeared into the forest. Ruby pulled up as Randy rode by and took the lead. As the group passed, she noticed Michael and Bruce shift their weight from side to side in the saddle.

A half mile up the trail, they rode into the first decent place to rest since the switchbacks. Ruby rode down to a small meadow where a couple of downed lodgepole pines were pre-arranged as a makeshift hitching post.

"Time for a break," Ruby announced.

She helped steady their horses as each guest rode in and dismounted. She held on to Charlie's reins as Luis stepped off. "How's that big gray behaving for you?"

Luis smiled as he expertly swung his leg across the saddle, set his boot on the ground, and stepped out of the stirrup. "Are you kidding? Charlie doesn't know how to misbehave. He's a good horse."

Michael rode Suzy, the beautiful sorrel, and Bruce rode Britt. They both dismounted like experienced cowboys. These men and their horses were becoming one. Still, everyone was happy to get out of the saddle and take a break.

"If your backside is still sore, try to walk it off. It's the best we can do until we jump into the lake tonight," Ruby offered.

With his dark skin, clear eyes, and six-foot frame—standing an easy six-three due to the heels on his cowboy boots—Luis looked like a romantic figure right out of an old western. In his clear management voice, he looked at Ruby and said, "I have a question for you."

"Sure, Darlin," Ruby replied.

"You, Alex, and Randy are all armed today. You have a pistol, Randy has a rifle, and Alex has both. Is there a problem? Should we be worried?"

Ruby tried to keep her smile. No, honey, don't worry." She locked eyes with Alex.

Alex, who had just settled Radar, walked into the middle of the group. "I'd appreciate it if I could take this one." He spoke in a loud, low, official voice. "You all know I'm here not only for pleasure, although I've had one hell of a good time." He almost smiled, but an intense look cast a shadow in his eyes. "I'm in charge of security, a job I'm trained for and a job I'm good at. Before we hit the trail this morning, I asked Randy and Ruby to carry their firearms. You've probably noticed that I've been on the two-way radio a lot today. I check in with our local law enforcement several times, and I update them on our progress, and they update me on any useful information they might have."

"Cut to the chase," Bruce ordered.

"I'm getting there," Alex said with a wrinkled brow.

Bruce sheepishly looked down at his feet.

"This morning, I was informed of some weird news—weird enough that I increased security. The Ninety-niners dropped a new video on social media."

Alex looked at each person, verifying he had their attention.

He continued, "They bragged that they had kidnapped Bruce. And they planned to hang him."

"What bullshit!" Bruce said awkwardly while he frowned.

"Are you sure they didn't say they planned to kidnap him?" Luis asked.

"Positive. The Ninety-niners specified they had kidnapped Bruce and said they were taking him to a ridgetop to do the deed."

"That's intent," Luis said.

"Sounds like bullshit to me," Ruby said.

"I can't disagree with that, Ruby. This could be a prank, but we must take it seriously. Luis is right; there could be intent. This morning, I advised Bruce, but he didn't want to abandon the tour; he wanted to keep going. Luis and Michael, I didn't advise you, and I should have. I apologize. This affects every single person here. So, I'm asking. We could be riding into trouble. Should we cancel the rest of the tour? We could turn around and ride back to Badger Lake. It's all downhill from here. We could make a good time. What do you think?"

"My answer is still no. I want to finish the tour," Bruce said emphatically as he crossed his arms.

"I want to keep going, too," Michael said. His voice quivered, but he appeared determined. "But moving forward could be dangerous."

"I agree," Luis added.

Ruby and Randy nodded.

"All right, that's what I expected," Alex said. "Michael, you're right; moving forward could be dangerous. So, we need to be security conscious. Keep your eyes open, and never walk off alone. Even if you have to take a leak, someone else must go with you. I'm serious."

Everyone nodded again.

"We have another safeguard that may give you peace of mind. Another group on horseback is following us, and they are prepared to catch up with us and help if we have a problem.

Ideally, we will never see them. But if we need them, they are right behind us."

"Did we hire them?" Bruce asked.

"No, they are good people who volunteered to help. They are a group of friends from Boise who like to ride horses. I have also been in radio contact with them. Be sure to voice your concerns."

"So, they aren't law enforcement or security?" Bruce asked.

"Take my word for it, Bruce. My understanding is they are formidable."

"Your word is good enough for me, always has been," Bruce said.

"Thanks, Bruce," Alex said with a little extra gravel.

Ruby broke in. "Alex, you are formidable. I feel safe having you with us."

"So do we," Luis said.

Michael nodded enthusiastically.

"So, gentlemen…" Ruby slapped her hands on her thighs. "We'll hit the trail in twenty minutes."

———

The incline lessened as the trees thinned and their ride smoothed out. It was easy riding compared to the switchbacks. The terrain flattened as they approached a creek that blocked their way. The current flowed fast and deep and looked like it would be difficult to cross. Ruby dismounted to look while Luis and Bruce took time to photograph the area.

Randy watered the horses, and Ruby walked downstream until she found a wide, shallow section of the creek that looked promising. The guys put their cameras away, mounted, rode downstream, and crossed the creek, following Ruby's lead. After one more rise, the trail leveled, and the riding was more comfortable. As the trail became broader, they made good time.

The landscape was mountainous to their right and, to their left, forested. They rode through several areas that showed signs of human life, fire pits, and messy campsites strewn with litter. At one site, they stopped and took a quick break while they cleaned up the mess.

After another small climb, the landscape and the trail spread out again. To their right, a steep, choppy cliff was fronted with rough-edged boulders. The boulders were likely rocks that broke away from the ridge over time. To their left lay a small, attractive, half-moon valley. The valley backed into a steep hillside lined with a lodgepole pine forest. The valley was thick with vegetation, including bushes, grass, and clumps of young trees. It was an inviting and exciting area with several game trails entering and disappearing into the forested hillside.

Ruby was discussing the local wildlife when Randy noticed movement ahead. "Hey, Aunt Ruby, take a look," he yelled, pointing up the trail.

A young man stood in the middle of the trail. He stood as straight as a military sentry, and his eyes were locked on them.

CHAPTER THIRTY-ONE

Ruby's eyes focused on the trim, muscular figure blocking the trail. The imposing young man took two strides toward her outfit and shifted into a balanced stance, squaring his shoulders. She felt she was about to be pounced on by a predator.

Ruby pulled on Blue's reins. He was a big gelding with a minor flaw; he could get skittish if scared. Ruby slowly leaned forward and patted his neck.

A few seconds felt like ages when Randy shouted, "Another one is behind us!"

Ruby turned her head to see a second young man blocking the path ten yards behind the pack horses. Simultaneously, two more individuals, a young woman, and another young man emerged from a cluster of thick bushes to her left, never taking their eyes off Ruby. Ruby checked their hands for weapons; she didn't see any firearms, but the young man had something strapped on his left side. It was maybe a knife, maybe something else. The man in front of her kept his right hand hidden behind his back. They weren't wearing masks.

Ruby straightened in the saddle and kept her eyes forward.

The men she was leading were vulnerable. They were being hunted. She watched the lead hunter's movements, looking for a sign of his intent. He took a step forward and then another. His right arm moved a few inches, revealing a hidden pistol.

That's enough. "Alex, we have a problem," she yelled.

Alex had been riding toward the end of the line; he was in front of Randy and behind Bruce. He lifted his rifle from his saddle holster, pulled Radar to his left, and expertly positioned himself at an angle, blocking Bruce. He waved and shouted, "Everyone, get behind me. Now!"

Bruce, Michael, and Luis maneuvered their horses behind Alex. Randy stayed back with the packhorses.

Alex scanned the trail and the rough terrain to his right and then the valley. He held his position.

Suddenly, a crack of rifle fire came from somewhere in the trees.

One shot.

The bullet struck Alex in his upper body, heart center. He lurched backward with a jolt and grasped his saddle horn. He looked at Bruce and struggled to mutter one word. "Run!"

Alex swayed forward and fell off his horse. His head impacted the trail, but his leg was snared. He hung from his left boot, which was stuck in a stirrup. Radar reared up, and Alex's boot broke free. He lay in the dirt, face down and motionless.

Bruce turned Britt's head toward the trees. Following Alex's command, he dug in his heels and urged her forward. Britt responded and surged to a gallop. The hills and mountains to the west swept back and formed a narrow valley covered with grass, bushes, and rocks. Bruce held onto the saddle horn as they charged across the valley. They fled up a path into the hillside pines. Within seconds, they disappeared.

Suzy, Michael's horse, whose regular job was to follow behind the horse in front of her, watched Britt gallop away. Suzy threw her head and tried to fight her bit. Michael grabbed his saddle horn, gritted his teeth, and kicked her. Seconds behind Bruce, the pair galloped across the valley and disappeared up the same path.

Radar nosed Alex. As the horse raised his head, his ears perked up when one of the runaway horses whinnied. Radar whinnied back. Two seconds later, carrying an empty saddle, he galloped after them.

The volatile reality impacted Ruby like an explosion. She almost fell off her horse when she watched Alex's awkward collapse. Her voice scratched out the first sounds and steadily strengthened with each word. "No! No! No!" Her hands shook as she reached into her holster. She grabbed her pistol, lifted it sky-high, and fired.

Blue reared up, spooked by Ruby's sky-shot. Ruby struggled to keep her balance while holding her reins in one hand and her pistol in the other. Blue surged forward, spun around, and collided with the young woman standing on the side of the trail.

The young woman wailed as she hit the ground. She landed face-first, ripping her cheek open. She tried to wipe the blood from her face with her right hand but smeared it into her eyes. She rose to her knee, kept her head down, hyperventilating, and she threw up.

The young man next to her knelt and wrapped his arm around her. He glared at Ruby and pulled a tall can from his belt. He ripped off its lid, aimed, and released a stream of pepper spray. His aim was hurried, so not much liquid hit Ruby, but it doused her horse, soaking his nose and eyes. Blue snorted, threw its head, and awkwardly leaped away from the vile stream.

A residual cloud found Ruby's eyes and lungs, and she coughed for a moment before regaining control of her breathing.

Blue wasn't as lucky. He bucked while Ruby struggled to stay in the saddle. With the reins in her left hand and her pistol in her right, something had to go. Her pistol flew out of her hand, bounced off a rock, and fired. It scared the hell out of her and her horse.

Ruby held on to the saddle horn and kept her balance. Blue stopped bucking, but he was too far gone for her to control. He galloped toward the tree line.

After galloping across the valley, Ruby gripped the reins with both hands and, with her full strength, turned her horse away from the trees and toward the open ground below the forest. Ruby felt her chest loosen as her spooked horse galloped over a knoll, but it quickly tightened back up when she encountered a large dead ponderosa pine that blocked their way. Partially collapsed, it leaned sideways at less than a thirty-degree angle. Ruby's frightened horse tried to jump over the massive tree, and reacting too late, they didn't make it. He lost his legs, fell, rolled onto his back, and in one continuous movement, rolled back onto his four hooves and trotted uphill into the trees.

Ruby lay motionless under the collapsed, dead, and rotting tree. She stared at the blue sky above and watched an eagle circle and fly west.

What the hell happened?

Then she passed out.

CHAPTER THIRTY-TWO

Brett led the riders on a pleasant yet rigorous ride. They had covered uncounted miles and closed some distance between themselves and the Starr Outfit.

They had pushed the pace most of the day, enough to warrant a break. They stopped when they rode through a valley and approached one of the many small creeks along the trail. Next to the creek was a wide, flat area with enough space to spread out. The stream slowed and created a small pool. It was an excellent spot to water the horses, and it was a calming landscape with towering ponderosa pines, lodgepole pines, lazy grass, and gently flowing water.

The horses were fed oats and set into a picket line where they could graze on the long grass, and then the riders heard gunfire— three separate shots.

DeShawn jumped to his feet and glanced at the horses. Mark had unsaddled them—they were covered with sweat and needed to cool down. A considerate idea suddenly turned into a mistake.

"That was gunfire; it couldn't be too far away. We need to ride out of here now," DeShawn said.

"Calm down. Let's take it one step at a time," Brett said as he walked over to the picket line. He slipped off Pepper's halter, slid on his hackamore, and led him toward the trail. "I've got my radio and my pistol. I'll ride ahead and let you know what I find."

With a quick leap, Brett swung his right leg over Pepper's back and sat bareback. Three seconds later, they charged up the trail at a full gallop.

Brett gritted his teeth and concentrated. If he had to, he'd hold on to Pepper's mane. Brett leaned forward, knowing his balance was necessary since riding wasn't easy without a saddle and stirrups. Still, he was invigorated, alive in a way that brought his senses to a high point, feeling and reacting to every movement Pepper made, knowing he was on a mission, a man and his horse.

Typically, when he rode bareback, he kept his posture erect and straddled his legs loosely and comfortably around his horse. Bareback riding was more about balance and movement than leg strength. However, the steep trail caused him to adjust as he struggled to hang on. He grabbed Pepper's mane when he slipped back on the uphill stretches. He weaved along the trail like the native Nez Perce weaved along the Palouse River at another time and place. Sometimes, he dreamed he belonged there.

The Trilogy Trail had climbed uphill since they started the day's ride. The first half of the ride had been slow and steep. This section of the track was faster but still steep in short stretches. Pepper hadn't slowed his pace since they had left the other riders behind and would run himself into the ground to please Brett. They had maintained a full gallop for too long, and Brett needed to take care of his horse. If he didn't, neither one of them would be much help to anyone. Ahead, the trail disappeared into the trees, and it was hard to tell what was coming.

Brett pulled back on the reins and panted, "Whoa, boy."

Pepper threw his head and charged forward.

"Whoa! I mean it. You've run enough. Calm down." He pulled back on the reins again.

Pepper slowed to a walk and turned his head back toward Brett. Pepper's look was puzzling.

Pepper had never stared at him like that. Maybe he was right. Perhaps he could handle it—he was an Appaloosa, after all. They had covered a lot of ground and had to be close. Those shots couldn't have been too far away.

"Okay, buddy, I'll trust you on this one. Let's go."

———

Luis knelt on both knees, closed his eyes, and silently prayed. He had turned Alex over onto his back to apply first aid, but Alex was gone. Luis bent over and tried to settle his stomach. He sulked for a moment, shook his head, calmed himself, took a couple of deep breaths, and approached Randy, who was working to calm the horses.

Randy found a good spot to set up a secure picket line and transferred the horses one at a time, and when he finished, he took a deep breath. Neither Luis nor Randy had seen horses run off like they had today; it was almost like a small-scale stampede.

"We need to cover, Alex. Do you have a spare blanket?" Luis asked.

"What? You mean he's dead?" Randy's eyes turned down into a crestfallen stare. He held his hands to his face and quietly cried. A moment later, he bent his knees and dropped to a squat while his wet eyes examined the long grass at his feet. He acted like a man who might throw up, but he didn't.

"I'm sorry," Luis said. He reached out and hugged the young man.

"He was such a good guy. He talked to me like a father. No, more like a grandfather. He cared about all of us." Randy dug through a pack, pulled out a blanket, and handed it to Luis.

Luis laid the blanket over Alex. "Would you like to say a prayer?" he asked.

Randy nodded, kneeled, and silently prayed.

When he was finished, they walked back to the horses. Randy asked, "Did you see where Aunt Ruby went?"

"No. I lost sight of her when she rode uphill. Everyone rode out of here at the same time. It happened too fast. Even the Ninety-niners ran off." Luis held out his hands.

"Should we ride out and look for her and the rest?"

"No, Randy. We need to be careful, and we need to slow down. If we leave now, it could make things worse. We need to stay put. If anyone tries to find us, they'll start here. If Ruby looks for you, she'll ride here first. Let's give them a little time to come back."

Suddenly, a riderless horse trotted out of the trees. It was Blue, Ruby's horse. He walked to the edge of a thick stand of lodgepole pines, turned, and stared at Randy.

Randy ran to the horse, and Luis followed. Randy seized Blue's reins and tried to lead him back to the picket line, but Blue wouldn't yield. He pulled Randy forward along the tree line with his nose to the ground. Randy struggled to hold on.

"Let him go. He acts like he knows where he's going," Luis said.

Luis and Randy walked behind the horse until they crested a small knoll. They looked downhill, and, to their surprise, they spotted Ruby.

Ruby was stuck under a fallen tree, her right leg unnaturally poked out beneath it. She lay flat on her back, and she was alive. The tree bridged a depression—leaving her trapped but not crushed.

Randy balled up both fists, shook them triumphantly, leaned over, and rested his hand on his aunt's leg. Her leg was warm.

"Aunt Ruby," Randy asked. "Are you okay?"

Ruby groaned an unrecognizable reply.

Luis knelt next to them and checked a couple of openings. "We need some help. This tree is too large. If we try to push it off her, the tree could shift the wrong way. If we had some extra muscle, we could shift the tree enough to slide her out, or if we had a lever, we could do the same thing. But we need an extra man or two. This is tricky. We'll have to be careful."

Randy frowned and said, "But we don't have any help."

"Not right now, but remember, another group is behind us. They could show up at any time. So, we need to get ready. Grab your axe. Let's find a lever. Ruby has been trapped too long."

CHAPTER THIRTY-THREE

B rett and Pepper galloped around a slight bend and found an attractive valley on their left.

Three things stood out as Brett rode into an expansive area. A blanket covered what might be a body. Five horses were tied to a well-set picket line. Brett was alone; no other human beings were in sight.

Brett rode Pepper to the picket line, dismounted, and left Pepper with the other horses. He was hesitant to look under the blanket; it somehow felt like he was intruding. But he had to know who it was. He pulled back the blanket to reveal an older man who lay with his eyes and mouth open in a frozen and silent yell. Brett could make a pretty good guess who he was, but he wasn't sure. Brett saw the wound in his chest and re-covered the man with the blanket. He whispered, "God be with you."

He pulled out his radio and spoke, "Agent Terry, Brett here, over."

"Brett, have you found them? Over."

"Yes, but the situation is undefined and unsecured. We have one dead from a gunshot wound to the chest. We have five horses secured, but no one else is here. Five people are missing, but they can't be far since their horses are here. I need to look around."

"Have you identified the deceased man?"

Brett scanned the valley from one side to the other to the tree line, looking for answers. The wind had picked up, and the clouds floated in an almost hurried path. Nothing stayed the same, and nothing made sense.

Suddenly, a young man jogged over a rise, and when he noticed Brett, he stared like a deer in headlights, but then quickly recovered from being stunned and ran toward him.

Brett rested his hand on his holster and answered, "I'm not sure who the deceased man is. There's a young man running down the hill in my direction. I need to get off the radio. We are going to need to alert the authorities. I'll call you back."

Randy was out of breath but relieved to find Brett. He quickly explained he was the Starr Outfit's wrangler, and that his aunt needed help. Brett followed Randy up the hill and over to where his aunt was trapped. A serious-looking man wearing a cowboy hat knelt next to a fallen tree. As Brett approached, the man shot Brett a stern look.

"Hi, I'm Brett." Brett leaned over and offered his hand. "I'm with a group of friends from Boise. We have been following you in case you needed help."

A slow smile appeared on Luis's face. He gripped Brett's hand. "Yes, of course—thank you. Alex told us about you. It's good you're here; we could use some help. Alex was shot, and our guide is trapped beneath this tree. She isn't crushed, so the best I can figure is to use a lever to lift the tree enough for her to crawl out." Luis suggested.

"It would be simpler and faster if we tied a rope to the tree and pulled it off onto the downslope," Brett said.

Luis raised his eyebrows slightly. "That won't work. I have an extensive enough engineering background to know that the three of us couldn't exert enough power to move the tree with a rope. However, we may be able to move it with a lever."

"Mr. Perez, I know who you are. I'm even a stockholder in your company, but I think we're talking about two types of power. You're talking manpower. I'm talking horsepower. We could tie a rope to the tree and let this horse pull it off."

Brett pointed at the saddled horse. "Randy, what's his name?"

"Blue."

"Can Blue handle a rope well enough to attempt this?"

"Blue is a great horse. Auntie's favorite, he can handle it."

Blue shook his head up and down.

If Luis was concerned about Brett, he wasn't anymore. He smiled. "Of course. What was I thinking? Horsepower indeed!"

An unidentifiable utterance came from under the tree, but it sounded positive.

Brett's radio squawked, "Brett, Tom here."

"Yes, Tom. Go ahead."

"I rode ahead of our group, and I'm here. Where the hell are you?"

"Ride across the valley to the tree line, turn right, and keep riding until you see us. Out."

Brett put the radio down and picked up the axe. He pointed at a section of the collapsed tree. "This section has almost completely snapped in two. Give me a minute to clean it up."

After a few well-placed swings, Brett had ensured that the tree was clear of any obstacles.

Suddenly, they heard the unmistakable sound of a horse. Tom crested the knoll, leaned forward in the saddle, and smiled. "Good! I found you. Can I help?"

"Your timing is perfect. Everyone, this is my friend, Tom." Brett said. "Tom, do you have your rope with you?"

"Of course."

Astride Blue, Randy secured the rope to his saddle, and Tom, riding Buck, took his position a short distance to the right. They both reined back until their rope's slack went taut. Brett knelt next to the uphill side of the fallen tree, ready to help when the tree pulled away.

Luis stood in front of the horses and analyzed their setup. He motioned Tom to move a couple of feet. "Okay, we're set. Now, together, on my mark." He raised his hand, swung it down, and yelled, "Go."

Tom and Randy rode forward. The tree rose up and slowly rolled over and downhill. It stopped after one and a half rotations and settled with a boom, sounding like a muffled bass drum.

Brett was ready to launch forward into the tree if it rolled back. Instead, he dropped to a knee, reaching for the blonde woman in the moist dirt and debris.

She pulled her arm away from Brett when he tried to assist, and she rolled onto her knees and rose to her feet, collapsing after two unsteady steps. Brett caught her and swept her into his arms. He had taken only a few steps when she opened her eyes. Her face was covered with grime, and her hair was laced with dirt and fragments from the rotting tree.

Still, Brett thought she looked familiar.

Ruby gazed into Brett's eyes, and she whispered, "Brett." She put her arms around his neck, pulled him close, and passionately kissed him.

Brett was stunned. But the kiss removed the foggy memory. When their lips parted, he whispered, "Ruby?"

Like she was given a strength elixir, Ruby erupted from her semi-conscious state. Her body stiffened, and she lucidly and angrily growled, "Put me down!"

"Wait a second," Brett said. He planned to carry her to a couple of blankets they had laid out.

"No! Now!" she ordered.

Brett carefully let her feet down and waited for her to be semi-stable before releasing his grip around her waist.

Ruby stood on her own. She took a few moments to steady her legs and slowly swung her arms back and forth as if loosening up or testing her stability.

Brett stood behind her with his hands out, ready to catch her if she fell.

She turned on her heel and wobbled a little.

Brett straightened up and gave her a reassuring smile.

Ruby smiled back and punched Brett in the face. Hard.

CHAPTER THIRTY-FOUR

After several gunshots and an unexpected exodus on horseback, the Ninety-niners regrouped. They had hopes of understanding the ramifications of what in hell had just happened. Bright sat on the ground, bleeding. Rage knelt beside her and rested his right hand on her shoulder; his eyes were fearful, angry, and confused. "Are you all right? You're bleeding. Did... did you get shot?"

"No, I scraped my face and was stunned for a minute. It's not a big deal."

Rage sighed. Then, his eyes turned cold as he spoke to the group. "Everything has gone to shit. Let's get the hell out of here!"

The group limp-jogged up the Trilogy Trail for a quarter-mile and turned onto an insignificant path that led to a small clearing in the forest where they had left their backpacks. Once on the path, they slowed their pace and kept their mouths shut. No one had much to say.

Bright wasn't the only one injured. When the outfitter's gun fell to the ground and discharged, Rage had dived for cover and cracked his knee on a good-sized rock. When the pretend hikers stopped to rest, he sat down on his pack, rubbed his knee, and shook his head. He couldn't believe their plan had gone from under control to total failure in seconds.

Digit approached him and asked, "How's your knee?"

"Don't worry about my fucking knee! It's not a problem," Rage snarled.

Digit held his hands up and walked away. After making eye contact with Bright, he sat next to her. The rip on her upper cheek wasn't deep, and her bleeding had slowed. It wasn't as bad as it looked. Digit poured water from his canteen onto a clean cloth, washed her face, and placed some bandages over the wound. "The swelling should go down pretty soon," he said while putting the wrappers in his bag.

Rage stood up and limped over to Digit and Bright. "Whoever shot the old guy blew up our mission," he said in a firm voice.

"I don't know about that. Once we were in position, we should have taken control." Torch said. "Rage, you should have taken the lead."

Rage snapped his head and yelled, "So, it's my fault? Bullshit! We were almost ready to take Arnold when the old guy was shot, and then it was too late. We couldn't kidnap Arnold after he galloped away on a horse."

"I guess that's true," Torch mumbled. "But there was a moment when we had a chance."

Rage stared at his feet and frowned.

"I have a question?" Bright's voice shook. "Do you think that old guy is dead?"

Everyone was quiet until Digit spoke up. "I was right behind him. He was shot in the chest. I think he was dead when he hit the ground."

A string of tears rolled down Bright's face. "I don't understand."

"I don't understand either. Everything happened so fast," Rage said.

"Too damn fast," Torch said as he raised his eyes.

"His death wasn't our doing." Rage leaned forward and stared at the dirt. "And the whole thing pisses me off."

"It pisses me off, too," Torch said.

"So, who shot that guy? Bright asked.

"Not us. I think the shot came out of the woods," Digit said.

"Do you think it was Fred?" Bright asked, wide-eyed.

"That's my question, too," Rage said.

"There's one way to find out." Digit pulled out their two-way radio and handed it to Rage.

Rage shook his head and hit the call button. "Fred, Fred, come in. Rage here." Rage paused for a minute. "Fred, Fred, come in."

There was no response.

Rage handed the radio back to Digit and said, "Let's try again later. We need to figure out what to do next."

Bright stood up and stuffed her hands in her pockets. "Arnold rode away alone. He could be lost," she said. "We should still try to capture him. I think he panicked. He's probably hiding in the trees."

"You're right," Rage said as his eyes lit up. "He's up in the forest. It's not far. If we hurry, we'll find him before anyone else. Let's hike up there and grab him."

The Ninety-niners renewed their mission's objectives with swigs of water and felt re-energized as they hiked southwest. They carried their guns but little else. Even with his bad knee, Rage limped in the lead. They stayed off the Trilogy Trail and hiked through the forest until they were sure they were close to where Arnold could be.

When they spotted horseshoe prints on an uphill path, they huddled together. "Let's start here. Spread out in an east-west line and march south. Let's snare him like a pack of wolves. If one of us sees him, we'll close in and hold him at gunpoint. No mistakes. No hesitation," Rage said.

They all nodded and headed out in their assigned directions. Radios would have helped them be more efficient. Instead, they would have to stay close enough to each other to communicate with hand signals. Their method was basic but silent.

Rage signaled everyone to come together after two hours without success. The forest was dense, too dense. They hadn't seen another trail, even a game trail. The Ninety-niners needed to adjust their search. They shifted their line toward the west, deeper into the forest, and searched toward the north. They marched along, looking for footprints, hoof prints, or any other sign of Arnold. They were losing light. Deep shadows developed as the sun swung toward the western horizon.

Bright hiked along the lower end of their search line when she heard a stick snap. She quietly slipped behind a tree. From behind her, a man on a horse rode through the forest. He pulled his horse to a stop as he spoke on a handheld radio. Sage slipped further out of his sightline and leaned against a pine tree. Somewhere nearby, a bird screeched. Bright closed her eyes and took a deep breath. After thirty seconds of silence, she peered around the tree. The man on horseback was still there. He stared at a device in his hand. She waited a few more minutes, and when she risked taking another peek, the man and the horse were gone.

Bright made her way to Rage, and when he spotted her, she waved her arms. Rage signaled the others, and within a few minutes, the group reunited.

They huddled behind a cluster of small trees. "What's up?" Rage whispered.

"I saw a man riding a horse through the trees. He carried a few gadgets, including a radio," Bright said.

"Gadgets like a phone or a GPS?" Rage asked.

"Probably a GPS. He kept looking at the screen while he sat on his horse."

"Could it have been Arnold?" Torch asked.

"No, it wasn't him."

"Did he see you?" Digit asked.

"No, I hid behind a tree until he rode away."

"Did you see anything else?" Rage asked.

"Yeah. He had a rifle."

"Shit! He's probably part of a search party. There could be more of them," Rage said.

"And if they're on horseback, we're at a disadvantage," Digit said.

"We can't compete with a search party on horses. I think we're done. Let's get out of here," Rage ordered.

"Agreed." Bright straightened her back.

Digit and Torch nodded and stood up from their squatting positions.

They hiked north. After a little effort, they finally found the clearing where they had left their backpacks and were relieved it was over.

It was time to radio Fred again.

―――――

A quarter-mile away, Fred rode his horse through the forested area. He had planned to scout the area, but he couldn't see through the trees. The slopes were gradual and fertile enough to support a dense forest. Lodgepole and ponderosa pines dominated the space, but the land was also covered with bushes and smaller trees. As hard as Fred tried, he couldn't see any movement, wildlife, hikers, or horses.

If Fred wanted to search for Bruce Arnold or the Ninety-niners, he would need to ride through the forest and scour the area. That wasn't going to happen. He couldn't take a direct role in Bruce Arnold's abduction or hanging. That was the Ninety-niners' job, and it looked like that plan got screwed.

Today was a bust. Only one person could have stopped the Ninety-niners: the Yoster security man, Alex Ford. When Fred recognized him, he had no choice. He had to eliminate him.

It didn't matter now.

They were at square zero. The Ninety-niners would have to take Bruce Arnold the hard way.

Fred considered his options as he rode his horse down a path that led him toward the Trilogy Trail. The kids would have to hold up their end of the bargain. If they didn't do what they came to do, they would learn the meaning of zero tolerance.

CHAPTER THIRTY-FIVE

As usual, Brett oversaw the pre-ride meeting. The men sat on a couple of logs, laid parallel to each other, and fashioned into benches, a remnant of what some ambitious vacationers made and left behind. Per Tom's request, Brett agreed to give him time to make sure everyone understood how to operate the advanced features on the new GPS units.

After a quick presentation, Tom asked. "Any questions?"

"Yeah, I can see where it shows where I'm going, but I'm not sure how this tells me where everyone else is," Mark stammered with a little frustration.

"Okay, let me show you," Tom said as he walked behind Mark and pointed at the GPS unit's controls. "You need to toggle over to the communication mode. See this setting?"

"Yeah, but—"

"Now, touch the links icon."

"Oh, okay, I got it. That's amazing," Mark said, grinning.

Tom owned the best outdoor sports outlet in the Treasure Valley. He was a good man to have around when they needed specialized gear. They were each equipped with state-of-the-art

GPS units. GPS technology wasn't new, but their small device's sophistication and ease of use were impressive.

Tom finished the tutorial and turned the meeting over to Brett.

"We're breaking the search area into four grids," Brett said. "Sage, you're taking section one, the northern grid. Tom, section two, north central. Mark, section three, south-central, and I'll take the southern grid. Everyone needs to ride through their grid as systematically as possible. We may find ourselves in rugged terrain, so we'll have to adjust as we see fit.

"According to the forecast, we may see some isolated storms with wind and lightning. We need to be careful; this is dangerous terrain. Call on your radio immediately if you need help. Keep track of each other on the GPS, and if you see any sign of the Ninety-niners, immediately alert the rest of us. Let's check in on the hour."

The Rider's Club had lost hope that the two missing men would ride back on their own; too much time had passed. Brett doubted Bruce and Michael had a plan when they rode off. They could be lost, hurt, or both. So much can go wrong in the wilderness.

Brett led the way as the Rider's Club and Sage saddled up and rode toward the path that entered the forest.

———

DeShawn stayed behind to manage their HQ. He was all business, dealing with a second death. Besides, he couldn't get the Colorado situation off his mind. DeShawn went over Colorado's story again and again. It didn't make sense. That guy must be a liar.

He had been on the radio with his boss and the Blaine County Sheriff. Their support could have been better. The sheriff had already officially declared Ranger Brooks's death an accident.

That conclusion made DeShawn's stomach churn. There was no way Brooks had died in a riding accident. Alex Ford's death was the second homicide in two days; at least, his murder was undeniable.

As the Rider's Club neared the end of their second day, they were a long distance from the Badger Lake Trailhead. DeShawn couldn't move Alex's body to the trailhead by himself, and he wouldn't walk away and let someone else handle it. He requested a helicopter, but the sheriff was worried about the weather and the precarious landing area. DeShawn insisted the valley was spacious enough for a helicopter to land, and he diplomatically told the sheriff to get off his ass and get one up here before it was dark.

———

Brett found hoof prints in his section. They didn't look fresh, and they were hard to follow. He tried to track them through several rocky areas that dotted the forest. The tracks turned north, crossed into Mark's section, and circled back into Brett's. They continued until they led to a rock-strewn clearing where a small cliff had eroded and pushed out most of the vegetation.

The wind picked up, and patches of the sky turned black. Brett felt and heard the first concussion of lightning. When he lived in Colorado, he experienced mountain storms and knew how violent they could be. He rode away from the trees and searched for shelter near the cliff wall. The next lightning strike was closer than the first, and Brett found himself in the center of a dangerous storm.

He dismounted, held on to Pepper's reins, and led him toward the cliff's edge. There wasn't an overhang, but it was as close as he could find. The sky opened with heavy rain. Pepper dropped his head and took the beating. Brett leaned against him and tried to give and receive comfort. The storm came hard and fast and, luckily, moved quickly. The wind swept the clouds to the northwest within a few minutes, and sunlight and blue skies reappeared as if nothing had happened.

When it was over, Brett moved away to a more open area. He radioed the others, "Brett here, are you guys okay? That was one hell of a storm."

"Mark here. I'm pretty wet, but I've seen worse."

"Sage here, lightning and thunder, but no rain. Okay, here, over."

"Tom here, no rain either, over."

"Good to know, everyone. Back to it, and check in on the hour. Over and out." Brett was soaked head to toe. He shook his head and rubbed Pepper's nose. "I guess that is what they call an isolated storm," he snickered.

He led Pepper alongside as he walked the perimeter of the rocky clearing. He had tracked a horse into the clearing and expected to track him away from it. They walked together as Brett examined every inch of dirt, sand, and vegetation. He would know which way to search if he could find a trace. But there was no trace to be found—nothing—except the mess left over from the storm.

———

Sage rode her search pattern, trying not to lose hope after the lightning and thunder. It was an instant panicked relief when a fully saddled, riderless horse, a pretty sorrel mare, appeared out of the trees. Sage slowly rode up to the horse and, in a calm voice, said, "Hi, honey." The horse reacted positively to her presence but shied away when Sage tried to ride close enough to reach her reins. The sorrel, a little spooked, turned west and trotted into the trees.

Sage followed, hoping to catch up, but the forest was thick and difficult to navigate. She led Tonto through twists and turns around large and small pines while trying to keep a western course. She hoped she was on the same trek as the sorrel, but after five minutes, she was done. Her methodology sucked. She faced a dense copse of lodgepole pines; the tall, skinny trees hardly left room for a horse to walk through.

"Well, that's why I haven't seen a hoof print for a while," she said to Tonto.

Sage took a deep breath and scanned the treetops. Through a gap in the trees, she could see a bright section of sky, possibly an area with a thinner accumulation of pines, maybe a clearing. She steered right and rode a circular course, forward and to the left, and as the forest opened up, Tonto increased his pace. It wasn't long before they rode into a clearing.

A small creek was flanked by a small oasis that opened before them. The mildly sloped terrain was smooth and covered with pine needles. It was an attractive spot reminiscent of a watering hole in a Daniel Boone movie.

Sage spotted a young man resting against a ponderosa pine. His arms were wrapped around his knees, and his head was down. When he heard Sage approach, he sat up in disbelief. His sad eyes were nested beneath a mop of messy brown hair. His dirty hands shook with a minor tremor. He quickly stood up and brushed his hands over his coat and pants, letting a small dust cloud loose. His cheerless face wore a mask of worry and fatigue.

Sage rode Tonto a little closer. "Hi, my name is Sage. I'm with a group riding the Trilogy Lakes Tour. We're from Boise; we're here to help." She smiled at the young man.

"Yeah. Okay, hi. Um, my friend. Alex..." He closed his eyes briefly, lifted his hands to his face, covered his mouth and nose, and quietly sobbed.

Sage's heart ached for the man. "Yes. I am sorry. I heard."

A few seconds later, he took a deep breath, opened his eyes, and said, "Excuse me, it has been a tough day. Alex told us about you and your friends this morning." He choked down another sob, took a deep breath, and said, "I'm kind of lost."

Sage held up her GPS. "Well, you aren't lost any longer. I have a GPS."

His face flushed with relief, and he weakly smiled. "I'm Michael. Sage, you are a miracle. Thank you."

"You're welcome." Sage smiled.

"I screwed up and now I can't even find my horse. I must look like a fool."

"I spotted your horse a few minutes ago, a pretty sorrel. Right?" She must be nearby, and Michael, you don't look like a fool."

Michael's eyes softened.

"Give me a minute," Sage said, holding up her radio. I'm calling my friends. I'll let them know I found you. Then we'll go find your horse."

Michael awkwardly stood while clasping and unclasping his hands. He acted like he didn't know what to do with them. He took a few paces in a circle and then noticed a large rock with a flat side. He moved in closer and saw what appeared to be words etched into it. He knelt next to it and read, "THE ANGEL WAS HERE."

Michael turned to face Sage as she finished her conversation, and before he could tell her what he saw, she told him the plan.

"A small game trail leads south from the creek. We should head out." She reached out to Michael with her right arm.

He awkwardly but successfully swung up and behind her onto Tonto's back and wrapped his arms around Sage's waist. After a dozen yards down the trail, they found fresh hoof prints.

"I've got an idea. What's your horse's name?" Sage asked.

"Suzy."

"Do you get along okay?"

"Yes, Suzy's a great horse, nice and friendly. She ran away when we had that thunder and lightning storm. It scared her."

"So, she'd probably react to your voice. If she's frightened, she may be happy to see you. While we ride down this trail, call out her name. Keep your voice calm and inviting. She may come to us."

"Suzy, Suzy," he called repeatedly as they rode down the game trail.

It wasn't long before they heard the horse's steps. Suzy trotted up and stood nose to nose with Tonto. Michael slowly slipped off Tonto's back. Suzy nosed Michael, and he easily grabbed her reins. Then he reached up and rubbed her nose and ears. She lowered her head and pressed into the rubs.

Sage checked her GPS and determined that if they kept a southeast course, they would find the trail she had ridden up on. It took them fifteen minutes until Sage found the trail and Michael's smile.

Sage turned to Michael. "So, should I call you Mike or Michael?"

"You can call me whatever you like," he said.

"Okay, Mikey, what did you think about Lake Sara?"

He turned toward Sage, wide-eyed. He gazed at her for a few awkward seconds. "It was great. The riding, fishing and camping, everything, and this wilderness is… *beautiful*."

"Yes, it is. I can't wait to see Kimberly Lake," she said.

"I was looking forward to it, too."

"So, Bruce Arnold invited you on this trip. You guys must be friends."

"I used to work for him. It's been a while, but we've kept in touch. I was surprised when he invited me. I've never called him a friend, but now… We've had a good time on this trip. It's been good for both of us to escape California."

"You don't work for him anymore, and he still invited you?"

"He wanted to get away from his company, so he said he didn't want to invite any of his employees. He said he invited us since we've had a good relationship."

"Are you worried about him?" Sage asked.

"Yes. I was pretty sick about everything until you showed up, and I'd bet Bruce feels the same way. I hope he's okay."

"Don't worry." She pulled back on Tonto's reins and stopped.

Michael pulled up next to her and peered into her eyes.

"We'll find him. Our friend Brett is looking for him, and *he* will never give up. He will find Bruce. Don't worry. It will happen," Sage said.

"Can I ask you a personal question?" Michael asked.

"Sure."

"You've been shadowing us for two days. Why are you helping us? Were you brought in by law enforcement or something? No offense, but you don't act like a cop. I don't understand."

Sage smiled and said, "I am not a cop. We were just doing the Trilogy Lakes ride, and we heard your party might need some backup. It was the right thing to do."

"We totally ruined your vacation. I don't think I have ever met anyone like you."

"Well, now you have."

CHAPTER THIRTY-SIX

Brett couldn't find a trace of the hoof prints he had been tracking before the storm. The heavy rain had power-washed the rocky surface clean. He was frustrated, knowing that his search was a bust and that his only step forward would be to start over. He turned Pepper onto a trail, and they worked their way downhill.

When he rode out of the trees, the valley below had four strips of bright orange tape laid out to mark the corners of a large square —not an ordinary sight in the wilderness. In the distance, Brett heard a faint flutter grow into a roar. Special Agent Terry's request for a helicopter came through.

Brett watched the helicopter land in the middle of the marked landing zone. Two men exited and ran low while carrying a stretcher. After a quick turnaround, the men hurried back with Alex Ford's remains secured to the stretcher. They slid the stretcher into the helicopter, lifted off, and flew south as quickly as they arrived.

Tom and Mark kept their horses away from the noise while they watched the skillfully piloted helicopter complete its mission. Brett rode over to them, and side by side, as if they were an 1870s posse closing in on a band of outlaws, the Rider's Club rode across the valley to where DeShawn waited.

Brett dismounted while he watched DeShawn check on Trixie, who was tethered to a makeshift hitching post. The helicopter's roar didn't bother her; she was calm and quiet as usual.

Brett put his arm around DeShawn. "Good job getting the helicopter. We didn't want to lose you. I was concerned you'd have to ride down to Badger Lake."

"I was worried, too, but my boss came through for me again. How did the search go?"

"We're still down one man," Brett said just as he saw movement in the trees.

Sage and Michael rode out of the forest and across the valley. Tom ran over to the pair and held their horses while they dismounted.

Brett turned around and yelled, "Sage, come here and bring Michael!"

Brett had to wait; Mark slowed Sage and Michael's approach.

"Michael, I'm Doctor Taggart. If I could have a few minutes." Michael turned his eyes toward Sage and asked, "You guys have a doctor?"

"Yes, and you haven't seen anything yet," Sage said.

"What do you mean?"

Sage pointed at DeShawn, who was talking to Brett. "See that guy who has his hand on the Palomino?"

"Yes."

"He is an FBI agent."

"You guys have an FBI agent? You're kidding, right?"

"No, I'm not kidding, and that's only the start. See the big man talking to the FBI agent?" Sage pointed again.

"Yes."

"He's Superman, and to top it all off," she pointed at Tom. "He's my dad."

Tom watched the exchange with a sly smile and stepped past his daughter. He reached out and offered Michael his hand, "Pleased to meet you, Michael; I'm Tom. Looks like my daughter may have figured out how to ring your bell."

Michael smiled and looked at Sage. "She figured that out right after we met."

Mark shook Michael's hand and asked, "Are you injured or have any other medical issues?"

"No. I'm doing great, thanks to Sage."

"Good. Let me know if I can help."

"Will do, doctor. Thank you."

DeShawn pulled Michael aside. He explained that he was friends with the Rider's Club but also on the job. He wanted to give him some time to rest, but he would like to talk more after dinner.

Brett raised his hand to get everyone's attention. "Everyone, listen up. The Rider's Club and the Starr Outfit have merged for the rest of the tour. Ruby and her group have ridden ahead and set up camp, and she's cooking dinner in her camp kitchen. Is that a good thing, Michael?"

"Yes, sir, that's an excellent thing," he beamed.

"I knew you'd say that. So, everyone, saddle up. Our new camp is ten minutes up the trail, less than a mile from Kimberly Lake."

Michael and Sage rode side by side as the six rode onto the trail. Brett rode up next to Sage. "I'd like to ride with Michael if that's okay."

"Sure," she said. She smiled at Michael and said, "Be nice to him. He's our leader."

She slowed down and let Brett take her spot.

Michael looked back at her with wide eyes.

She gave him a reassuring nod.

"I'm thrilled we found you today, but we still haven't found

Bruce. I'm planning to ride back and take another look. You might know something that might help with the search," Brett said.

"I'm happy to share—anything to help. I'm worried about him. What would you like to know?" Michael stroked Suzy's neck.

"First, I'd like to understand Bruce's state of mind. Randy said that he rode away, and seconds later, you followed. What motivated you to react?"

"Alex…" Michael took a big swallow before continuing. "This morning, as a precaution, he set up a few code words to help us react quickly during a risky situation. Right after he was shot, Alex said, 'Run,' and we ran." Michael turned his head and wiped his eyes with his forearm.

"Wow," Brett whispered. "His last word?"

"Yeah. Right before he fell off his horse," Michael said slowly.

The sound and rhythm of the horses' hooves on the trail bounced off the trees. The sound of the tack and rings hitting leather calmed the men as they collected their thoughts.

Brett finally broke the silence. "After you rode away, did you have a plan to follow?"

"I wish we did; maybe I wouldn't have gotten lost if we had one. I'm sure Alex would have led us to safety."

"Did you ever catch up to Bruce?"

"I hesitated after I looked down and saw Alex on the ground with a chest wound—I knew he must have been dead." Michael closed his eyes and cleared his throat before going on. "I followed, but I never caught up with Bruce. But I did spot him for a moment. I climbed, looking for better trails, and searched for him. I thought I was in trouble when the forest thinned out. It became rocky and hard to navigate. That's when I saw Bruce ride by above me, maybe on a cliff. I led Suzy up through the rocks until I found a trail. I wasn't sure if it ran along the upper part of the mountain or downhill toward Badger Lake or into a cliff. I didn't know and wasn't comfortable guessing. I didn't see Bruce again, and I didn't want to try to ride down the ridgeline alone. I wanted to find Ruby and the rest of our group. So, I turned around and tried to backtrack until I became disoriented and lost. I was in real trouble when I lost Suzy, but it all worked out when Sage found me."

Brett collected his thoughts and said, "It sounds like when you broke above the tree line, there was a trail that runs along the ridge, and Bruce was riding on that trail."

"That sounds right," Michael said.

CHAPTER THIRTY-SEVEN

Brett led the Riders into the campground that Ruby had expertly laid out. Even their tents and gear were organized and staged.

Randy helped with their horses and politely offered directions on organizing and stowing their gear. He held Buck's reins as Mark dismounted. "I'll take him from here," Randy offered.

"Hold it. This is usually my job. You can't handle all these horses by yourself."

Another cowboy approached Mark and introduced himself. "I'm Luis. That's why I'm here. Randy needed an assistant, and I volunteered."

Mark smiled at Luis. "Well, then. Thanks."

After Michael slid off Suzy, Ruby approached Michael and hugged him so hard that he lost his breath. She quickly wiped her eyes, and without saying a word, she returned to her camp kitchen and worked on dinner.

After the horses were secured, Randy built a fire in an existing pit. A few fallen logs lay nearby for seating, but it wasn't enough, so he set up some camp chairs.

Michael and Sage sat next to each other. Like everyone else, Luis was excited to see Michael, but there was a shadow over the campers. Everyone was worried about Bruce. DeShawn, Tom, and Mark joined the circle. DeShawn engaged Luis with some small talk while Michael and Sage talked in hushed tones and scooted closer together.

Brett and Ruby kept eyeing each other but kept their distance. Nothing had been said since she hit him, and they needed to talk. Brett wanted to make things right, but he needed to ride back to the northern search area and find that trail above the tree line. Bruce could be up there, alone, afraid, or hurt, and there was only one way to find out.

Brett checked in with the Rider's Club, saddled Pepper, and said his goodbyes. Before leaving, he walked by Ruby's kitchen, but as he approached, Ruby turned her back to him and looked away.

Undeterred, Brett circled to meet her face-to-face and stepped close to her. It was a risk since her first punch had blackened his eye. He planned to duck if she tried to hit him again. "I'll be late for dinner. Michael spotted Bruce on a trail above the tree line where we didn't search. I'm riding up there to find him."

"All right, I'll hold dinner for two." She said without expression.

"When I get back, we should talk."

Ruby didn't answer.

Brett didn't mind missing dinner to find Bruce; it gave him more time to sort out what he would say to Ruby later.

Innocent, fluffy, scattered clouds lightly covered the sky. The angry black clouds that had soaked him earlier had erased the crime scene and left the earth renewed, but there was still much to do, and the sun was dropping toward the western mountains. The temperature had started its nightly fall, and even though Brett was adequately insulated in his Blue Levi's coat, he felt the cold pierce the marrow in his bones. He shivered.

The Trilogy Trail led back to the valley in a wide, smooth, and downhill grade. After a quick and easy five minutes, Brett and Pepper rode up the thin trail where Bruce and Michael entered the forest. The trick was to find the trails that led to the ridgetop. He tried to stick to a rigid search pattern when he searched earlier, but with dusk coming fast, it was time to find the easiest way to navigate through the stand of pines.

The first trail they intersected turned south and snaked toward the valley. The second trail also turned south and joined the first one downhill. The third trail cut northwest and climbed uphill. He felt like he was making progress. The trail split after a five-minute ride, and Brett turned Pepper up the steeper northwest branch. They had less than two hours of light left. It needed to be enough.

The trail disappeared into a scree field as they broke through the tree line. Brett led Pepper around the rocks and through an opening. On the broad summit, they found the elusive ridgetop trail. It ran north and south. Brett instinctively turned Pepper south. The northern route looked like it would run out quickly.

Brett held Pepper back while he took his time scanning the rocks on his right and the forest on his left. He kept their pace slow and easy. Bruce could be lying in a pile of dirt or riding his horse down the trail.

He was wrong on both counts.

He found Bruce leaning against a tree. His horse stood fifteen feet away. Bruce nodded at Brett in an almost too casual manner, and then his eyes fell, focusing on his right boot.

Brett dismounted and quickly knelt in front of Bruce. "Bruce, my name is Brett. I'm with the group trailing behind you and the rest of the Starr Outfit. I'm here to help." Brett pointed at the buckskin mare. "You have a good horse; she hasn't strayed. How about I grab her and let's ride out of here?"

"Ride where? It doesn't matter where I go. I create hate everywhere," Bruce lamented.

"If that's true, you'll need to find a way to change the hate into something else."

"Oh, that's easy for you to say, mister. You don't know me and don't know how fucked up my life is."

Brett grabbed the reins of Bruce's horse and said, "I know who you are, and I know you're intelligent. So, it all comes down to courage. You need courage to change."

Bruce glanced at Brett with a slight scowl. "I'm sure a big man like you has plenty of courage, but I'm not a big man."

"Truth be told, I have a personal issue I've ignored for years. I have to work up the courage to deal with it. Pretty soon, in fact. I can't hide from it. So, we have something in common. We both need to suck it up."

Bruce chuckled. "Now I'm intrigued. How can an old personal issue arise in the wilderness?"

Brett had asked himself the same question. Although discussing his personal affairs wasn't something Brett wanted to do with anyone, especially with a billionaire target. But maybe discussing it would distract Bruce from his self-imposed hell. Brett held his left index finger beneath his left eye. "You see this black eye?"

"Yeah."

"Ruby Starr."

"She hit you?" Bruce stared in disbelief and almost chuckled.

"It was a right cross, and I deserved it. I need to talk to her tonight. I've put this off for years."

"Well, I can't see how anyone could have a problem with Ruby. She is a hard-working, intelligent woman who always smiles and has a heart of gold. You must have done something wrong. If she punched you, you probably deserved it."

"She didn't smile when she punched me, but other than that,

you're correct. I have a code I live by, and at times like this, it helps me keep perspective and gives me direction. Can I quote you a line that relates to both of us?"

Bruce looked at Brett with a confused frown. "I think we may be talking about different problems. But, once again, I'm intrigued."

"Live each day with courage."

Bruce mounted his horse, and the two men rode the trail back toward camp. It was ten minutes into the ride when he finally broke the silence. "So, this code of yours... it isn't yours?"

"That's right. It was originally The Code of the West before the State of Wyoming adopted it as its moral code."

"I'm surprised. I didn't know that. Can you quote another line?"

"Sure, *'Remember that some things are not for sale.'*"

"Man, you've got me on that one," Bruce said.

Brett and Bruce rode downhill toward the valley. Brett's conversation relaxed Bruce and kept him from brooding, but he did spend some time self-evaluating.

"I think part of my problem is I distance myself from everyone except my wife. I need to separate myself to secure my interests," Bruce said.

"I get it. Your interests are so significant; everyone wants a piece of you. It must also seem you don't control your interests; rather, your interests control you."

Bruce pulled the reins and stopped. He stared at Brett quizzically. "Exactly, you sound like a man who has been through a similar situation," he said, nudging Britt back into a walk.

"I played a lot of football back in the day, and the more I played, the bigger the game became. It became more important than everything else: my personal life, family life, finances, and health. I lost control of everything until one day, I woke up and walked away."

"I've felt that way. Sometimes, it all doesn't seem worth it. I'm thankful I have a loving wife. Without her, I don't think I could survive. I got involved in tech as a teenager, and now it's all I know. Everyone I deal with is an employee, an attorney, or a business associate. I can't say I have ever had a true friend."

Brett pulled up and looked at Bruce. "You have some now."

CHAPTER THIRTY-EIGHT

When Brett and Bruce rode into the camp, a small cheer erupted. They were late—but hopefully, they weren't too late—Brett and Bruce were hungry. Ruby left the kitchen, ran past Brett, and almost knocked Bruce over with one of her cherished bear hugs. When she finally let him go, Bruce shot Brett with a knowing look.

Brett shook his head.

Randy and Luis stood close by, waiting to shake Bruce's hands. After everyone greeted Bruce, Luis and Randy unsaddled Britt and led her to join their small but growing herd.

"You guys made it in time for dinner. Let's get you something to eat," Ruby said.

Ruby hauled up enough food to feed a small army with the help of a couple of pack horses. The Rider's Club benefited from the changeover, a culinary upgrade. Ruby's dinner included steaks, potatoes, corn on the cob, and peach cobbler for dessert.

Brett savored each bite of dinner, and when he took a bite of the peach cobbler, he closed his eyes, escaping into the flavors. When he opened his eyes, reality slapped him sober. He was happy they found both men today, but he wished he could have done more. If he had, maybe Alex Ford would be alive.

Then his mind drifted to Ruby and what could have been.

The campground was large and reasonably flat; a trickling stream ran through its eastern edge as it slowly flowed toward Kimberly Lake. Ten tents sprawled along a stretch backed by lodgepole pines. The horses were to the north, the fire pit was mid-camp, and the camp kitchen was to the south. Across the stream, a trail led to their portable outhouse.

After dinner, DeShawn was all business. He interviewed Michael and got a play-by-play recitation of the encounter with the people who stopped them on the trail and the shooting. After forty-five minutes, he went over everything with Bruce. Both men were more than cooperative; they were appreciative and happy that Agent Terry was so thorough.

Mark checked up on his three patients, Ruby, Michael, and Bruce, starting with a physical checkup and then offering to help with their mental stress. Alex's death had shaken all three.

Bruce said he felt like he had lost a close family member. He regretted their past and wished he had treated Alex more like a friend or an uncle. Mark validated it was hard to take and would hurt for a long time.

Ruby admitted she was lucky she didn't break her leg, arm, or neck when she was thrown from her horse. She was bruised but not broken, and based on her positive attitude, Mark gave a positive prognosis. He offered her pain pills, but Ruby passed.

Michael thanked Doctor Mark for his attention but reassured him he was physically and mentally okay. He took Alex's loss hard and understood he would carry it with him forever, but that was grief, not a medical problem, and dealing with a loss was personal.

The sun dropped behind the western mountains, and with it came a quick drop in temperature. The higher altitudes meant colder nights, but the flames from the fire pit helped; they were warm, comforting, and hypnotic. A bottle of whiskey appeared after most of the group settled around the pit. Tom, Mark, and Luis slowly sipped from their camp cups. Neither Sage nor Michael drank whiskey, and unfortunately, there wasn't a bartender mixing gin and tonic.

Bruce stood and smiled at Tom. "Save a little for me. I need to make a phone call."

As Bruce padded into the darkness, Tom asked Luis, "He's making a phone call?"

"Yes, he calls his wife every night. He has a satellite phone."

"Of course he does," Tom said, shaking his head.

Sage and Michael scooted close together as the night cooled. "Where do you live in California?" Sage asked.

"Sunnyvale."

"You're not too far from me. I live in San Francisco."

Michael couldn't hide his excitement. "Really? That's only about an hour away. That's great. What do you do in the city?"

"I'm an account manager at a digital marketing company. It's a lot of work, but it's going okay." Michael was transfixed by the light from the campfire that sparkled in Sage's eyes.

"That's a great field with multiple sectors transitioning their dollars to digital advertising." Michael smiled.

Luis leaned over into the couple's space and added, "I agree; a high percentage of our marketing is going in that direction."

Sage smiled politely at Luis and then pressed her shoulder closer to Michael. "You said you left Yoster. That had to be difficult. It was probably a pretty good job."

Michael nervously scratched his nose. "Yes, it was, but I'm young, and I wanted to have a new experience. So, I moved on."

"Where do you work now?" Sage asked.

After a short pause, Michael replied, "Lane Technology."

"I've heard about them. Lane Technology is a great company. Do you like working there?"

Michael paused for a second and quietly cleared his throat. "Well, yes, I do."

They sat in silence, letting the flames warm their cheeks.

Sage announced. "Ruby has hot water on her stove; I'll be back in a few minutes. I'm going to make a cup of tea."

While she was gone, Luis leaned close and whispered, "Michael. I don't think she knows who you are."

Michael nodded and smiled. He patted his heart twice and took a deep breath.

Luis leaned back and returned the smile.

Bruce returned from his phone call when Sage returned with her tea and re-joined the others. The glow of the campfire wrapped around the group. Its warm flickering light turns strangers into companions, bound by a quiet magic under the stars. It was distracting.

No one noticed. They weren't alone.

———

A man in dark clothing stood in the trees above them, studying the camp. Satisfied, he turned, hiked back to his horse, and rode away.

CHAPTER THIRTY-NINE

B rett skipped hanging out with the group at the fire pit. Instead, he decided to take a brisk hike down the trail that led to Kimberly Lake. He didn't care about the hike or Kimberly Lake; he needed time alone. He needed to walk, and he needed to think.

Brett took pride in his strength and confidence, but this evening, he had neither. He was afraid—not of Ruby—*well, maybe a little*. He worried he might not say the right words the right way. He felt he was years and years too late. Still, he wanted to tell her he cared and wanted another chance. He touched his bruised eye, and a twinge of pain shot through his skin to his nose. Ruby had the combination of beauty, femininity, and tenderness, along with the explosive power of a midwestern tornado.

How could I be so clueless not to know Starr Outfitters was hers? When Bruce Arnold's staff vetted the outfitters, they picked the one owned by Ruby Starr. Of course, they wanted the best. Brett should have known.

After he left Wyoming, he tried to keep track of her. When he spent his weekends tackling running backs in the NFL, she rode horses, barrel racing on the rodeo circuit. He let the distance get too far. While he lived in Denver, she married another man. After Brett learned about that, he tried to keep her out of his thoughts. That was tough.

After some time, an old friend told him she got divorced, but Brett never followed up. He selfishly wished it was true but never did anything about it.

Brett blew out a fast breath and turned around. He wouldn't have felt more confident if he had walked through the Idaho wilderness for a month. His confidence level was stuck at zero. There was no reason to be optimistic after the way he treated her. He needed to suck it up. Now was as good a time as he would find. He had waited long enough.

Brett had thought about this conversation all day long. Still, it was hard to know what to say. He decided to stick with the basics. First, he would apologize. Second, he would stick to the truth. It wasn't a complicated plan and was probably a poor one.

Brett trudged back into camp. Ruby stood beside the stove, heating a pot of hot water and coffee. A bright lantern hung nearby. She had removed her apron and replaced it with a light coat. She wasn't wearing her cowboy hat, which helped the lantern's warm light highlight her suntanned skin and blue eyes. Her long blond hair was tucked back in a ponytail. Her tight jeans enhanced her curves. Brett took a deep breath and strolled toward her.

After hearing his footsteps, she addressed him without looking up from the stove. "There you are. I wondered if we were still on for *our talk*."

Brett stopped five feet short of her, and Ruby stepped back and stood her ground. They faced each other awkwardly in the camp kitchen, like two knights readying for the joust.

"Hi, Ruby." Brett slumped, attempting to meet her stare, and he shivered slightly. His brown and orange flannel shirt was too lightweight for the cold evening. Hunched over, he resembled a tired mountain man. He took a deep breath. "I've been walking around tonight, thinking about what I would say to you."

Ruby crossed her arms.

Brett took a deep breath and exhaled the words, "Ruby, I'm sorry."

"It's been a long time, Brett." Ruby didn't blink.

"I know, but it doesn't change how I treated you. You didn't deserve it."

"I can't lie; I thought about it for a long time, and it finally occurred to me why you left me. You were moving up, and there was no place in your world for a Wyoming girl like me. I get that. I do. What pissed me off was how you dumped me. You ghosted me, which means you had no respect for me at all! You walked away without a word. One day, we were a couple, and the next, you were gone." A tear slid down Ruby's cheek.

Brett closed his eyes briefly. "You're right, of course. My world changed when I was drafted, and I wasn't mature enough to handle it. Suddenly, there were agents, sponsors, press, and public relations people. I was caught up in it and overwhelmed, but that doesn't make my behavior acceptable. There is no excuse, but I know now what I missed. When I finally realized it, the damage was done. I lost you."

"Well, Brett." Ruby took a single step toward him. She shoved her hands into her apron pockets and looked either confident or angry. It was hard to tell. "I also owe you an apology. I'm sorry I punched you in the face. I shouldn't have done that. So, let's call it even and let it go. We'll be together for the next few days. Let's put this behind us and do the job."

Brett took a small step forward and looked at Ruby. "Okay, but there is something else. When I was in Denver, I realized how much I'd screwed up. You should know I tried to track you down, and I found you. But I was too late. You were married."

"That doesn't make me feel better at all. Time passes, and people get married. That's normal. You did the same thing, right? You moved on."

"I've had some girlfriends, but no—not even close. When I heard you had gotten divorced, I had some hope. But I didn't act. Are you with anyone now?"

"No, I'm not. My marriage didn't last long—less than a year. Jake was nice but not much of a husband, and we never had kids." Ruby cast her eyes sideways and quickly sniffed.

"It's not too late to have a family."

"It's possible, but I'd be a pretty old mom." With a questioning glance, she chuckled. "Why? Are you volunteering?"

Brett smiled and stepped closer to Ruby. "I screwed up, but my feelings have never changed. We were good together. Time and all of my mistakes haven't changed my feelings for you. Ruby, you are still the love of my life."

She stepped up to Brett and stared deep into his eyes. After an uncomfortable silence, she hissed between her teeth. "Damn you. Where do you get off saying that kind of bullshit? You're twenty years too late, and I don't trust you!" She bent over and grabbed a fist full of pine needles, threw them into his face, turned, and marched away.

Brett stood alone, stunned, and watched Ruby stomp away toward her tent. Once she closed her flap, he gazed at the stars above the tree line, smiled, and muttered, "Same old Ruby."

CHAPTER FORTY

DeShawn patrolled the perimeter of the camp, building a mental image of the area, section by section. He pushed aside his nervous energy, and his FBI training took over. He was troubled by their chaotic day and the death of Alex Ford, and now their risk level grew while they camped in an exposed public area. Their camp was set up for convenience and comfort, not for defense. He was grateful that their tents were in a tight formation, but the bottom line was they all needed to avoid or secure the fringe areas.

DeShawn sat at the fire pit, and he passed on the whiskey. He needed to be clear-headed. He strategically positioned himself to watch while pretending to be relaxed. He wasn't on vacation. He was on assignment and refused to let his guard down. If he was acting like an old crab, so be it. He was there to keep his friends safe, all of them. That was his job.

Regardless of the risks, the Rider's Club and the Starr Group planned to keep their trip moving forward. The group was behind schedule; they would spend less time than was originally planned at Kimberly Lake. It was a sacrifice—one that they all accepted. They were here first and foremost for the ride through the wilderness, and missing a little scenery wouldn't bother them. There was plenty left to see. They planned to stick it out and enjoy the rest of the ride.

The group of riders believed they had a solid plan, but it wasn't one DeShawn agreed with. Every day was more dangerous; two men had been murdered, and another survived a gunshot wound. That should have been enough for them to fold up their tents and go home. They should have bailed on day one. Now, they were in danger out in the middle of nowhere. Colorado's warning should have been enough. To DeShawn, Colorado was trouble, but he couldn't prove it. And the Ninety-niners were still out there; another kidnapping attempt could come anytime.

Not long after DeShawn sat down, the campers were ready to call it a night. The whiskey had calmed their nerves, and everyone was content to turn in. Brett and Ruby silently sat on opposite sides of the fire like two magnets with their poles facing each other. They were pushing apart, turned away from each other, and neither smiled. DeShawn knew that all it would take was for one to flip, and they would snap back together.

DeShawn explained his security plan. He wanted to post armed guards throughout the night.

"I'll stay up for the first watch and let everyone else sleep. I'm not tired," Brett said.

"I appreciate that. I want to work in pairs, starting at ten tonight and rotating out every two hours. Ruby and Brett, you're first watch. Mark and Randy, take over at midnight. Sage and Tom take the next shift at two. I will take the four o'clock shift. Sunrise is around quarter to six. Does that work for everyone?"

Luis spoke up. "When is my shift?"

"Luis, you don't have a shift," DeShawn said.

"I want to contribute. I don't want to be babysat. Michael and I should be part of the team and contribute."

"You're capable, both of you, and you *are* part of the team, except the game here is to protect the potential targets, and you, Michael, and Bruce are the targets. I appreciate your offer, Luis; you're one hell of a good man. Anything else?"

Ruby kept her head down and stared at the fire. Her smile had disappeared.

DeShawn stood up and stretched his back. "We're not sharing firearms or radios. Everyone on guard duty needs to carry their own. If you see trouble, radio in; Brett and I will come running." DeShawn glanced at Brett.

Brett caught his eye and nodded.

———

Mark and Randy emerged from their tents and stepped to the fire pit at twelve o'clock sharp.

"Hi, guys," Mark smiled.

Ruby and Brett sat close together on one of the log benches. They had shifted the bench to an angle where they could enjoy the fire's heat while keeping their eyes away from the flames.

"Did you get any sleep?" Ruby asked.

"Not really. I'm a night owl. But I relaxed and read a little," Mark said, squinting at Brett.

Randy came from behind Mark and yawned. He carried a two-way radio and his Winchester rifle.

"I stocked up on firewood, so you should be in good shape," Brett said.

Ruby stood up, hugged her nephew, and kissed him on his cheek. "Goodnight," she said. Brett and Ruby left together. They walked close together and leaned toward each other.

Mark watched with a glint in his eye. Their body language had changed. It was a complete reversal since DeShawn's safety meeting.

A few minutes later, Mark and Randy sat in camp chairs beside the fire. Randy pulled over another chair and used it as a footrest. He leaned back as if he was in an overstuffed recliner.

Mark shook his head. He stood up, picked up his rifle, and said, "I'm going to walk around, stretch my legs, and check out the camp."

He patrolled the camp's northern edge, checked the horses, circled toward the east side, and walked south along the creek until he passed the camp kitchen and circled back north. The wind had picked up enough to make some tree branches shiver. The stars were spectacular. To the south, Jupiter chased Saturn across the sky.

He paused when from somewhere ahead, he heard something reminiscent of crinkling plastic. Mark noticed movement from one of the tents, and he tucked himself against a tree, hoping he would disappear in the dark. The front flap opened on one of the tents. Mark watched Ruby slip out of her tent, secure the front flap behind her, and pad to a different tent under a pine.

He smiled as Ruby crawled into Brett's tent.

———

Time crawls by when you are on guard duty. Mark and Randy were ready to retire when Tom and Sage took over at two in the morning. Randy nearly fell out of his chair at one point. When it was time to head to bed, he sat up, checked his watch, and mumbled goodnight. Mark slapped Tom on the shoulder and walked toward his tent. The zipping of the tent flaps sounded like an avalanche in the silence.

After a few minutes. Tom poked at the fire, and Sage took the first patrol around the camp. Sage was in her element. The moonlight highlighted the forest behind the camp, casting a beautiful effect that wasn't easily replicated. She walked the short circuit around the camp, gazing at the sky, looking for shooting stars. The breeze had pushed in some cloud cover, and most of the stars were blocked from her view. After she made the round, she sat on the campfire bench, keeping her eyes away from the bright light of the flames.

A movement on the peak of a towering tree caught Sage's eye. A large owl dove off the top limb and sailed straight down as if in free fall. It leveled a few feet above the ground and disappeared into the dark—a night hunter making a kill.

Sage stood up when she saw movement from somewhere in the tents. Alerted by Sage's attention, Tom stood just as a tent flap opened. Sage and Tom watched someone struggle to crawl out with a flashlight in hand. After stumbling, he walked toward the fire pit.

He held up his hands. "Don't shoot!" Bruce smiled. "With all this security, I thought I should let you know. I'm taking a quick trip down to the outhouse." He walked past the fire pit to where he could cross the small creek and hike down the hill.

Sage grabbed her rifle and followed. "Hold up, I'll come with you," she said.

Bruce stared at her as if she was an employee who had irritated her boss. "Come on. How about a little privacy?" he asked.

"Sorry. I'm following orders."

"Okay." Bruce shook his head.

"I'll stay back far enough to give you some privacy."

"Thanks."

After he crossed the creek, Bruce walked down the path that led to the portable outhouse. When Randy had set up the outhouse, he picked a spot surrounded by trees for privacy. It had been used enough to wear a slight path, but a good flashlight helped in the dark. Bruce had one, but it didn't benefit Sage from her distance behind.

The cloud cover thickened its blanket over the sky, reducing any light that might have helped Sage find her way. The light from the crescent moon was a diffused glow. Sage tried to watch her step as she followed Bruce's point of light. It was too late to turn back for her flashlight.

With a small jump, she cleared the creek, walked downhill, and followed Bruce. Her footing was solid regardless of the hillside's dirt, coarse sand, and rocks.

Sage stopped about twenty yards back when she noticed Bruce's light had stopped moving. Sage held her position, and after a few minutes, Bruce climbed out of the outhouse enclosure. Sage heard what sounded like him stumbling.

She called out quietly, "Bruce! You okay?"

There was no answer. Sage braced to charge down the hill and see if Bruce was all right when a tree branch snapped behind her.

Bruce's flashlight went dark.

Neither of them was ready for the attack.

CHAPTER FORTY-ONE

S age's face slammed into the dirt. The wind was knocked out of her. Stunned and out of breath, she felt a knee dig into the middle of her back while her arms were pulled back and cinched tight. Her face was pushed into the dirt. Lightning bolts of pain exploded through her back and shoulders. Sage closed her eyes, gritted her teeth, and tried not to cry out.

"Don't make a sound," a woman whispered. Then she spoke to someone else, "Be careful; you'll break her arms."

Sage stopped struggling and kept her eyes closed. She felt a warm stream of blood flow from her nose, and she choked on dirt and dust as she fought to breathe.

She felt a hard, cold tool press against her right cheek. She assumed it was the muzzle of a gun.

Then a man spoke, "If you make a sound, I swear I'll kill you."

She didn't doubt it since two men had been murdered since they left Sun Valley. Sage closed her eyes, forcing herself to remain calm and think.

Two people held her down. The Starr Outfit said they encountered four aggressors earlier—three men and one woman.

These must be the same people. There should be two others, both men. They must have grabbed Bruce.

They pulled Sage to her feet, and she squinted to see where Bruce had gone. She saw movement; one figure was hunched over while another held him as a third figure hit the hunched-over figure. They had Bruce. His knees buckled, and he fell forward. The man holding him pulled him up to his feet.

A hand in the middle of Sage's back gently pushed her forward. A feminine voice whispered, "Watch your step."

———

Fred viewed the kidnapping through low-light binoculars from a high angle uphill. He quietly took a deep breath and let it out slowly. The screwups made it work. They were back in business.

He had played the part of the supportive uncle, giving helpful advice, but now he had to play a new role as the unforgiving father. He needed to maintain control. The Ninety-niners needed to act out his plan, or he would have to deal with them and move forward himself.

Earlier, Fred had caught up to the kids in a secluded meadow by a small creek. Fred rode into the meadow, interrupting their rest. They had just sat down and leaned against their packs. They looked comfortable.

He frowned as he dismounted, and he yelled, "What the hell was that?"

"What do you mean?" Rage jumped to his feet.

"I mean, you screwed up!"

"How do you figure? You shot that guy on the horse. Didn't you?" Rage snarled.

"Yes," Fred said without blinking.

"Then you're the one who screwed up. That's why everything fell apart." Rage snapped.

"The man I shot was Alex Ford. He may be older, but he was a legendary lawman. When he pulled his horse out of line and shielded Arnold, he already had you. I gave you an opportunity, and you guys stood there and watched. You lost control of the situation. And then, you let Arnold ride away and didn't try to stop him." Fred jammed both of his palms into Rage's chest and knocked him on his ass. Fred pointed his finger at him and ordered, "Stay down."

Before Rage could react, Bright stood up. "It's my fault," she said, her voice quaking. "I was in the best position to stop him and didn't even try."

"Why didn't you?" Fred asked in a pseudo-soothing tone.

Bright looked down. "The other night at the Sara Lake overlook, we had a moment, and well… it affected us. We questioned our ideals and decided to try a passive approach."

Fred blinked at Bright momentarily as he tried to decide what to say. He threw his hands up and let them drop, slapping against his legs. "I guess it's time for me to leave. I'm done here. I believed you were serious about the cause. I guess I was wrong." He turned and walked to his horse, which grazed on the meadow's long grass.

Rage stood up and said, "Wait. Really?"

Fred started messing with the gear on his horse. "You planned to make an example out of Arnold, one that would change the world. He was there for the picking, and you let him go. You talked about hanging him on a mountaintop, and *now you are pacifists*?"

Bright and Rage exchanged looks.

Digit finally spoke up. "I told you guys when we were at the lake. I don't give a shit about billionaires. I don't know why we should."

Bright raised her hands. "Bruce Arnold is a pig. We need to make an example out of him, but we aren't killers."

Fred turned around to face the Ninety-niners. He decided they needed some inspiration–maybe some motivation. He held his pistol low.

Bright spotted the gun and instinctively took a couple of steps back. She looked at Rage, who stared back at her.

Fred ejected the magazine, looked at how many bullets were loaded, and slammed the mag back into the handle. He pulled the barrel back and pointed the gun at Rage.

"I think you kids have lost sight of your mission. Maybe you need to be reminded that this isn't about you and your personal ideals. It's about improving the world by eliminating problems like Bruce Arnold."

———

The man holding Sage whispered in her ear, "I'm going to let go of your arms. If you try to get away, I'll shoot you. Do you understand?"

"Yes."

He loosened the restraints, and she slowly swung her arms in a circle, trying to work the cramps out of her back.

"Keep walking," he ordered.

They walked through the trees for a few minutes and then turned onto another trail. Sage guessed they had hiked east and were now on a new trail bearing north. She kept her eyes trained on markers to memorize their route. If she could see the North Star, it would help her find her bearings, but the cloud cover hadn't cleared.

Bruce stumbled ahead of her, flanked by his captors. He walked with a slight limp. Sage hoped he didn't get beat up too badly.

They hiked for over a half-hour when Sage decided she had to escape. It was worth a try. The cloud cover had increased. It was so dark that she could hardly see the trail. The Ninety-niners had difficulty finding their way, and in an attempt to remain stealthy, they didn't use flashlights. Sage's captor gave her too much room.

Sage seized the moment. She faked a fall, ran several steps, tripped, and accidentally fell into a cluster of dense bushes. She crawled forward, trying to disappear by keeping her head down; she pushed into the branches like a dog rousting a fox.

Her captor was slow to respond and spun around, looking at where he thought she had fallen.

After a few feet, the bushes thinned, and Sage broke into an open area where she could be exposed, but there was a taller thicket on the other side. She waited until she thought her captor was looking the other way, and then moved quickly across the gap and crawled into the tall thicket. As the branches parted, they scratched her hands and both sides of her forehead. She sat motionless and felt the blood dripping down her face. She curled up as much as possible and tried to control her breathing. She prayed she was well hidden.

The man growled. "I'll find you, bitch. If you stand up now, it will go easier. If not, I'll kick the shit out of you."

"Shut up!" The woman said in a loud whisper. "Keep your voice down."

Sage could hear the urgency of their movements as they searched. They came close once but instead focused on a stand of trees further away. After a few minutes, she heard another male voice.

He spoke forcefully. "Let's go. It doesn't matter. We have Arnold. We don't need her."

CHAPTER FORTY-TWO

S age hid in the bushes and tried to keep her breathing under control. It wasn't easy. Her shoulder ached, and her face and hands were bleeding. She felt like she had lost a fight.

She hadn't heard any voices or footsteps for five or ten minutes. It was hard to tell without her watch. It was missing, torn off her wrist, and she lost track of time as she curled up and shivered. She hoped that one of the Ninety-niners wasn't sitting, watching, and waiting for her to show herself. They would have found her if it was daylight, but the dark sky worked in her favor. She rubbed her coat sleeve over her face in an attempt to wipe the blood from her eyes. The scratches should heal soon enough, but her shoulder might be another issue. It made an unnatural popping sound when the kidnapper hooked her from behind and lifted her to her feet. And twice, her shoulder folded under her weight while she crawled through the bushes.

Sage prayed she had waited long enough and took a deep breath. She listened for a few seconds more before climbing to her feet. She stood like a deer entering a meadow, looking for movement. She surveyed the area—no kidnappers were lying in wait.

Sage walked down the mild slope and ripped her pants when she stepped through the thicket. No wonder the Ninety-niners didn't see her; the bushes covered the hill like a blanket. After finding the trail, Sage started the problematic hike back to camp. The trail's condition was poor. Sometimes, she stopped and questioned her direction. Twice, she caught her foot on a rock or a root and fell. It wouldn't be nearly as difficult if she had a flashlight.

A familiar copse of lodgepole pines stood alongside the trail, like the forest they had crossed when they hiked away from the outhouse. She hoped she had found her way back.

———

Back at the camp, DeShawn approached the firepit and found Tom sleeping in the chair. Irritated, DeShawn kicked his chair.

Tom woke in a fog. "Hi. I guess I dozed off."

"Where is Sage?"

"Oh, a…she went down to the outhouse with Bruce?"

"How long ago?"

"A few minutes. Bruce had to go to the can, and Sage went with him to stand guard. She took her rifle." Seeing DeShawn erased Tom's fuzzy mind. He stood and stretched, looking around the campground.

DeShawn grabbed a couple of pieces of wood from the pile and dropped them on the fire. He leaned his rifle against one of the log benches and sat down. "Your fire is burning low. You need to keep feeding it."

"I was." Tom frowned while he gazed at the fire. "Maybe I've been asleep longer than I thought. What time is it?"

DeShawn checked his watch. He grabbed his rifle and

flashlight and charged toward the path leading to the outhouse, with Tom on his heels.

The area around the outhouse was quiet. DeShawn called out their names. Neither Sage nor Bruce responded. He walked up the path and swung his flashlight back and forth as he searched the hillside. He spotted an object. DeShawn bent down and picked up Sage's rifle.

"Shit," he said. He pulled out his radio and called Brett.

Brett bounded down the path. DeShawn held up Sage's rifle. "They've got them both," he said.

Brett felt like someone had kicked him in the stomach. Tom fell to his knees. His hands were shaking, and he looked sick. Brett struggled to keep his anger in check. He took a deep breath. "They've crossed the line again. I've had enough. How about you?"

Tom gritted his teeth. "I'm going to kill them."

DeShawn patted Tom on the shoulder.

"Where do you want to start? Should we wake everyone?" Brett asked.

"Before we do that, let's treat this as a crime scene, make a full sweep, and see if we can find anything," DeShawn said.

"Can I help?" Ruby asked. She had followed Brett down the hill. She nodded at Tom, who was seething.

DeShawn asked. "Are you familiar with the area?"

"Yes, I am. There isn't much around this spot. That's why it's a good place to set up the outhouse. Toward the lake, there's a trail." She pointed. "It is about fifty yards east. I'd look there."

Using their flashlights, they walked through a growth of pines, finding crushed foliage and footprints. They crossed through the forest and intersected a trail of fresh prints leading north.

"Okay, they took them through here," DeShawn said. He

asked Ruby, "This trail doesn't look like it is used much. Do you know where it leads?"

"It runs roughly parallel to the Trilogy Trail. There is a branch that splits off from it and leads down to the lake. Backpackers always stray off the main trails; sometimes, they get into trouble. These side trails aren't maintained at all."

Brett ran back to camp and woke Mark and Randy. "You need to get up right now. There is an emergency. Meet us at the fire pit."

It didn't take long for both men to get up.

"Sit down. We've got a problem, and we need you here," Brett said.

Mark leaned toward the fire, warming his hands. He spoke in a quiet voice. "What's up?"

Randy sat in a chair, half awake.

Brett took a deep breath. "Bruce and Sage have been kidnapped."

Randy woke up. "What the hell?"

Mark stood up and looked at Tom, who trembled with rage.

"While Sage and Tom were on guard duty, Bruce walked down to the portable outhouse, and Sage went with him. They both were taken." Brett said.

DeShawn broke in. "I woke at four, ready to take over, and Tom had dozed a little, so they couldn't have been gone too long. I searched the area by the outhouse. I found Sage's rifle." He held it up in his right hand.

"Okay, I've been calm long enough. Let's get these assholes!" Tom's hands were shaking.

"I know, my friend; we need to remain calm. First, follow me; we need all our eyes on this," DeShawn said.

DeShawn led with Tom a half step behind, followed by Mark and Brett. After hiking part of the way down the hill, DeShawn stopped. "I found Sage's rifle here." He pointed to an area ten feet off the trail. They continued downhill and walked around the area next to the outhouse. "We can't figure out where Bruce was captured. It's hard to see if a struggle took place. Ruby knows of a trail about fifty yards over there." DeShawn pointed. "Some foliage was disturbed. Our kidnappers may have come down that trail."

"So, you think they came through here, kidnapped Sage and Bruce, and returned on the same trail?" Mark asked.

"That would be my bet. We'll have daylight within an hour. We'll be able to see much more then," DeShawn said.

"It looks clear enough to me. Let's saddle up and go get these bastards!" Tom yelled.

"Hold up for a second. We need to go about this the smart way." Brett said.

"I sure as hell know where I'm going. I'm going up this trail, and I'm going to get my daughter back." Tom turned on his heel and marched back toward the outhouse.

Brett followed behind him. "Okay, I'm with you, but we need to make a plan. We need to bring our rifles, food, and water. But we have a problem. If they're smart, the Ninety-niners will set up a diversion and send us down a false trail. We need to work together and be prepared. The Ninety-niners are on foot, and we are on horseback. We'll run them down if we're ready to ride at first light. Is that okay, Tom?"

A teary-eyed Tom choked down a sob and said, "You're right. We need to go about this the smart way."

"That's exactly what we'll do. Together, we'll take care of this."

The four men hurried to the campground and went to work.

———

For the third time, Sage walked through a stand of lodgepole pines. They all looked alike, especially in the dark. Finally, she spotted their portable outhouse. She closed her eyes and said a silent prayer. When she opened her eyes, the outhouse was still there. She let out an audible cry of relief and marched forward.

As she passed the outhouse, she looked for her rifle. She had lost it when her attackers took her down. It should still be there. She searched the area and found nothing. Worried they picked up the rifle, but not able to do anything more, she gave up and walked uphill, frustrated and pissed.

When she walked into camp, her dad and the guys circled the firepit, talking. She closed her eyes, silently thanked God, and approached the Rider's Club. "Dad, I can't find my rifle. Could you help me?"

Tom whipped around, shocked and unable to speak. He choked on his words and instead hugged his daughter.

They fell into each other's arms.

————

Sage leaned forward toward the heat; her father's arms were wrapped around her as if he was afraid to let her go. Mark had cleaned Sage's face, arms, and hands. Her shoulder was dislocated, and he popped it back in place. He was worried about infection and was more than a little irritated that someone would intentionally mistreat her. His inspection was cursory, and he planned to give a complete examination after sunrise. His biggest concern was her shoulder. He suspected the injury was more than a dislocation, possibly a deep soft tissue injury or a break.

Sage told her story while Tom bit his lip. Brett and DeShawn asked for details.

"You're sure there were only four of them: three men and a woman?" Brett asked.

"Yeah, I heard one of them mention that they were Ninety-niners."

"But you didn't see a fifth or someone on a horse?" DeShawn asked.

"No. Only four. Was there another?"

"DeShawn and I figure that there must be a fifth—our shooter. Alex Ford was shot by someone positioned up the hill in the trees. He was murdered by someone we have never seen."

Ruby jumped in. "I agree. Only one of the Ninety-niners had a possible angle when Alex was shot. The young woman. She was ten yards away, right in front of me. I would have seen her shoot, and it would have been loud. I heard a rifle shot a long distance away, like an elk hunter."

"Or a sniper," DeShawn added. "He was probably hiding in the trees, and we were too busy looking for Bruce and Michael to investigate."

"If he was that precise with his shot, it was probably the same person who shot Colorado in the back," Brett suggested. "Colorado was tight-lipped when I talked to him, but he alluded that Ranger Brook's death and everything else is related. He also warned me that there were more targets, and we were one of them. He said we need to watch our backs."

CHAPTER FORTY-THREE

The diffused sunrise came with a cold breeze. The cloud cover had intensified throughout the early morning, and dark clouds threatened rain. Brett looked at the angry sky and hoped it wasn't a bad omen.

Michael and Luis approached the fire pit, and Sage kept her head down while Brett broke the bad news. Bruce had been kidnapped. The mood turned as dark as the sky; it was as if hope was taken away with the sunlight. A hawk cried in the distance.

Ruby announced that breakfast was ready. The dreary morning came with some urgency, so an early breakfast, especially one cooked by Ruby Starr, couldn't hurt, but it wasn't enjoyed leisurely.

Michael carried a plate of two breakfast sandwiches and a cup of black coffee to Sage.

She tried to smile, but even that hurt.

"I can't imagine what you've been through. Are you all right?" Michael asked.

"I'm a little beat up. Don't look at me. I'm not very pretty this morning."

Michael was silent for a few seconds. He pushed a strand of

hair behind her ear and gently took her hand. "You're wrong. You're beautiful." He pressed his lips to the back of her hand and looked into her eyes.

Sage would have blushed if her face wasn't already red for all the wrong reasons. She was beat up, but Michael's gesture sent a surge of electricity through her. A tear slid down her cheek. "You probably say that to all the girls."

"No. I've never said that to any girl except you."

Sage tried to smile again. "Do you have a girlfriend?"

Michael chuckled. "I lead a boring life. All I ever do is work or attend never-ending meetings and then work some more. As much as I have dreamed about it, I've never had a girlfriend."

Sage smiled, and it felt like all the pain instantly vanished for a moment.

The combined group's attitude brightened after breakfast. They migrated back to the fire pit to discuss their next steps.

Brett smiled at Ruby.

She winked.

"Thanks for breakfast, Ruby," Brett said as the meeting started.

Everyone smiled and murmured their thanks.

Agent Terry's rigid posture had everyone on edge. "Since everyone is here, I'd like to update you. I've been on the radio with my boss. Two SNRA Forest Rangers and a Blaine County Sheriff will be here soon. They're on horseback and hope to be here later this afternoon or early evening. Depending on the severity, this new weather system could impact their timetable. We also have a helicopter on call.

"The Ninety-niners have claimed responsibility for Bruce's kidnapping. They blitzed multiple social media sites with their posts. They made the same claims before, but this time, they had still and video images of Bruce. They also restated that they found Bruce Arnold guilty of crimes against the impoverished and 'sentenced him to death.' They said he would be hung in front of the world on a mountain peak. They didn't say which one."

Mark interrupted. "I've studied the maps in this area and believe they might choose either Lookout Ridge at around 11,000 feet or Monroe Peak near 12,000. Both locations would give the Ninety-niners a dramatic backdrop for their videos."

Ruby stood up. "I'm not sure if you plan to evacuate us, but I'd like to stay up here, and I'd like to go get Bruce and bring him back. We're closer to finding him, and he's one of us."

"I agree," Luis said. "We should be able to catch up with the terrorists. We're on horseback. They're hiking."

A murmur collected around the fire.

"Hold it! I agree with you. My boss could override me, but I'm the officer in charge right now. If Bruce is going to get rescued, we're in the best position to get the job done. We should go after him. I already told my boss that we would try."

"Did he agree?" Mark asked.

DeShawn's shoulders dropped an inch for only a moment. "He didn't like the idea but didn't say no."

DeShawn looked at Brett, who returned a quick nod. Then Brett slowly stood. He looked at each of his friends. "I'm impressed we're such a like-minded group. Last week, we were strangers. Today, we are friends. There is a code I live by. It helps me navigate the complexities of life. I want to share a line that reflects where we are today... *Do what has to be done.*"

Everyone nodded.

Brett continued, "DeShawn and I have come up with a plan to rescue Bruce. We'll break into two groups. We need to keep a group here to secure a base camp. It may not be just Bruce that these people will target. Luis Perez is an internationally known technology executive and a man who knows how to work with a horse."

Luis smiled.

"And, of course, Michael Lane of Lane Technology."

Sage snapped her eyes at Michael. "What the hell?" she whispered.

Michael closed his eyes, dropped his head, and stared at the dirt.

"Ruby, Sage, and Randy will also stay behind at base camp. This group needs to maintain a high level of security. The five of you should be a strong team. The camp will also be our communications hub. You'll work with the forest rangers and the county sheriffs who are en route. And... if we need help, we'll contact you. You're our backup."

Sage, Ruby, and Randy nodded.

"Agent Terry, Tom, Mark, and I will saddle up, track the Ninety-niners, and rescue Bruce."

"Let's get going. We've burned too much time already," Tom ordered.

"Hold up a second. I'm coming with you guys," Sage said.

"No, you're not," Tom said.

"Are you and Brett trying to leave me behind again?"

Mark jumped in. "We aren't excluding you. Your dad would have included you, and Brett would have, too. Sage, you may have a broken shoulder. It needs rest. You're not ready to jump on a horse. As your doctor, there is no way I'll let you go! It's about time someone listened to me. You don't have to prove yourself to us; you have already done that."

"We need you here, and you need to take care of yourself," Tom said as he pulled his daughter in for a hug.

"Okay, I guess that makes sense," Sage said into her dad's shoulder.

Michael stepped next to Sage, and they watched the Rider's Club saddle their horses. "I didn't want you to find out about Lane Tech that way. I wanted to tell you."

"Did you assume I knew?" Sage asked.

"I did initially, but when you asked if I liked working there, I guessed you didn't."

"You could have told me, then." Sage faced him.

"I know, but I didn't want to sound arrogant. I wanted to tell you when we were alone."

"I can see that," she said under her breath.

"This trip has been a good experience for me. When I started my career, I learned the creative side of technology, and I loved it, but now it's all business. Being out here has helped clear my mind and helped define my priorities. This wilderness is beautiful and inspirational. So are you. When I'm with you, everything else has meaning."

CHAPTER FORTY-FOUR

The Ninety-niners were smothered by darkness without a moon or a star to light their way. Rage had done his best to lead the Ninety-niners uphill on a seldom-used trail. He still limped from his knee injury but did his best to ignore the pain. Torch tried to use his flashlight, but Rage pulled it away. Even a weak lamp could signal their presence. They were lucky to have captured Arnold, but they were stupid to have lost the woman. Now, they needed patience; sunrise would be here soon. Even the thick clouds wouldn't hold back the morning light.

Digit hiked behind Rage, followed by Bruce, Torch, and Bright. After the woman escaped, the Ninety-niners needed to ensure they didn't screw up again, so they wrapped a rope under Bruce's arms, looped it around his neck, and wrapped it around Digit's and Torch's waists.

The thick brush beside the trail made it difficult to search in the dark, and they spent too much time searching for the woman. If she returned to her camp, she could give away their location. The Ninety-niners silently considered that she may have lost her way, got injured, or died. They really didn't like any of those outcomes, but they didn't want to get caught either.

Bruce Arnold had taken several hard falls along the trail. He had turned his right ankle and collapsed like a basketball player, landing awkwardly after rebounding a ball. The hurt ankle slowed the caravan, and they weren't quick to begin with. He wasn't a twenty-something like the rest of them, and now he was limping.

The sky turned purple and blue in the east when they were ten minutes short of their camp. They were grateful for the light—they had all tripped and fallen more than once.

Cold, tired, and sleep-deprived, their initial stamina had all but drained completely. Digit set up the internet uplink while Torch shot group pictures and videos with Arnold in the starring role. After they uploaded their images, they heated water on their camp stove, made hot coffee and tea, and ate granola bars for breakfast.

They circled a small fire and warmed themselves while Bruce remained tied to a tree close by. It was time to relax and enjoy their success. After yesterday's debacle, they were on track again. The next task would be bigger, yet.

Fred rode into their camp and tied up his horse. He scanned the camp. When he saw Bruce asleep against the tree, he snarled. He walked up to the fire and made eye contact with Rage.

"Were there any issues?"

"Not really; you were right about their location. We hung out until Arnold came out of his tent and grabbed him. The hike back was difficult, but the markers we set along the trail kept us from getting lost. The plan worked, and we're dog-tired," Rage said. He chose not to reveal their mishap with the escaped woman.

"Yeah, I bet." Fred gazed at the dense clouds that were turning from gray to black. The storm clouds blew across the sky and pushed against the mountains. "It looks like we could see one hell of a storm. These mountain storms can be dangerous. You may be stuck here for a while. I'd reinforce my shelter if I were you."

Fred found a spot next to the campfire and congratulated them all. The pot of coffee beckoned, and he grabbed a cup. "Will you make another social media post?" he asked.

"We already have, and we attached images of Arnold," Rage said.

"Great job," Fred said.

"If this storm is as bad as you think, could it ruin our plans?" Bright asked.

"It depends on how long it lasts. We could lose half a day or more, but the group behind us will have to deal with the same storm. I'll ride back and see where they are at. Keep your radio handy. I'll update you."

The tired Ninety-niners exchanged wary looks.

Fred finished his coffee, walked over to his horse, and rode away.

————

On the lower part of the Trilogy Trail, Colorado drank cold creek water and relaxed while taking his sixth break on his hike to the Badger Lake Trailhead. He had started at dawn, hoping to take advantage of the cool morning and avoid as much of the coming rainstorm as possible. In the north, the higher mountains were undoubtedly getting hammered.

As he practiced breathing and tried to will his body to heal faster, he sat in one of the most beautiful meadows he had ever seen. A creek meandered through a flat area, creating several deep pools surrounded by wildflowers and green grass. On his uphill hike, he had stopped here and relaxed for a few minutes, which made the meadow an important landmark in tracking his progress. He woke at dawn this morning and knee-crawled to a small creek, filled his water bottle, and chewed two pieces of beef jerky. It wasn't much, but it helped fill his stomach. He rested for ten minutes and self-assessed his fitness level, which wasn't great but was better than the day before.

He took the antibiotics and the anti-inflammatories and left the pain pills. He needed to be fully alert while he worked through the uneven, downhill terrain. But if his back and ribs hurt too much, the pain pills were there. He still had half a flask of bourbon. If he made it back to the cabin in Bellevue, that would be his reward.

The trekking poles that Tom gave him were a godsend. He might not have been able to get off the ground without them. He had improved his technique; when he stood up, he transferred his weight from his legs to his arms and shoulders, then back to his legs and feet, rising in one smooth movement. He also improved his hiking technique by swinging and planting the poles in perfect time with his steps while he hiked. Yesterday, the poles helped, but his walking speed was limited; today, he hiked at a near-normal speed.

Colorado was pleased with his progress. He knew exactly how far it was to the trailhead, and he figured he would make it before losing daylight. Yesterday, he made progress. Today, he had made a lot more. There was one difficult section left. The trekking poles should keep him stable.

After reaching the permit station, it would be an easy downhill hike back to the Badger Lake Trailhead. His Chevy Blazer waited for him. He envisioned it all in his mind: driving back to Bellevue and crashing at his cabin.

Colorado felt like he was back from the dead.

CHAPTER FORTY-FIVE

The Rider's Club pulled out their rain gear and prepped for the wet ride. A light rain had started, and the storm clouds to the north promised a lot more.

Brett announced, "Everyone, gather 'round. We should be able to catch up with the Ninety-niners within three to four hours. Once we spot them, we'll assess the situation, make a quick plan, and rescue Bruce. Anything else?"

"Yes," DeShawn said, opening a duffel bag and pulling out four Kevlar vests. "Put these on under your rain gear."

"Are these back in style?" Mark asked with a grin.

"Not funny. We needed these last time," Tom said.

"I'll never forget it," Mark said.

Last summer, when the four of them tried to arrest a group of criminals, gunplay erupted, and the bullet vests saved both Brett's and DeShawn's lives. It was time to wear the vests again. They weren't looking for a fight or an arrest. This was a rescue mission, but it was better to be safe than sorry.

"While we're at it, let's do a quick radio test," Tom said. Their slick headsets were voice-activated models that made conversation easy. Tom kept them charged with his solar backup battery. After a quick soundcheck, he was satisfied they were good to go.

While they prepared for the trip, Randy saddled the horses. Brett, who preferred to saddle his horse, walked over to Pepper and checked Randy's work.

"Is everything okay?" Randy asked.

"Looks good," Brett said, smiling. "I'm pretty fussy, and you saddled him exactly as I would."

Randy put his hand on Pepper's shoulder. "If he were my horse, I'd be fussy, too."

As the Rider's Club mounted their rides, they noticed a fifth horse was saddled and staged with the others. Brett recognized the brown quarter horse and silently questioned Randy.

Randy looked Brett in the eye. "I'd like to ride with you today. You may need someone with you that is familiar with the trails."

Brett put his hand on Randy's shoulder. "You are a fine young man. We need you here while we're gone. Without you, we could be shorthanded. We may need you to track us down if we need backup."

"Okay." Randy sighed. "I've explored these trails a few times. Riding up that trail, you'll run into several branches that could lead you in circles. The Ninety-niners might even leave fake tracks to slow you down; besides, this rain could wash away their tracks. In less than a mile, you'll need to find the trail that runs parallel to the Trilogy Trail. It would save time if I led you to it."

Brett made quick eye contact with DeShawn, who returned a quick nod.

"Okay, you're with us. But just to guide us to the trail, and then you're back here. Understood?"

"Yes, sir."

"Gentlemen, we will use the same rules of engagement we used last year," DeShawn announced. "When we encounter the

Ninety-niners, Brett and I will take the point. Mark and Tom will back us up. Do not fire unless you are fired upon or have received permission from Brett or myself. Agreed?"

"Agreed," Tom said.

"Agreed," Mark said.

Randy stood straight with wide eyes. "Agreed."

DeShawn returned to his duffle, pulled out another vest, and handed it to Randy. "Put this on under your coat."

Randy took the vest and stared at it briefly. "Cool."

"It isn't cool. You're around six feet tall—this vest only covers part of your upper body. If you are shot in the chest, the vest can prevent a bullet from ripping through you, but the impact will knock you on your ass and could bust your ribs. The vest does not make you invincible. So do not take any unnecessary risks. Remember our rules of engagement, and be careful," DeShawn explained.

"I will be," Randy said reverently. After the warning, he unfolded the vest nervously.

"Let's ride," Brett said. He held on to his hat and checked the stormy sky. Even with the sun rising, the sky remained a depressing gray, and the gray clouds wouldn't last long—one after another was turning an angry black. "We need to move out. Let's get Bruce before this storm breaks loose."

Brett led the men down the hill and past the portable outhouse. After passing through the trees, they found the trail they had checked out earlier. The rain had already washed away some of the footprints. Brett looked at Randy and smiled; bringing him along would be a good call.

The rain went from light to steady within fifteen minutes. Small streaks of sunlight slipped through gaps in the clouds, and as time passed, the gaps disappeared, and the diffused light made everything a shadow. The Rider's Club wore similar gray rain slickers that covered them past their knees. Randy wore a water-resistant all-around outdoor coat that cut off at the waist. His jeans were already partially soaked, and if the rain kept coming, his coat could go that way, too. All the riders wore cowboy hats that helped keep the rain off their face, necks, and, to a lesser degree, shoulders.

Brett leaned forward and ran his hand down Pepper's neck, and rain poured off the rim of his cowboy hat and splashed onto his saddle. Brett never liked riding horses in a rainstorm. Pepper didn't seem to care.

After following the trail for two hundred yards, it split three ways, and footprints led right. Brett turned toward Randy, who rode right behind him.

"Keep going straight," Randy said.

Brett stared at the footprints. His gut said they should turn right, but he didn't have experience on these trails. They rode straight ahead. Not one of the trails was dominant. All three would be better categorized as paths. Ruby was accurate when she said none of the trails were maintained.

The riders stayed on the middle trail, intersecting with others. At the last intersection, they turned left.

Randy announced to Brett and DeShawn, "We're about there."

They rode through a dense section of mixed pines. The rain came down harder, and their visibility narrowed. The trees opened into a flat, rocky area below a steep hillside. The trail ran toward the left side of the flats, then rose to the top after a switchback.

"This is it," Randy said. "From here, this trail runs parallel to the Trilogy Trail. The Ninety-niners should be somewhere up there." He pointed uphill.

Randy rode into the flat, rocky section. Brett and the other three riders followed close behind.

Just then, a rifle was fired from somewhere uphill. Two more shots followed.

The riders turned their horses toward the trees in search of cover. Brett and Randy were out in the open and brought up the rear. Brett rode into the trees, jumped off Pepper, grabbed his rifle, and looked for a defensive position.

Randy's horse followed Pepper into the trees. But Randy didn't step off his horse; he fell off. He lay on his stomach, alone, in the open. He tried to push himself to his knees and collapsed.

No more shots were fired.

Brett walked through the trees and leaned against the protected side of a ponderosa pine. He was covered with blood.

Mark scrambled to meet him. "Let me look at that," he said.

"It's not as bad as it looks. I was grazed and might need stitches, that's all. Can you put a patch on it and sew it up later?"

Mark grabbed his med kit and quickly cleaned and bandaged Brett's wound. That will get you by for the time being. But you need to be careful."

Brett nodded and said, "Thanks."

They grabbed their rifles and moved forward.

DeShawn's voice came through the headsets. "Stay down!" He crawled to a small opening, pulled out his binoculars, and scanned the hillside.

"Riders, I don't see anyone, but I bet he is set up by those rocks next to the trail," DeShawn said. "I have my eyes on that position. On my mark, light them up, and I'll see if anything moves. Ready, fire."

Six quick shots sent chards of rocks flying.

"We have movement. Someone is up there," DeShawn confirmed.

Three more shots volleyed from the hilltop. They were all off-target.

"He just reminded us that he has the high ground," DeShawn said. "Riders, on my signal; fire into that position again—three rounds. I'm going to get Randy."

"Let me do it," Brett said.

"Nope. You've already taken a hit. It's my turn. I'll move out as soon as you start firing." He got into position and yelled, "Fire!" The headsets weren't needed.

Multiple sets of bullets were fired at the outcropping while DeShawn exploded off the line. Running low to the ground, he scooped Randy's limp body off the dirt, threw him over his shoulder, and turned toward the trees. He leaned forward, steadied the extra weight, lifted his knees, and charged ahead. DeShawn had to make a quick choice. He could run straight back into the woods and the safety they provided—doing so would expose his back—or he could run at an angle toward the woods, making himself a tougher target. He chose to run the angle.

Several bullets whistled through the gap between the hill and the trees.

DeShawn was a step away from the trees when the bullets struck him.

CHAPTER FORTY-SIX

Brett held a defensive position. DeShawn and Randy were down, in the open, exposed. DeShawn was quietly moaning, and Randy lay dead still but was breathing.

"This is too damn much!" Tom whispered through clenched teeth. His hands were shaking, and he was breathing hard. He was itching to get this guy.

"Calm down. The sniper could still be out there. Give me a minute; I'll take a quick look. We need to assess the situation." Brett moved to the edge of the treeless area and pulled out his binoculars.

Randy tried to crawl onto his knees.

DeShawn, lying next to him, whispered, "Don't move. Stay here."

Randy slowly collapsed onto his stomach.

Brett glassed the hillside. In a low voice, he whispered into the radio, "DeShawn, I don't see any movement on the hill. But we should wait a few minutes before we try to pull you in."

A long five minutes later. DeShawn asked Randy, "Can you crawl to the trees? It's about ten feet."

"I don't know," Randy said shakily.

"When I say go, let's give it a try. Just ten feet. Okay?"

"Okay."

"Go."

DeShawn tried to crawl forward. His breathing was ragged, and his right arm was useless. He groaned as he tried to make progress but couldn't get far.

Randy crawled about two feet, moaned, and rolled onto his side.

Tom couldn't take it any longer. "Damn sniper! I've had enough of this bullshit." He marched out of the trees, wrapped his arm under Randy's shoulder, lifted him to his feet, and carried him back to where Mark waited with his med kit.

Brett glared at Tom. "What the hell? You could have been shot."

Tom stared at his rifle lying on the ground. He picked it up, took a deep breath, turned, and walked away.

"I can't move. My right side is worthless." DeShawn muttered.

Brett made eye contact with Tom and said, "Let's go. Now!" The pair moved together, carefully pulled DeShawn to his feet, and led him into the trees. They held on to him until he could stand on his own. Then, he leaned against a tree and threw up.

Mark hustled over. "Sit down before you collapse. You've taken a hell of a hit, and you're bleeding."

"Leave me alone," DeShawn said. "Take care of Randy. He should be your priority."

"He's okay, so don't give me that shit. I'm your doctor." Mark carefully removed DeShawn's blood-soaked coat. He pulled out a syringe and slid it into DeShawn's injured shoulder. DeShawn took a deep breath and settled.

The riders decided they had better take a different approach and regroup.

An hour later, as the rain slowed, Brett led the ride back to their camp. Randy wore Tom's slicker over the top of his coat. The kid was tough, and he paid for it by taking a bullet. When Mark examined him, he said Randy didn't have any internal damage, at least on his first check. The kid would have a nasty cantaloupe-sized bruise on his chest. The Kevlar did its job.

DeShawn's unnatural color made him look like a ghost on a horse. He leaned forward in the saddle, kept his eyes down, and held a weak grip on the saddle horn. His balance was awkward.

The reins slipped from DeShawn's fingers while the horses kept an easy, comfortable pace. Tom grabbed the reins and led the pair down the trail, and Mark rode within arm's length the rest of the way.

————

The Rider's Club limped into camp late in the morning.

Ruby had set up an impressive tarp system that kept the campers dry and comfortable. She even had a portable outdoor wood burning heater that provided enough heat to keep the chill off. The area extended outward from her outdoor kitchen.

With the cold wind and rain, a hot lunch was called for. Ruby went with beef stew and campfire biscuits. She had coffee and hot cocoa simmering on the stove. Everyone was eager to hear the lunch bell.

Mark confirmed Randy's original diagnosis; Randy was bruised and had no significant injuries. Mark wrapped Randy's chest to help support and protect the right side of his rib cage. He gave him a pain pill and ordered rest. Mark smiled when Randy followed his directions. He was a fine young man.

Brett felt defeated and was quiet after their morning disaster. He wondered how everyone else felt. They had made good and bad decisions but should never have walked into an ambush. He was supposed to have an analytical mind. He should have seen the attack coming. Brett sat alone in the rain and tried to sort it out.

Tom was ready to fight. He lost his smile, paced around the kitchen area, and never let his daughter leave his sight. His emotions bounced like a ball on a Ping-Pong table. One minute, he was mad as hell; the next, he was ready to cry. His frustration was contagious. He needed to settle down.

Mark examined both Brett and DeShawn. Brett's injury was inconsequential. After Mark had cleaned and bandaged the wound, stitches were not needed. However, DeShawn's injury was severe. His shoulder required surgery.

DeShawn's Trilogy Lakes Tour was over.

The Rider's Club was at an impasse.

Brett checked their supply of whiskey. It might be an excellent night to have a drink.

————

After dinner, the entire camp sat around the firepit. It had stopped raining. The forest smelled fresh and clean, and the campfire was a warm contrast. All day, Brett stewed about what to do. He worried about his friends, the Starr Outfit, and Ruby. He didn't want to let them down. He feared they were all engaged in a losing scenario. The obvious way to rescue Bruce Arnold was to chase the Ninety-niners and their sniper uphill. But riding uphill into a tactical disadvantage couldn't work without people getting hurt or killed. Brett wasn't confident he knew the next move. They needed to find a workable plan tonight. Hopefully, Bruce was still okay.

Tom sat like a rocket ready to launch, and he admitted that he needed to calm down. But he had a tough time doing it. Michael and Sage sat together, and Ruby sat next to her nephew.

They all welcomed a break from the rain. They sipped coffee or tea until Brett pulled out a bottle of Jack.

Ruby responded by bringing out a clean set of camp cups and a canteen full of water. "We don't have any ice, so if you want to dilute your whiskey a bit, we have clear, cold mountain water."

"You make that sound quite appealing," Luis said.

"If we run low, I've got some backup bourbon in the kitchen," Ruby said.

"I brought a bottle of scotch I'd love to share," Luis added.

"If you brought it, I bet it's the good stuff," Mark commented.

"It is."

Randy grabbed one of the camp cups.

"Excuse me, young man," Mark said. "No booze for you. At least until you're off your pain pills."

"Shit," Randy whispered under his breath.

Tom broke in. "I don't think drinking will help any of us. I want to get the son of a bitch who shot at us. Randy's lucky he's here right now. Enough is enough. We need to get up in the morning and go after them."

"I agree, but we need a new plan. We were sitting ducks this morning. We have a fifth enemy out there or more. And they're watching us," Brett said.

"When Alex was shot, the Ninety-niners were near us, but the shooter wasn't. He was watching from the trees. He fired from a distance, just like this morning," Ruby said.

"Our shooter is either the fifth Ninety-niner or someone else involved. And he moves fast; maybe he's on horseback," Mark suggested.

"Which means he'll be watching and waiting for us. If he's on horseback, he might be mobile enough to check both the trail we rode this morning and the Trilogy Trail. And Brett may be right. There could be more than one shooter out there," Tom said.

"What do you think, Brett?" Mark asked.

"This morning proved we are at a tactical disadvantage. The Ninety-niners have the high ground; if we follow them, they'll always have the high ground. I don't know how to get around that problem. It's driving me crazy. I'm afraid we're done."

"We can't give up. Where's your football playbook? If we can get around or through these guys, we'll gain the advantage," Mark said.

"If this were a football game, it would be time for an end run. But we can't sweep around them and take the advantage. We'd need a third trail, which we don't have," Brett said.

"That's not completely true," Ruby offered.

"What do you mean?" Mark asked.

"Brett, remember the trail where you found Bruce? People call it the Ridge Trail."

"Yeah, but it ran out going north."

"True, but that is only the first problem."

CHAPTER FORTY-SEVEN

Fred rode his horse up a narrow ridge leading to an overlook. He had stopped the group who tracked him, which was a relief. He didn't mind a good fight if he had an advantage. After taking out two of them, they were smart enough to turn around. Good for them. He had no desire to kill them all. Killing one or two was enough. Fred just wanted the rest of them to back off.

The gray, depressing rainy day had turned positive. Fred was pleased that the social media posts were making an impact. It was a significant achievement. His job was almost done.

Fred pulled out his radio. "Rage, come in." Fifteen seconds passed.

"Rage here, over."

"The rain is too much for your pursuers. They are spending the night at their campground, over."

"Good. What's your recommendation, over?"

"Looks like the rain may not be done with us tonight. Some heavy stuff is forecasted to blow through this evening. It is a dangerous mess out here, but we'll have less rain tomorrow. Let's wait out the storm and plan to travel at first light. Over."

"Will do, over and out."

———

Bruce heard a shuffle before Rage unzipped the door of his tent. "Get out of there," Rage shouted.

Bruce poked his head out of the tent and crawled through the opening. Once out on the damp dirt, he waited for his command. Rage pointed toward an empty spot between Digit and Torch. Bruce crawled between them, turned, sat, and stared at the ground.

"It's lunchtime," Rage said. He handed Bruce a combination bowl-cup and a plastic spoon.

Bruce observed as Digit grabbed a plastic package full of hard noodles. He opened the package and dropped the noodles into a bowl while Rage pulled a pot off the fire and filled Digit's bowl with steaming hot water.

Bruce watched Digit, hoping for some guidance.

"You have to cook your own. Put the noodles in the bowl, and Rage will fill it with hot water. Let it sit for a few minutes, and stir in the powder," Digit said.

"Okay." Bruce turned the package of noodles over and read the directions, confirming what Digit had said. He would have passed on the unappetizing opportunity, but he was hungry, and Digit's bowl of noodles smelled good. Bruce dropped the noodles into the bowl and held it toward Rage.

"You've never made ramen noodles?" Digit asked.

"No, I haven't," Bruce whispered.

"A mega-rich guy like you probably never cooks anything. Am I right?" Digit asked.

"Yes, I haven't cooked anything for a long time."

"Who cooks your food—your wife?"

"No, we have a personal chef."

"Good God!" Torch exclaimed as he shot Bruce a look of disgust.

Bruce opened the seasoning packet and stirred it into the mixture. He scooped up a mouthful with his spoon and slid it into his mouth. He held the noodles in his mouth briefly before swallowing, then ate a second spoonful. Bruce looked at Digit. "This is good."

"It is, isn't it?" Digit smiled.

Torch chuckled.

———

Colorado exited the Trilogy Trail and limped into the parking area. He moved slowly. His shoulder ached, as did his side, back, and everything else. He made it. It had been a hell of a day.

His Chevy Blazer waited patiently. His hidden key was right where he had left it. He tossed his water-soaked coat, trekking poles, and half-assed waist pack into the passenger's side of the SUV. He turned the key and waited for the heat to kick on.

Colorado would never forget the moment when Tom gave him the trekking poles. He wouldn't have made it without them. So many times, he slipped or stumbled on the downhill hike, but he never fell, never hit the ground. Thanks to the poles, he had the leverage he needed to stand up after he took rests. Even with them, the three-hour hike took more than six. Slow and steady was his plan, and his plan got him out alive.

Colorado drove out of the parking lot and turned right on State Highway 75 toward Ketchum and the Bellevue motel. He had reserved a cabin for an entire week, just in case.

Colorado was dog-tired. He'd sleep well.

———

Bruce carefully watched the four Ninety-niners. Dinner that night consisted of dehydrated chicken and rice poured out of plastic bags. He thought it was okay but not as good as the ramen noodles. Bruce was taken aback by their almost adolescent approach to things. The Ninety-niners were quiet and sleepy after the meal. It was dark, and Bruce was tired as well. It had been a long day. Before they decided how his sleeping would be arranged, Bruce caught Rage's attention.

Rage stared daggers at Bruce. "I've got a question for you."

"Go ahead," Bruce encouraged.

"How do you justify having billions of dollars when millions of people are in poverty?"

"I don't think I can justify it, so honestly, I rationalize it." Bruce's blunt answer was like a belly flop off a high dive.

"So, you know you are, in fact, immoral as you continue to build your wealth."

"Part of the problem with great wealth is you reach a point where your money makes more money, and you can't spend it fast enough. You can become a slave to greed. It almost becomes a game. One you want to win, but in reality, you lose."

"Bullshit."

"My wife and I can't go out anywhere without a security detail. I used to get a business proposal and determine if it had merit. Now, I get a thousand proposals a day, so I can't deal with them. I have to turn that over to others."

"Why don't you give your money away?" Bright asked.

"I do give away a lot of money. I have an entire department in charge of it. Even when I give millions of dollars away, at the end of the day, I have more than I started with, and it doesn't solve the world's problems."

"If you are looking for sympathy, you won't find it here," Rage said.

"I'm not looking for sympathy. I have my own problems; I'm

here now. Since I've been on this trip, I've had time to think. When I was younger, my ambition drove me, and I enjoyed the challenge and what it could do for my family. But I have lost focus. My wife will hardly leave the house, and I rarely leave the office. But I call her every night, and we talk for maybe fifteen minutes. It's the best time of the day."

He sighed, and the Ninety-niners exchanged glances.

Bruce continued. "I've thought about walking away. But it's too late. You're giving me another way out. Maybe it's for the best."

Digit pulled out a hand-rolled cigarette and lit it. He inhaled, held it for a few seconds, and exhaled. The smell traveled toward Bruce, and he recognized it wasn't a cigarette but a joint. Torch took a hit and handed it to Bright; after her turn, she passed it to Rage, who took a hit and passed it back to Digit. Digit gazed at Bruce. "How about you, old man? You want a hit?"

"It's been a long time," Bruce said.

"You've smoked dope? No way." Rage said.

"When I was your age, we smoked weed, too. I'm not too old to remember." Bruce reached out with his right hand. "Give it to me. You can call it my last wish."

CHAPTER FORTY-EIGHT

D ew covered almost every surface. A few stars shined through random gaps in the cloud cover. A steady rain kept everything wet all night, but at least it hadn't snowed. It was hard for everyone to leave the comfort of their tents and sleeping bags, but Ruby's pancakes beckoned.

After a satisfying breakfast, the Riders lingered at the camp kitchen table, where Ruby spread out her outfitter's map. Bright lanterns on each side of the table provided enough light to see the map's details.

Encouraged by Ruby's plan, Brett allowed some hopeful optimism to dry up his soggy attitude. He needed to check the details. Her map resembled the SNRA maps they had seen before, but this one had extra lines indicating trails and an abundance of notations.

Ruby pointed at their current campsite. "We're right here, off the Trilogy Trail. Following the trail south leads you to the valley where we ran into the Ninety-niners. If you ride up through the forest on the valley's west side, you can access the Ridge Trail."

"I see a lot of broken lines on the map. Does that signify there are gaps in the trail?" Brett asked.

"Yes, this is rough country. Sections of the trail run along ridges of solid rock, and with yesterday's rain, the rock floor will be swept clean, and in spots, the trail will vanish. It will show up again when you clear the rock surfaces, but it can be hard to find. You might lose it if you don't ride the correct line."

"We should spread out on a ridge like that. Three sets of eyes are better than one," Mark said. He looked at Brett. "Does that make sense to you?"

"Yes, and we'll go live on the radios if necessary."

Brett studied the map. "On the northern sections of the Ridge Trail, there isn't a branch leading down to the Trilogy Trail. This must be rough country."

"High, fragile country would be more accurate. There are escarpments, plateaus, cliffs, and canyons. The only way off some steep sections is to climb down with mountaineering gear or ropes," Ruby said.

"Which won't work with horses," Mark said.

"Right. The geology is fragile and dangerous in some spots. You'll have to ride around those areas. Further north, a branch leads to the Trilogy Trail, just south of Lookout Ridge."

"Yeah. Have you seen where it connects?" Brett asked.

"No. The trail must come down through a canyon or a forest. I've never seen it from below. You'll find your way; this is *Angel* country."

"What does that mean?"

"Nothing, it's just a myth," Ruby said.

Brett shook his head and leaned on his clenched fist. "Assuming the map is right, we might beat the Ninety-niners to Lookout Ridge and take the advantage. We could have the high ground."

"That's what we need," Tom said.

"What about visibility along the way? Are there viewpoints where we can see what's below us?" Brett asked.

"There are several spots overlooking the entire valley."

"So, we might see them coming? Assuming they hunkered down last night like we did." Mark said.

"Yes, and there is another advantage. Since the Ridge Trail crosses rocky terrain, its surface varies from solid rock to sand. After all the rain we've seen, the other trails will be muddy, making riding difficult and backpacking horrible," Ruby said.

"I feel pretty good about this. Anything else?" Brett asked.

"Yes, one more issue, which may be a problem. The trail loops west to avoid a section riddled with dangerous geography. That adds over a mile to the ride, and there aren't any shortcuts. If you keep a decent pace, you could make up the difference," Ruby said.

"The Ninety-niners are backpackers. I didn't see any horses. Ruby's right; the muddy trails should slow them down," Sage agreed.

"Remember the fifth man? Their shooter is probably on horseback. He moves too fast to be on foot. We'll need to be careful," Brett said.

Brett leaned out to look at DeShawn, who sat in a camp chair along the edge of the group. His right arm was wrapped around his body.

Brett asked, "DeShawn, do you have anything to add?"

"Yes. A few things. First, I wish I was going with you…" DeShawn's voice trembled—he looked down for a few seconds. Then he raised his eyes. "Brett, you usually share your code with us, and there is a line that hits hard this morning. *Always finish what you start*. Well, I've failed you, and I'm sorry. However, I believe in you guys. You don't need me—the three of you are strong—you can handle anything. You have proven it before, and you'll prove it again today. It's who you are."

Brett knelt next to DeShawn and grabbed his left hand. "You've never failed us and never will."

DeShawn awkwardly grabbed a canvas bag with his left hand. "Here's my satellite phone. If you need help, my boss's number is in its memory—call him. He will answer, and he will help. He has unlimited resources. If they don't throw me into the hospital, I'll be available, too. I've been on the radio with the county sheriff. They're on the trail and should arrive here today. They'll probably fly me out of here."

The dawn's first light started to build from the eastern horizon, and a lingering cloud dropped a light rain. Another system looked like it was growing. Brett hoped this system would blow over. They didn't want to have to fight their way through another mountain storm.

Ruby gave Brett a goodbye hug. "I wish I were riding with you," she whispered.

"I wish you were, too. Don't worry. I have confidence in the men I'm with. They are good men—the best."

They embraced again. "I love you; please be safe." Ruby kissed Brett's cheek.

"I love you too," Brett replied, feeling more determined than ever.

Sage hugged Tom. "Be careful, Dad."

"I will, honey. You, too, keep your eyes open around here, and take care of DeShawn."

Randy and Luis saddled the horses, packed a light load of supplies, and saddled Britt, the buckskin mare Bruce rode. Bruce would need his horse.

"Okay, we need to stay alert and work as a team. Wear your vests and your radio sets, and have your firearms loaded. Questions?" Brett asked.

They all just shared looks of determination.

"Okay, let's make that end run," Brett said.

Tom's irritation hadn't recessed. Sage getting nabbed brought his feelings to the surface, and his friends being shot had cemented his anger. He was too quiet. Which wasn't like Tom.

Mark pulled him aside and asked, "Are you all right?"

"I'm fine. I want to kick some ass," Tom mumbled.

"I can see that, and I know you. When you're upset, you're not at your best."

Tom frowned. "I told you I'm fine. Take care of yourself."

Mark grabbed Tom's arm with a vise grip. "Look at your hands. They're shaking."

Tom stared into Mark's eyes.

"We may ride into difficult and dangerous situations," Mark said. "I don't want to ride with the angry, agitated Tom. I want to ride with Tom, who spotted a shooter and calmly warned DeShawn over the radio. I want to ride with Tom, who fired his rifle and made a lifesaving shot. We all need him."

Tom took a deep breath and smiled. "You're right. I appreciate it."

"Take three more slow, deep breaths."

Tom took three deep breaths and closed his eyes.

"You good?" Mark asked.

"I'm good. Let's ride."

CHAPTER FORTY-NINE

Torch unzipped the front flap of his tent, crawled outside, took a deep breath of the cold mountain air, and shivered. He wondered why it was warmer in a tent with sides slightly thicker than a sheet of paper. Design and body heat, he guessed. He zipped up his coat and pulled a tight-fitting beanie over his head and ears. He raised his eyes toward the cloudy skies, hoping it wouldn't rain, and questioned why he volunteered to be the first one up. He had never been a morning person; unfortunately, nobody else was either.

It had been a late night. He had planned to crash early and blew the opportunity, but it was worth it; last night was illuminating.

Torch stumbled as he walked to the fire pit; he knelt beside the dormant campfire and searched for hot coals. A tiny whiff of smoke drifted from the old fire as he stirred the ashes. He exposed a few glowing embers, added several pieces of fuzzy kindling, and blew as the flames grew. He added some larger kindling and smiled as last night's campfire was resurrected. No one else could have pulled that off.

He rubbed his hands together, held them toward the campfire, and remembered why he volunteered to be the first one up—it was for moments like this.

Bruce surprised Torch when he was the next one out of his tent. He already wore his heavy coat. Bruce nodded as he walked toward the trees.

"Good morning," Torch said sternly to Bruce.

Bruce hesitated for a moment and turned his head. "I need to take a leak." He marched into the trees and out of sight.

Torch wondered if he should have stopped him. *He better come back*, he thought. If he didn't, all hell could break loose, and it would be his fault.

After taking care of business, Bruce returned to the firepit and sat next to Torch. "Boy, the fire feels good," he said. He rubbed his hands together and held them toward the growing flames. "I don't like the look of those clouds; it looks like more rain."

Rage stepped out of his tent, his bald head covered with a tight beanie. He plopped down next to Bruce and didn't say a word.

Torch was nervous, and his voice cracked. "I let him walk into the trees—he needed to take a leak."

Rage gave a curt smile and puzzled eyes. "Well... that's where I'd go to take a piss. Wouldn't you?"

A few minutes later, the other two Ninety-niners emerged. Torch set a pot of water on the fire, and as it started to steam, they filled their mugs. Bright wore an oversized black coat with a hood. She leaned forward and looked at Bruce. "We're out of coffee, but we have tea bags. Do you like English breakfast tea?"

"One of my favorites," he said.

The steaming water worked to cook the instant oatmeal in addition to the tea. Torch wished he had added more water to his. It was thicker than what he ate at home, but he washed it down with a gulp of tea. It felt like more of a feeding than a meal, but having something warm in their stomachs was all they could ask for. Most of them drank another cup of tea before breaking down the camp.

Bruce collapsed his tent and slid his mummy bag into a stuff sack. "Bright, do you have an extra backpack? I want to carry my share."

She sorted through their backup supplies and found a medium-sized daypack. "We have this one, but you won't get much into it."

"I could carry your backpack, and you could carry the daypack."

"That's a nice offer, but I can handle my pack. You need to take care of your ankle. It doesn't make sense for you to carry any extra weight."

"My ankle feels better." Bruce offered.

"Good. Let's try to keep it that way. You don't have a raincoat, do you?" Torch asked.

"Not with me, but I have my heavy coat," Bruce said.

Bright handed him a small plastic package. "This is an emergency rain poncho. It will go right over your coat and keep you dry."

Bruce held the wallet-sized package in his hand and scanned the directions. "Thanks, I've seen these. This could make a big difference."

Rage walked away from the group while he talked on the radio. The conversation was quick, as usual. When he returned, he said, "I got the morning report. Our route is clear, but the trail is a muddy mess. We'll hike on this trail for a couple more miles; then, a branch will take us back to the Trilogy Trail. Fred said he would mark the turnoff for us."

Bruce didn't ask questions.

After everything was packed, Torch put out the fire while Bright, Digit, and Rage patrolled the area and cleaned up. They didn't want to leave any signs that they had been there. They were all getting the hang of camping.

Rage sat on the log next to Bruce. "If your friends catch up with us, what's their plan? They carried guns when we ran into them last time. Will they attack? Will we have to fight?"

"I don't think they will shoot and ask questions later if that's what you're worried about. But remember, you kidnapped me. That will affect their mindset. A couple of strong, serious men won't be afraid to act, but these guys are good people who would rather talk than fight."

"Are they your professional bodyguards? Can you order them to back off?"

"I brought one professional security man. He was the one who was shot. You remember him, don't you?"

"I remember—that wasn't supposed to happen." Rage winced and shook his head.

Bruce sniffed. "The group we merged with is from Boise. They are on vacation, riding their horses through the Trilogy Lakes Tour. They are good people trying to help."

"Tell me about them."

"There are three friends that ride horses together. There is a doctor, a businessman, and a retired football player. They call themselves the Rider's Club. The football player is a kind of philosopher. He lives by an idealistic code. Like I said, these are good people trying to help."

"But they're carrying guns?"

"Probably."

Rage stood up and said, "Okay," and walked away.

A faint roar of thunder sounded in the distance, but light rain had already started to fall—it was not as heavy as the day before.

Rage said, "Put on your rain gear and grab your packs. We need to get ahead of this storm." He nudged Bruce and asked, "Are you still ready for this?"

"I want to get it over with," Bruce said.

"Okay, let's go."

CHAPTER FIFTY

Colorado snapped his head off the pillow. The distinct sound of a vehicle was unmistakable; even in a dead sleep, he heard the squeal of tires—an accelerating engine—and it instantly cleared his mind. He was in Bellevue, in bed, at a motel, but his instincts weren't easily shut off. He rolled onto his side and squinted at the clock on the nightstand. The digital display read six-thirty. He had slept for eleven hours—a new record.

When Colorado drove into town, he was exhausted. He ordered a burger, fries, and a milkshake at the local drive-in. He checked back into his little log cabin at the cabin-themed motel. The room was comfortable. Even the furniture and bed frame were fashioned out of logs. He related to the environment since he lived in something similar to the Colorado mountains. Or he used to. He sat in a comfortable chair and ate his dinner. He saved most of his milkshake for dessert and savored every drop. After dinner, he took two of the pills the Doc gave him. He again passed on the pain pills, opting for two drinks of Tom's bourbon. With a bit of ice from the machine at the office, he made bourbon on the rocks —pretty damn good—even the bite.

The motel room's bed was large, soft, and forgiving. Colorado fell asleep a few minutes after he laid his head on the pillow, and he had never slept better. He would have still been out cold if that noisy car hadn't driven by.

He sat up in bed and took an assessment of his injuries. His ribs still hurt, and his shoulder ached, but not like they did yesterday. Colorado evaluated everything that had transpired, and a good night's sleep helped bring clarity.

He stood in the shower and let the hot water slowly make him feel human again. He leaned his forehead against the shower wall and let the hot water soak into his sore muscles. He took one of the tiny shampoo bottles from the sink and washed his hair. The dirt and grime swirled down the drain. Then he washed his body from head to toe. He stepped out of the shower and breathed in the steam. It felt good to clean up.

The bandage on his ribs came loose in the shower. He secured it with some tape from his suitcase—a short-term fix. He pulled out his beard trimmer and cleaned up his beard, sideburns, and mustache. When he finished, his beard was short and well-defined. His hair was a medium shaggy length. He combed it into an acceptable shape and trimmed the rough edges around his face and ears.

He walked to the motel office and grabbed a cup of coffee. When he returned to his room, the morning news was on the TV; it was just white noise. At a quarter to eight, he got back into his Blazer, drove the four blocks to Aspen Urgent Care, and waited for them to open.

———

Dr. Eiriksson smiled as he walked into the examination room. "Good morning, Mr. Wilson; I understand you need me to look at a rib injury?"

269

"Yes, I was sent here by Dr. Mark Taggart." Colorado handed him Mark's business card.

Dr. Eiriksson scanned both sides of the card. "Dr. Taggart and I are colleagues and friends. The nature of his note suggests this is a sensitive and private issue."

"Exactly. I have a meeting this afternoon, I can't miss. I want to function and look like I don't have an injury. Dr. Taggart suggested a local anesthetic, along with a rib brace."

"Understood. Let's take a look."

Colorado removed his shirt, and Dr. Eiriksson removed the bandage. After a few minutes, he said, "You have taken a big hit; your ribs are a mess, and I'd bet your back is hurting. Did Dr. Taggart prescribe any medication?"

Colorado handed him the pack of medications Mark had given him. "I've only taken half a pain pill, but I took the others yesterday and this morning."

"All right, sir. I need to take an x-ray, and then we'll see how we can help you."

———

Later that morning, Colorado had the best breakfast in town. He wore dress shoes, dark chino pants, a button-up shirt, and a navy windbreaker. He slipped on a black, logo-free baseball cap and oversized sunglasses.

He stepped into his Blazer, took a deep breath, and said aloud, "Let's go."

CHAPTER FIFTY-ONE

The Ninety-niners started their morning hike with fresh legs and a positive attitude, but the trail's condition could have been better. Last night's rain had left it wet enough to compromise their footing. They hiked uphill in single file, with Rage leading the group and Torch bringing up the rear. Rage was worried; the trail was muddy, and they might have missed the turnoff.

The trail's grade flattened as they entered a bowl-shaped valley. They were excited to leave the steep climb behind until they encountered water pooling along the trail. The thick mud clung to their boots. Stepping to the trail's edge didn't help—tall, wet grass encroached on both sides.

Digit tapped Rage's shoulder and pointed to their right. "What the hell is that?"

A pair of antlers rose above the grass and moved toward them.

"My guess—a moose. Let's move it, everybody. I mean, run!" Rage yelled.

After a five-minute gut-wrenching scramble, the antlers turned away. Rage, breathing hard, stood with his hands on his knees. He was tired and irritated. They needed a break. But they couldn't sit down in the mud. Why did Fred send them up this trail? The recent rainfall didn't create this mess. This wasn't just a muddy trail; they found themselves in a wetland that would be challenging to hike through on a sunny day. Drainage, possibly from one of the lakes, saturated the area. This soggy terrain made them appreciate the uphill climbs where their boots weren't sucked into the mud.

Rage turned toward Bright. "Fred said he would mark the turnoff, but he didn't say how he'd mark it. We may have missed it. Have you seen anything?"

"No, and I've been looking."

"If we're walking twenty-minute miles, we should have seen it by now."

"We're not walking twenty-minute miles. This mess has slowed us down."

"Shit!" Rage yelled as he stomped his foot, splashing mud all over his jeans.

They trudged further, and finally, Digit shouted, "Hey Rage, there is a shirt draped on that bush. I bet it's our marker."

————

Tom and Brett shared the lead, and the Rider's Club kept a steady pace along the Ridge Trail. Brett thought they needed to maintain their pace since their wide-sweeping course would add miles to their journey. They focused on beating the Ninety-niners to Lookout Ridge.

After the first mile, they found a viewpoint that overlooked the valley and a section of the Trilogy Trail. They would have been able to see for miles, except the steady rain cut their visibility. But they saw enough—an empty trail cut in and out of the forest below them.

In contrast, the Ridge Trail skirted along a jagged ridge with an impassable rim. The mountains to their west rose higher with every mile they covered. The forest density thinned, and snow-covered peaks rose above the tree line. The constant rain and wind gusts affected their visibility and pace, and as they gained elevation, a snow-rain mix developed. Sometimes, bouts of sideways precipitation burned their eyes.

"It is a good day to wear goggles. Too bad we didn't bring any," Tom joked.

The riders answered with polite chuckles.

Their horse's footing was sound. The trail's surface ran from sandy to rocky to solid rock, with all variations in between.

While they were planning, Ruby said there were two ways to climb up to Lookout Ridge. The backpackers preferred the direct approach, where they climbed the face of the ridge. The climb was covered with unrelenting switchbacks. There was no way to avoid multiple rest breaks on the rise. The switchbacks would test the physical condition of every hiker; they would suffer leg and thigh burn—some more than others.

The outfitters rode up the horseback loop that weaved up from the west. The trail covered more than five times the distance of the direct approach, but the horses made up the time at their consistent pace. No set rules split the backpackers and the horseback riders, but combining the two groups on the switchbacks would be too tight.

According to Ruby's map, a trail would split off from the Ridge Trail a few miles ahead. It would lead downhill into the valley and connect with the horseback loop. Brent's end run would be a success if the riders found the split before the Ninety-niners began their climb up the switchbacks.

As the Riders rode along the ridgetop, the sandy and rocky surface gave way to a section of solid rock, and all traces of the trail disappeared. If there was any sign left, the rain had washed it away. This was the first break on the trail, and the Riders weren't surprised. Brett pulled up and turned toward the group. "Let's spread out and try to find the trail. Mark, ride up toward the tree line. I'll stay close to the rim. Tom, position yourself to balance out the line between us. Let's go live on the radios."

They spread across the ridge and kept the same directional bearing. After a half mile, Mark called in. "Mark here, I found a trail, but it's way up by the trees. Brett, you need to look at this. Over."

"We'll be right there, over."

Brett and Tom rode together and pulled up beside Mark and Rondo. A faint trail was detected in the dirt. It ran northwest, away from the ridgeline and higher into the mountains—the wrong way.

Brett grabbed Ruby's trail map and shielded it from the drizzle with the brim of his cowboy hat. He studied the map. "I think we should follow this trail. The map shows a turn to the left. This must be it. It's hard to appreciate the scale when you look at the map, but if we stay on the ridge, we might find ourselves at a dead-end, and then we'll have to backtrack."

"Can I look? Mark asked." He studied the map briefly and said, "The map makes this turn look like a short detour, but from here, it looks like a long run to the west."

"I agree, but a user added the detour after the map was printed."

"Why don't we spread out, split the difference, and see if we run into another trail?"

"Sounds like a good idea," Tom said.

"It is a good idea, but I think we need to follow this trail," Brett said.

"Why?" Mark asked.

"I don't think we should split up, and I've got a gut feeling this is the right way. I don't understand it and can't explain why, but I'm sure."

"That's it?" Mark asked.

"Yeah."

Mark stared at Brett, and neither man spoke for almost a full minute.

"That's good enough for me," Mark said.

"Me too," Tom said.

"Let's go," Brett said.

The trail swung toward the west, higher up the mountain, away from any eastern overlook. A large rock formation with a natural overhang rose on their left as they rode. Scattered boulders were strewn beneath the overhang, most likely remnants of landslides that had come down over time. The overhang also covered a level shelf where a couple of scrub pines grew from crevices. It would make a good shelter.

"Let's get out of the rain," Brett said.

"Sounds good," Mark replied. He looked happy to get out of the rain. They needed to give their horses a break, and the Rider's Club needed a break, too. They rode through the boulder field and climbed onto the shelf. The overhang was wide enough for the riders and their horses to fit beneath easily. It was the type of formation where they might expect to find historical artifacts, but they only saw a rusted soda can. The shelf provided a break from the rain-snow mix and the wind.

Mark stood beside Brett and gazed across the valley while Tom settled their horses.

Brett anxiously paced the space and then suddenly froze.

Mark noticed the change in his mood. "Are you all right?"

Brett didn't respond. He stared straight ahead with dull eyes.

Mark turned and tried to see what was so interesting. He couldn't see anything, just an overcast sky. "Brett, what are you looking at?" Mark asked.

"What?" Brett asked, confused.

"Are you all right?"

"Yeah, I kind of spaced out and had a weird feeling; it felt like someone was watching us."

"Are you dizzy?" Mark asked.

"No, I'm fine. Did you hear anything?"

"Like what?"

"Never mind," Brett said.

Mark grabbed Brett's arm and said, "If you're not feeling well, let me know."

"I'm fine." Brett raised his right arm and flexed his biceps. Then he smiled and walked away.

Mark looked out into the landscape and muttered, "What the hell?"

Lightning struck in the east, several miles away. The entire weather system had shifted in that direction. Dark clouds built against the eastern mountains, away from where they rested. It was an excellent time to be west of the Trilogy Trail. Brett took a deep breath and smiled; for once, they had dodged a significant storm.

Tom needed to take a leak and walked past the left side of the overhang. A minute later, he yelled, "Hey guys, look at this!"

He pointed to hoof prints in the sand next to the shelf.

Brett dropped to a knee and studied them. "These were made by a horse not too long ago."

"More like in the last five minutes," Tom said.

"You're right. It rained hard ten minutes ago. How could we have missed a horse?" Mark asked.

Brett walked alongside the hoof prints. He stopped and said, "Come here and check out the trail."

The hoof prints were clear for twenty feet, and then they disappeared.

CHAPTER FIFTY-TWO

"This trail is a hell of a lot better," Rage said as they hiked along the branch, leading them to the Trilogy Trail. They walked uphill; the track was wet, even muddy, but it was nowhere near as messy as the trail they had left behind. Some sections were broad enough to hike side by side, and when they ran into a muddy area, they could step over or around it and keep a steady pace. Bruce and the Ninety-niners were glad to be out of the damn wetland.

"It's better, but I'm tired. I think we all could use a break," Bright said.

"See that tall ponderosa pine ahead? It's big enough for us to sit under and get out of the rain," Rage said.

"It looks like a good spot."

The group was happy to follow. Everyone needed to get off their feet. They had been marching since they left their camp this morning. The rain was steady, but sunlight was beginning to break through the clouds to the west, a hopeful sign.

Bruce kept up with everyone until he stumbled and rolled his ankle again.

Rage stepped under the ponderosa pine and sat next to him. "You're limping?"

"My ankle is tender, but it's not as bad as it was yesterday."

"This may be a problem. You're starting to slow us down, and we have a long way to go. You need to keep up."

"Understood," Bruce said. "Do you have a first aid kit?"

"Yeah, I've got a small one in my pack." It was a backpacker's kit in a lightweight roll-up pouch. Rage grabbed the first aid kit and unrolled the contents between them. "Here's some ibuprofen."

"Ibuprofen will help, but I don't see anything I can use to wrap my ankle."

"I've got an idea. I have an extra hiking sock; if you stretch it over the top of yours and lace up your boot extra tight, the increased thickness and compression could act like a wrap and improve your ankle support. Do it quickly, before your ankle swells."

"It's worth a try," Bruce said.

They sat beneath the tree's canopy and drank from their water bottles. Everyone grabbed a granola bar. Bruce stood on the cinched-up boot and tested his ankle by strolling in a circle. He waved at Rage and gestured a thumbs up.

The wind and rain picked up; a clearing to the west lured them closer, but they hadn't yet reached it. A bolt of lightning struck close by. It sounded like a mortar shell landing in a war zone.

"Get away from the trees!" Rage shouted. They scattered and came back together in a clearing fifty yards away. After a quick huddle, they hustled up the trail when another strike hit a tall pine behind them.

———

The Riders rode up the Ridge Trail, which improved in condition as they approached the thin line of trees above them. The sun was high in the rain-free sky. Cumulus clouds moved toward the east, driven by a consistent wind that dried everything it touched. Patches of snow were scattered in the shadows, signaling they had reached the snow line.

Brett worried about the hoof prints next to the overhang. *Could they be from the shooter?* He didn't think so. Whoever killed the forest ranger and shot Colorado in the back wouldn't come within spitting distance and disappear. He wouldn't have wasted the opportunity. It had to be someone else. There had to be a rational answer. Brett looked up the trail and tried to keep his mind on the ride.

The Rider's Club kept riding west. Every step the horses took brought them further away from the rim. Brett stopped and pulled out Ruby's trail map. This was the third time he checked it. The dotted line on the map hadn't changed; the trail led west-northwest until it looped back to the east. How long should they have to ride in the wrong direction? They had ridden this way for almost an hour—they had lost too much damn time. They could fail if they didn't start closing the distance soon.

Brett pulled up and let Mark and Tom draw even. They weren't smiling, and Tom always smiled when he rode Buck. "Let's give this route fifteen more minutes; if it doesn't swing back by then, we'll cut the corner and ride toward the ridgeline."

"Sounds good," Mark said.

Tom smiled after that.

Five minutes later, the trail turned as they rode around an impassable ravine. Their pace quickened as they rode downhill, and the area's geology changed. The surface became rocky, bordering on solid rock. Mark looked away as he rode next to a deep, three-foot-wide crevice. It seemed to come out of nowhere.

Rondo saw it, and he didn't like it. He reared up and almost threw Mark, who was lucky to stay in the saddle.

"Are you okay?" Tom asked as he rode up.

"I'm fine, but a little embarrassed. This area is unstable as hell. I need to watch where I'm going."

The central Idaho mountains were prone to earthquakes. A couple of years ago, a high-magnitude quake originated near their location. It not only registered as far away as Boise, but it rocked Boise hard. It must have hit this area with all its force. Brett considered riding off the trail to check out the damage but decided against it. He didn't want to waste any more time.

The ridgetop widened to their right, and their trail turned another twenty degrees east. According to their trail map, they had made progress. The route would continue east until it split. One fork would turn to the north, and the other traversed the side of the mountain on a gentle downhill course until it intersected the Trilogy Trail and the horseback loop.

The riders were getting close. Lookout Ridge should be an easy ride from here.

Brett stayed in the lead as they neared the rim. They all pulled up at the edge of the ridgetop and checked the view. Brett sat in the saddle, stroked Pepper's neck, took a deep breath, and said, "Oh shit!"

———

The Ninety-niners hiked up the Trilogy Trail alongside a creek that weaved through a gorgeous valley. The group was unrecognizable as kidnappers. They enjoyed the scenery and talked as they kept a reasonable pace. Bright and Rage hiked side by side as Torch took the lead. Since the trail wasn't technical, they were back to rotating positions. The storm blew over, and they stopped for lunch, finding a shady area to the right of the trail. With clear skies, the temperature moved to the mid-sixties, which made it warm for backpacking, but it was not uncomfortable. Most of the group enjoyed a mild sweat and the second wind that came with it.

Bruce leaned against a tree and elevated his bad ankle during the lunch break. After lunch, he took a few more ibuprofen. He winced whenever he miss-stepped, but it didn't happen often. He kept an eye on the trail's surface, the ups and downs, bumps and rocks, and anything that could trip him or make him stumble. If he took another fall, that could be the end of his hiking. Rage had already taken the daypack away from him and distributed its weight among the others.

After they hiked for an hour after lunch, they approached an extensive set of switchbacks. It was the last challenge that would lead them to Lookout Ridge. Rage found a good spot for them to stop and take another short break. "We're close to Lookout Ridge," he said. "The climb will be challenging, so we'll take extra breaks from here on out."

He checked his watch and frowned. "Somebody needs to keep track of the time. My watch hasn't worked since those lightning strikes. Damn it."

"The lightning must have fried your watch," Digit said.

"Is that possible? Rage asked.

"Absolutely." Digit said.

"I'll keep track of the time," Bright said. "We're making good progress, and I've been checking the trail behind us. I haven't seen anyone."

"I'd bet someone's coming, especially after our last social media post. We've made good progress since it stopped raining; if someone is behind us, they're a long way back. If we keep our pace, we should stay ahead of them. So, let's get back on the trail in five minutes." Rage said.

———

Brett stared at the view below him. A steady wind blew in his face. The trail they planned to ride down was gone, missing, erased from existence, and replaced by the biggest landslide he had ever seen. A section of the mountain had separated and fell away. He had seen something similar in northern Idaho, where part of a mountain had broken free and buried a highway, but that happened due to erosion, and the slide took a year to clean up. That landslide was minor compared to what they saw today. The reality of their new problem sucked. When the side of the mountain slid away, so did their hopes of beating the Ninety-niners to Lookout Ridge.

Brett dismounted. It was time to make another new plan. He wondered how they could move forward. *How can we find something positive in this hopeless moment? How can we finish what we started?*

He pulled out Ruby's trail map and studied it again. There had to be another route. He sure as hell didn't want to backtrack. From here, the Ridge Trail continued northwest to the edge of the map. Once again, the wrong way. Lookout Ridge and Monroe Peak were to the northeast. Christine Lake was to the northwest. *So, where does the Ridge Trail go?* The answer suddenly became obvious—Christine Lake.

That was their choice. Ride to Christine Lake or backtrack to the Trilogy Trail. Brett held his breath and thought. He didn't like either alternative. They would run out of time either way.

Tom and Mark grabbed their binoculars and glassed the area below them. Sections of the Trilogy Trail were visible as it snaked through the mountainous area. A ridgetop ahead led to a peak that reached out and held onto the clouds. Lookout Ridge and Monroe Peak were both breathtaking, but they were beyond their grasp.

"I guess this is why Ruby never saw where the trails merged,"

Mark said. He rested a hand on Brett's shoulder. "We'll find a way. We always do. We can't ride downhill from here, but the trail continues north. It must go somewhere."

"That's what I'm looking at." Brett held the map lower so both men could see it. "The map doesn't show any detail past this intersection, only a faint line leading to the edge of the map."

"So, are we lost?" Mark asked.

"Yes, kind of. We can backtrack or continue riding northwest on this trail; I don't know?"

"What would you guess?"

"If we keep riding northwest, we'll end up at Christine Lake."

Mark stared at the map. "Christine Lake is miles to the west. This trail would have to take a hard left-hand turn."

Brett looked at Mark with a quizzical look and then looked down at the map again. "Maybe it connects to the Trilogy Trail, but on the other side."

"The other side of what?" Mark asked.

"The other side of Lookout Ridge. Suppose we rode up the Trilogy Trail as we originally planned. We'd ride up to Lookout Ridge on the trail below us. Then we'd ride across Lookout Ridge and head west toward Christine Lake."

"So, this trail could be a shortcut to Christine Lake or a bypass to Lookout Ridge?"

"Yeah, but the question is, where does it tie into the Trilogy Trail? We'd be in trouble if it ends near Christine Lake. But if it ends near Lookout Ridge, we could turn right and ride up Lookout Ridge's west side. Riding forward is a high-risk move. Backtracking is the safest move, but we'll lose a day. It's a tough call."

Hey Brett, Mark, come here!" Tom yelled from the edge. "Take a look at this."

Tom handed Brett the binoculars. "Check out the trail leading toward the switchbacks. There's a group of backpackers."

Mark spied on the group. "There's five of them. I wish I had a high-powered scope, to be sure. They could be Bruce and the four Ninety-niners. If they are, they'll beat us to Lookout Ridge."

"We should assume they're the Ninety-niners, and if they are, we need to keep moving; we're too far behind. And we might have to backtrack," Brett said.

"Hurry," whispered a feminine voice.

"Did you hear that?" Brett asked.

"Hear what?" Mark asked.

"Hurry!" Brett heard louder this time.

"There it is again. A lady's voice," Brett said.

"Look!" Tom squinted, furrowing his brow and pointing up the trail.

Brett gawked.

In the distance, a lady sat bareback on a large black horse. She was dressed in a simple tan outfit, had long, flowing white hair, and her skin glowed when the light hit her. She looked *angelic* and otherworldly. She waved at the four men who stared at her. She was about fifty yards ahead on the Ridge Trail.

Brett wished she was closer, but... he sensed something. A chill ran up his back.

She waved again. Not *a* greeting but instead as instruction—a *"come-this-way"* wave.

Tom grabbed his binoculars and tried to get a better view. He was too late.

She rode up the trail, over a rise, and out of sight.

"Who was that? What just happened?" A wide-eyed Mark asked.

"I'm not sure. I mean, I don't know." Tom said.

"Brett, what did you hear?" Marked asked.

"I heard her. Didn't you?" Brett asked.

"No, but my hearing could be better," Mark reassured him.

"I might have, but I'm not sure. I was on the edge in the wind," Tom said.

"Do you think she wants us to follow her?" Mark asked.

"I'm not sure, but yeah, it seems like it," Brett said.

"If she rides around here, bareback on a black stallion, I'd bet she knows where she's going," Tom said.

"No kidding," Mark said.

"I don't know, but I feel like we should follow her up the trail," Brett said. "What do you think?"

"I'll support any decision you make. But I wonder. We're out in the middle of nowhere. Have we lost our minds?" Tom asked.

"We haven't lost our minds if we all saw her," Mark said.

Brett folded up the map. "Okay, guys, here is the plan. We'll ride up this trail until it ties into the Trilogy Trail on the backside of Lookout Ridge. Then, we'll ride up to Lookout Ridge from the northwest side. I think it will add a few extra miles to our ride. Hopefully, we'll get there in time to make a difference."

"How many miles do you think it will add?" Tom asked.

"I don't know," Brett said.

"I know this is an unusual situation, but we have some good things going for us," Mark said.

"Let's hear them," Tom said.

"Our trail is in good shape, and I bet the Christine Lake section of the Trilogy Trail will be even better. We've got a long way to go, but we'll be able to keep a steady pace."

"Thanks, Mark. I appreciate the optimism." Brett said. "The horses have rested long enough, and I think that woman wants us to hurry. Let's go."

———

Fred rode along the southern edge of Lookout Ridge. He pulled out his binoculars and glassed the area behind him; there was no sign of the cowboys. They had backed off after he pinned them down this morning. It was typical. People act pretty tough until bullets fly, then fold up like a flower after dark.

He watched the Ninety-niners climbing through the switchbacks. They were struggling. The tight switchbacks were muddy, making every step challenging. They still had a long way to go, and it would take some time.

Bruce Arnold was the critical player; the rest were expendable, but Fred was proud of the Ninety-niners. They had made progress.

He turned his horse uphill toward Monroe Peak. It was a steep climb, and it was going well, all due to his horse. While he rode across Lookout Ridge, he checked every entrance. He was alone.

Perfect!

He only had one job left.

CHAPTER FIFTY-THREE

Brett couldn't complain about this part of the trail; it was a pleasure. They had left the steep rocky sections of the Ridge Trail behind. Their path had narrowed and was smooth and comfortable. The mountainous terrain's rugged ridges and landslides had been replaced by rolling hills covered by a dark green forest. A calm came with it.

They rode at a good pace. For every hill they climbed, a longer downhill stretch followed. The overall course was downhill, making their horses eager to run. The riders decided there was no harm in carefully letting them loose. After every long run, they eased up and let the horses walk until they caught their wind.

Tom commented that he had never seen a trail showing less use; there were no footprints, hoof prints, or wildlife tracks. They guessed the rain must have washed the trail clean.

Brett tried not to think about the mysterious white-haired lady riding bareback on the black horse. Mark believed the horse was a stallion. It could be, but Brett questioned that, along with everything else. He didn't see the pair well enough or long enough to know. Based on her presence and a wave of her hand, the Rider's Club had abandoned all rational thinking and followed her lead. Brett's military and law enforcement training took a back seat when he backed the decision. He hoped he wouldn't regret it.

Tom and Buck took the lead. Buck, as always, was eager to run and fought the bit when Tom pulled him back for a breather. The quarter horse was in his element.

Tom stopped. "Hey, Brett, check this out," he yelled.

Brett rode up and saw what had caused Tom's concern. The trail split. One fork turned right, and one continued straight.

"Was this on the map?" Tom asked.

"No, it shows this trail as one thin line." Brett wasn't comfortable making another uninformed call. "The right fork leads north-northeast, which is the direction we want to go, but either fork could be a wrong turn. We don't want to run into a dead-end. Maybe we should take a break, and I'll scout it."

"Brett, look." Tom stared uphill to the left.

The mysterious white-haired lady on the black horse was in front of them again—she was closer this time. Spotlit by the sun, she gazed at them while astride a black stallion, and her eyes begged them to *hurry*.

Brett stood in the stirrups, hoping to get a better look. He tried to take in every line on her face, the curve of her jawline, and more, but her eyes demanded all his attention. They spoke to him. They spoke of care, calmness, courage, confidence, and compassion.

She waved again. It was definitely a *"go-this-way"* wave.

Tom turned Buck uphill onto the trail's left fork, trying to ride closer to her.

A gust of wind came from behind her, and her hair rose from her shoulders. The dirt surface of the trail was delicate and full of dust, easily caught in the wind. A small dust devil developed behind her. It weaved downhill, moved past, and crossed in front of her. She smiled as the air currents calmed and the dust devil faded.

The lady and her horse were obscured momentarily—a second at most. Her stallion rose onto his back legs, and his front hooves clawed the sky as he turned. When his hooves touched the trail, they galloped away over the rise behind them.

Brett remained transfixed. He had never seen anything like that. When the stallion rose and turned, she moved with the horse perfectly. She didn't grab, shift, touch, lean, or change her posture. Every movement was perfect.

Brett was envious; she was a better rider than he could ever be and better than he had ever seen.

A few seconds later, Tom pulled up to where the lady and her horse had stood. He shook his head. There was no sign of her.

Brett dropped his reins and closed his eyes.

"Are you all right? Did you hear her again?" Mark asked.

"I didn't hear her. I felt her. We're running out of time."

———

The day was long, and the summer sun stayed high. With a brisk wind, the riders were invigorated. The Ridge Trail rolled through gentle hills as it approached the lake country. The downward track gave the riders an expansive view of three iridescent lakes. If the riders weren't on a mission, they would be off their horses, taking pictures. There was no time for photography. Hopefully, they would return someday.

Mark yelled, "Hold up for a minute; I've seen those lakes before. I rode down to them the last time I took the tour. They're the Tear Drop Lakes. We're close to Lookout Ridge."

With renewed anticipation, the riders crossed a gentle hill and turned downhill through a draw that intersected an established east-west trail.

Tom smiled and checked both ways as if he was searching for someone.

Brett rode alongside him and said, "I don't think we need *her* help. This has got to be the Trilogy Trail." He turned in his saddle toward Mark, who answered with a firm, approving nod.

The Rider's Club turned onto the trail. After a couple hundred yards, they pulled up next to a branch trail that led downhill to their left. Two weathered signs stood in front of it.

The first sign marking the downhill trail read:

Tear Drop Lakes - 3 miles

The second sign, with an arrow pointing west, read:

Lookout Ridge - 2 miles
Monroe Peak - 3.5 miles

The Riders collectively took a deep breath. Brett had believed they were back on the Trilogy Trail, but he was thankful that the sign confirmed it. He stroked Pepper's neck. "Only two miles left. You can do this in your sleep."

"Wait a second," Tom said. "Someone is coming." He pointed at the trail that led to the Tear Drop Lakes."

"Spread out, men. Get into a defensive position," Brett ordered.

An average-sized, fit-looking young man hiked into view. He had the trim muscle tone of a rock climber. His short, dirty blond hair looked like it hadn't seen a comb for a week, but his braided, foot-long goatee was undoubtedly his signature look. He wore hiking boots, lightweight shorts, and a tie-dyed tee shirt. He looked like a throwback from the sixties.

He grinned at Tom, raised two fingers, and said, "Peace, man."

"Peace," Tom said and smiled. "You're the first person we've seen all day. It's good to see you. My name is Tom, and these are my friends. We're a riding club from Boise."

Brett and Mark smiled and nodded.

"It's good to see you, too. I'm Larry. That's a big horse you're riding. He looks serene and gentle."

"He's always happy when I take him out for a ride. What are you doing up here?" Tom asked.

We have a campsite about a mile downhill. We're becoming one with nature."

"That's wonderful. I hope it's going well. So, you're not alone?"

"My girlfriend is in the trees. She's concerned about your guns."

Brett said, "We understand, and I'm sorry if we scared her. We don't like carrying them, but we're on a rescue mission and brought them as a defensive measure. We're trying to help a friend. Your girlfriend isn't in any danger."

"I can tell you have a good heart." Larry turned his head and yelled, "Crissy, these guys are good people. Come out."

A young, athletic-looking woman stepped out from the trees. She wore blue and red trail shoes, purple and gray tights, and a black short-sleeved shirt. She had a lovely smile and bright green eyes. Her face was partially hidden by a tight black beanie pulled down to her eyebrows, covering her hair and ears.

"Hi guys," she said. "I hope your friend is safe." She moved next to Larry and smiled at the group. Her voice was soft and musical.

"Hi," The Rider's Club replied together.

"You have beautiful horses," she said.

"Thank you," Brett said. Then he turned to the riders, "Relax guys. We're okay here."

"You're welcome to come to our camp for tea," Larry said.

"I wish we could, but we need to keep moving. Have a wonderful day. Peace and love," Tom said as he flashed the peace sign.

"I hope everything goes well for you," Crissy said.

The riders turned toward Lookout Ridge and rode away.

After they had covered about fifty yards, Tom said, "Did you see the hair sticking out the back of her beanie? Was it white?"

"I don't know, but let's not go there now. The next two miles are uphill, and we need to make up time," Brett said.

———

The Ninety-niners' climb up the switchbacks was taxing as they hiked turn after turn up the narrow trail. The bottom third of the rise left mud caked on their boots, making each step awkward and heavy. When they reached mid-mountain, the trail surface evolved from mud to sand and dirt, making a significant improvement. Their pace was slow, but their stride became measured and consistent with the improved footing. When they hit the top third, their legs were dead. They had to take another break.

"We can't keep taking these long breaks," Rage said as they all sat down and leaned back into the uphill side of the trail. They pulled out their water bottles, drank, and took deep breaths. Each of them spent some time massaging their legs.

"We need the rest," Bright said. "It's been a hard day."

Digit chimed in, "My uncle told me a story about a similar hike. He said they counted their steps. They kept smaller goals and rested quickly after completing twenty-five to fifty steps. The small goals were attainable and led to larger ones. I guess it helped a lot."

After their rest, they tried Digit's counting method, and it helped. Rage led and counted out loud, and after they completed each increment of twenty-five steps, they stopped for a minute or two, took a few deep breaths, and started the count again. Even with the rests, the trail took its toll, and the group spread apart as they neared the top. Bright and Bruce fell behind, both struggling to catch their breath. They eventually caught up with each other, and Rage panted, "We're almost to the top. One more count might do it. Come on. One, two, three…"

On the twenty-first step, the Ninety-niners climbed onto Lookout Ridge. They ripped off their backpacks, threw them to the ground, and collapsed. Bright giggled as she lay flat and stared at the blue sky. "I think this may be my greatest athletic moment," she breathed.

"No shit," Digit added.

"We should be proud of ourselves," Rage said. "To climb here after what we had already been through today is an achievement." Rage asked Bruce, "How's your ankle?"

"Not good at all, but I'll survive. I'm glad I made it."

"You toughed it out."

"Thanks."

After they rested for about fifteen minutes, they were ready to take in their surroundings. Lookout Ridge spread out in front of them. Kimberly Lake was to the south. The view of the lake was beautiful but minor in scope compared to the extensive wilderness surrounding it. The elevation had added up. The Trilogy Trail snaked through the mountainous country. Viewing it from where they stood made it seem insignificant.

The trail crossed Lookout Ridge at a lazy diagonal angle. The ridgetop rose higher as the path crossed it. Lookout Ridge's surface was covered with dirt, sand, and rocks. The rocks ranged in size from a pebble to a good-sized refrigerator. Even at the high altitude, plant life was abundant. Grasses, sedges, flowers, mosses, and dwarf shrubs thrived in the hostile environment.

They followed the trail across and through the ridge. The

uphill grades and uneven footing were tricky, but after what they had been through, it didn't feel like as much of a challenge. When they approached the north side of the trail, they experienced *the top-of-the-world view* Lookout Ridge was known for. Straight ahead lay a series of mountains that they could not see beyond. They had seen photos but were not prepared for the massive scale.

After the trail crossed most of the ridge's length and width, it dropped over the edge on a steep slope and continued downhill. The Ninety-niners beheld three beautiful lakes set thousands of feet below and miles away. Christine Lake was hidden from their view within the landscape of countless mountains. It's too bad their hike wouldn't take them there, but they had pressing business.

Two old signs stood at the edge of the trail. The first pointing downhill said:

Tear Drop Lakes - 5 miles
Cristine Lake - 9 miles

The second sign, pointing ahead, said:

Monroe Peak - 1.5 miles

The Ninety-niners had a decision to make. Should they shoot their video on Lookout Ridge or climb higher to Monroe Peak? It was a long uphill climb in front of them. The Monroe Peak Trail ran straight up a smooth hillside for over a mile and disappeared near the summit. The illusion made the trail look like it ran into the sky. Monroe Peak was impressive, but Lookout Ridge would be hard to beat. Any spot along their current viewpoint offered an excellent background for their video.

Bright, almost jokingly, said, "Hey, we've traveled this far; we might as well check out both."

The others shrugged and decided to head uphill.

Due to his ankle injury, Bruce stayed behind with Torch. The rest of the Ninety-niners lightened their load and left their packs. After hiking a quarter-mile, Rage spotted a man riding downhill on a horse. Digit pulled out his binoculars and checked him out as he rode closer.

The man took off his hat and waved.

It was Fred.

CHAPTER FIFTY-FOUR

Tony Levitt wrapped up his business meeting in a private conference room inside the Sun Valley Inn. He stood up from the conference table and shook hands with the young man he had worked with for the last few hours. "I appreciate your service. Your crypto transaction system is the best in the business; we'll make a lot of money working together."

"I'm sure we will, Mr. Levitt. It is our pleasure to work with you." The young man spoke perfect English, but Tony could still hear his slight Eastern European accent.

Tony walked into the reception room just off the Inn's front entrance. He checked his watch, stood straight, and surveyed the room.

His slim, middle-aged frame stood just short of five foot ten. He had perfectly cut and styled dark brown hair that matched the color of his eyes. He wasn't someone who worked out in a gym but was driven in all aspects of his life with a work ethic that kept him physically and mentally fit. Tony wore a long-sleeved gray button-up shirt, black slacks, and black shoes. Typically, he wore a black shirt, black tie, and a black coat, but since the Cottonwood Financial Conference was a casual event, he left the coat, shirt, and tie in his room and stepped out of his comfort zone by wearing a gray shirt.

The conference had ended the day before, but Tony planned to stay two extra days to wrap up some additional business. The meeting he just concluded fell into that category. Today had been a long day, and with his work winding down, Tony was ready to walk back to his rented condo. It was time to relax and drink a glass of his favorite red wine.

When Tony finished his meeting, his assistant was absent. Unacceptable. He wondered if he was hiding at the adjacent bar watching a game again.

Tony walked through the reception area and turned at the bar's entrance. Only two men and a bartender were in the establishment; Tony's assistant, Adam, was not one of them.

Tony paused and scanned the reception area again.

"Can I help you, Mr. Levitt?" A clerk at the front desk asked.

"Yes, have you seen my assistant, Adam?"

"He was here earlier. You might check the patio or the bar. Or he might be outside stretching his legs. He usually stays close by."

After checking the men's room, Tony walked out front. Several guests enjoyed drinks on the patio, but Adam wasn't there. It was comfortable outside, and with the day winding down, Tony figured he would wait in comfort. He pulled up a chair on the deck and waited. A waiter brought him a glass of sparkling water. Tony leaned back, took a sip, and relaxed.

The bright blue sky was painted with a scattering of innocent white clouds. There was no wind, and the mountain air tasted clean and crisp. Across the walkway, an expansive area was covered with perfect grass except for the extensive, beautiful flower-laden landscaping. In the middle of the lawn, a sizable reflective pond was home to several swans and a larger number of ducks.

The Sun Valley Company operated various businesses, including two local hotels, the Sun Valley Lodge and the Sun Valley Inn. The company also ran several condominium developments. Of the three choices, some of the more high-profile customers preferred the privacy of the condominium option. The closest and most expensive units were a short walk from the Inn. Tony rented a comfortable two-bedroom unit there.

After he had drunk half of his sparkling water, Tony became restless and bored. He didn't understand the appeal of Sun Valley. *Why would anyone want to sit and watch ducks swim in a pond?* He sure as hell had no interest in playing golf, shooting clay disks with a shotgun, or hiking on some unpaved trail. He also didn't get the attraction of Idaho. He'd rather be in Vegas or another big city with more action.

He walked toward the rest of the village, scanned the area, and turned back. He still didn't see Adam. Adam was supposed to provide security. Tony wasn't comfortable walking from place to place alone. He had enemies who would like to isolate him, especially in the evening. *Then again, who would follow me to this backwoods bullshit place?*

Tony turned down the walk toward his condo. He walked through a stylistic archway, an artistic feature designed as a tunnel carved through the Inn's walls. It was approximately forty feet long, meant for pedestrian traffic only, but tall and wide enough to handle an oversized pickup easily. Tony paused before going through it. He analyzed the security risk. A twelve-year-old girl rode past on her bicycle and through the archway. Tony smiled, shook his head, and followed her through. *No problem*.

A few minutes later, he entered the Rose Wood condominium complex. A footpath surrounded by hanging flowers and tall pine trees led to his condo. Tony frowned as he walked down the path. He was irritated, disappointed, and angry with Adam. This was the second time Adam didn't wait for him outside of a meeting, and now he was probably somewhere in the village wasting his time. If he wanted to make a negative impression, he had been successful. *How is it that Adam cannot understand simple instructions?*

Tony checked the path at the door of his condo, both in front and behind him. He entered the entry code. As the door lock opened, someone grabbed his left shoulder.

"Adam, where in the hell have you been?" Tony said as he spun around.

"Guess again," said the man standing in front of him.

Tony stared at the man, waiting for his brain to process what he saw. Even hiding behind sunglasses and a baseball cap, he recognized him. "Joe Colorado?" he asked.

"It's just Colorado."

"But you are…?"

"Dead?"

Tony stared at Colorado with haunted eyes. "No, of course not." Tony smiled and reached out with his hand. "It's good to see you. I want to buy you a drink. It's been a long time. Let's walk over to the Sun Valley Bar."

"I already had a long conversation with your man on the mountain. He's a coward. He put a bullet in my back."

Tony's hands shook. "Colorado, please. We can work this out. I didn't authorize a hit on you. You've been working on a hundred-million-dollar operation. I can guarantee you a minimum of seven figures."

"Bullshit. Remember your zero-tolerance policy. It looks like you'll miss your parole hearing. Let's take a walk."

Fifteen minutes later, a Chevy Blazer drove out of Sun Valley Resort, past the Sun Valley Golf Course and the Trail Creek Camping and Hiking area, and continued up the unpaved road toward Trail Creek Summit and Copper Basin beyond.

Then it disappeared.

CHAPTER FIFTY-FIVE

Fred tied a loop around a jagged boulder and created an acceptable tether. "I'll be back soon," he said to his horse.

They were a hundred feet below Monroe Peak's summit. The ride uphill had been smooth and easy. A novice hiker wouldn't have any trouble with the trail until they neared the summit, where it became somewhat technical. Fred didn't have a problem; he skillfully climbed up to the forty-foot diameter peak, the mountain's namesake. The view to the north was spectacular but comparable to the same sight a thousand feet below on Lookout Ridge. Both views offered a top-of-the-world feeling, but Monroe Peak was unique, with a great element. It has a 360-degree panoramic view. Fred extended his arms and slowly spun around. "Wow," he whispered to himself.

He stepped back into the saddle and started the long, gentle downhill ride when a gust of wind lifted the cowboy hat off his head and carried it away. Fred jumped off his horse, scrambled downhill, and caught it before it took flight toward Montana.

With his hat secured, Fred leaned back in the saddle and enjoyed the ride. He spotted the Ninety-niners hiking in his direction. He could ride downhill a hell of a lot faster than they could climb up. Their legs had to be tired after climbing the switchbacks. He hoped they'd spot him and take a break; he'd catch up to them soon.

Fred smiled as he rode up to Bright, Rage, and Digit. "It's good to see you guys. You're right on schedule. That climb up the switchbacks had to be tough."

"It was hard but worth the effort. We're feeling pretty good about it right now." Bright grinned.

"I've been on the lookout and haven't seen anyone tracking us. There was a group I was concerned about, but they must have dropped back. It looks like we're in good shape. You should be able to shoot your video, complete your mission, and get the hell out of here."

"It is a beautiful day, and the light looks perfect. We need to unload our gear, set up, do a quick run-through, and we'll be ready to go," Digit said.

"Where's Arnold?" Fred asked.

"He has a sore ankle. He's downhill, taking a break. Torch is with him," Bright said.

Fred pulled up his binoculars and scanned the trail below. "I see that asshole. He's flat on his back, lying against a pack. Shit, he might be taking a nap."

"Hold on a second—"

"Shut up," Rage whispered as he stared at Digit.

Fred didn't seem to notice.

"Fred, what do you think? Should we shoot our video on Lookout Ridge or Monroe Peak?" Bright asked.

"Either one is good. I'd recommend Monroe Peak since it's more isolated. No one should interrupt us up there, but it is windy on top right now. Do you think the wind could hurt the audio quality?"

"We want our message to be clear. I want to stay out of the wind," Digit said.

"Then we should shoot on Lookout Ridge," Bright said.

"I agree. It's Lookout Ridge," Rage said.

Fred led the way on the easy trip down to the ridge. He turned to the Ninety-niners and said, "I need to take care of my horse." He rode toward the horseback loop, the same trail he rode up to Lookout Ridge. Two hundred yards below the ridge, a creek ran downhill and pooled up on the trail's uphill side. Next to it lay a grass area ideal for resting a horse. Fred removed his horse's saddle and bridle, fed him a few handfuls of oats, gave him a quick wipe down with his blanket, and scratched him behind his ears. The horse leaned into his hand while Fred gave him a little love. It was too bad he couldn't take this horse home; he would be missed.

Fred picked up his rifle and checked to make sure it was loaded. Then he inserted a magazine into his pistol and slipped extra ammunition into his vest.

When he walked back up the horseback loop, he found the Ninety-niners sitting in two groups on a flat section of the lower ridge. The area was spotted with grass and bushes. In the spring and the first summer months of every year, vegetation claimed more of the rocky surface.

Fred joined Rage and Bright, who sat on the ground and leaned against their backpacks. Fred didn't have a pack, so he picked a decent spot and collapsed. He crossed his legs and tried to make himself comfortable.

"I have a concern about the video," Fred said. "Executing Arnold on camera may be too graphic, and the horror of it could turn the public against our cause. Why don't you shoot a video where Bruce stands on the edge of the ridge? You could put a rope around his neck and announce that he has been found guilty and will be executed. Then fade out and leave the rest to your audience's imagination."

Rage started to laugh and covered his mouth.

"What is so funny, smart ass?" Fred asked as his eyes flared.

"You keep telling us what to do, but you're not our boss," Rage replied.

"What the hell are you talking about? I've cleared the way for you every day."

"You ran us through a mud hole this morning."

"I sent you through the safest route available. Did you run into any opposition? No! I probably saved your ass."

Rage stood up, poised to throw a punch. Fred sprung to his feet, keeping his rifle in his right hand.

"Hold it," Bright said. "This is no time for a fight. Settle down." She turned toward Fred. "Your suggestion does make sense, but we've changed our minds. We've decided to take another direction."

———

The Rider's Club ran their horses up the continuous incline. Brett was concerned that Pepper led too fast of a pace, but all the horses kept up. The riders took great pride in their horses. They were motivated and tireless, and Britt—Bruce's horse—ran with the rest as if she were a wild horse running with the herd.

Brett was sure they were close to Lookout Ridge but didn't want to run the horses into the ground. They were already covered with sweat. Fortunately, a stream flowed along the left side of the trail. It ran hard and fast with the runoff from the last two days of rain. Brett flashed a halt signal and pulled off. "I don't know if we'll be able to water the horses for a while, so let's give them a drink here."

Mark pulled alongside. "Everybody, just give them a quick

drink. After we pushed them this hard, we need to let them cool down before they have their fill."

Tom stepped off Buck and led him to the water. He smiled, pulled off his cowboy hat, and threw it into the air.

"What's that about?" Mark asked.

"We have done some real riding today!"

———

Fred didn't back down from his defensive position. He wouldn't kill Rage unless he was forced to. Right now, he was more concerned about their *new direction*.

Bruce Arnold, looking irritated, stood up and limped over to Rage, Bright, and Fred. He grabbed Rage's arm and raised his voice. "Don't believe a word this man says. He has lied about everything. He works in our public relations department and is full of bullshit."

Bruce faced Fred. "Did you think I wouldn't know you in a cowboy hat? I wasn't even near you and still recognized your voice."

Fred took two steps toward Bruce. Bruce inched back. Fred lifted his rifle and drove the rifle's butt through the bridge of Bruce's nose.

Bruce collapsed onto the ground. Blood covered his face.

The Ninety-niners looked at him unconscious in a pile of rocks.

Bright pushed her hands into Fred's chest. "Leave him alone! Leave him alone!" She shouted, "You could have killed him!"

"It wasn't a killing blow. Arnold will live. I'm done taking shit off that asshole."

Digit and Torch lifted Bruce off the ground while he slowly regained consciousness. He tried to walk, but his legs gave out. They half-walked and half-carried him back to where they had left their backpacks. They tried to stop the bleeding and cleaned him up the best they could. Some blood continued to ooze from a gash on the bridge of his nose, but most of the blood poured out of his nostrils. Bruce pinched his nose with his left hand and tried to breathe through his mouth.

Rage leaned over Bruce and whispered, "Don't worry, I'll deal with that asshole."

Rage, Bright, and Fred calmed down enough to talk. "Do you work for Bruce?" Bright asked Fred.

"Not anymore and never again. Arnold's the most corrupt man I've ever known. So, tell me about your *new direction*."

"We have a new plan," Rage said.

"Which is?"

"We're going to let Bruce go. He's—"

"Shut the fuck up! I've had enough of your shit. I guess your last social media post will have to do." Fred shouted.

Fred slid his rifle onto his hip as if he were in a cowboy western, then he pulled the trigger and blew a hole through the middle of Rage's chest.

CHAPTER FIFTY-SIX

The horses were watered, and the riders were ready for one last push to Lookout Ridge. Brett had stepped back into the saddle when he heard the distinct sound of a rifle firing—only one shot.

"You guys heard that, right?" Brett asked.

They couldn't miss it.

"I heard it," Tom said. "We need to check it out before we ride into trouble."

"You're right. Give me a few minutes; I'll ride up and see how far it is to the ridgetop."

Brett put Pepper into an easy lope. The trail was sandy and smooth until it narrowed into a tight, steep hairpin curve and almost disappeared. After Brett had led Pepper through the curve, the trail ran straight and steep until it topped out on Lookout Ridge. No wonder the gunfire sounded so loud. Lookout Ridge was right on top of them.

"We're within walking distance," Brett whispered as he stepped out of the saddle.

"Leave the horses here," Mark said. "We've pushed them enough. They've done their part."

The riders agreed they would be better off on foot if there was trouble on the ridge. Mark set up a picket line in an area with grass and plenty of water.

The Rider's Club took stock of their situation. During the long ride, they had discussed several approaches they might take if they found the Ninety-niners holding Bruce Arnold on Lookout Ridge. After looking at several alternatives, they agreed on Brett's plan.

"Okay, guys, double-check your gear. Put on your vests. Make sure your firearms are loaded and ready. Bring your binoculars, and Tom, bring your camera and an extra battery. It's a short walk. We need to keep our noise down. We'll regroup on top," Brett said.

Tom jumped in. "We need to check our radios. Set them in the sensitive mode. We will probably be able to hear each other whisper."

Brett smiled, "Good call, Tom. Anything else?"

Tom and Mark shook their heads.

"Let's go," Brett said.

———

Bright stared at Fred with bloodshot eyes. She couldn't stop her ragged weeping. Her legs trembled, and her stomach churned. She bent over and spat out a mouth full of vomit. After three deep breaths, she stood erect. With tears streaking her dirty cheeks, she tried to speak and choked on her words. After three more deep breaths, she asked, "Why?"

"Shut your fucking mouth!" Fred yelled. He pointed his rifle at her. "Are you carrying a gun?"

"No!" she wailed.

"Any other weapons?"

"No."

"Spin around and let me check."

He checked her pockets, belt, pant legs, and boots with his left hand while he kept his pistol jammed into the back of her neck.

"Okay, sit down over there." He pointed to an open spot on the rocky surface, away from Rage's body.

Fred searched both Digit and Torch. He disarmed Digit, who was carrying a pistol, and Torch, whose only weapon was a pocketknife. Digit, Torch, Bright, and Bruce sat eight feet apart with their backs to each other. Fred pulled a sleeping bag from Rage's backpack and threw it into Bright's lap. "Cover him up."

Bright stumbled to Rage. She sobbed harder when she saw his unblinking eyes. She fumbled with the zipper and finally unzipped the bag to its full width. She carefully covered his body and closed her eyes. She respectfully stood silent over her friend and sobbed until she was ordered to return to her spot.

"Listen up," Fred yelled in a clear, loud, slow voice. "Don't move—stay exactly where you are, even if you have to piss your pants. Do not speak, cry, or make a sound of any kind." He stood in front of Bruce. "Understood, Bruce?" Bruce nodded.

Fred moved to Torch, Digit, and Bright and repeated the question.

No one was stupid enough to challenge him.

"Now that we're all calm. If anyone can't follow my simple instructions, I will kill Bright."

Fred's statement washed over each of the remaining Ninety-niners and Bruce.

Exhausted from the traumas that they had been through, fear was no longer their expression. They instead looked physically sick.

Torch stared at his feet, turned his head, and quietly cried.

"If you cooperate, I will spare her life. If you don't, you will all die one at a time. Whether you leave this place alive or dead is up to you."

Fred picked up his bag, removed a satellite phone, turned it on, and typed in a code. After a moment, he said, "Situation gold. Location: Lookout Ridge. Execute—out." He then terminated the call.

———

The Riders entered the ridge from the north side and encountered rough and rocky terrain. They slipped behind a scattering of boulders, pulled out their binoculars, and glassed the ridgetop. They spotted the group on the lower end of the ridge. Five people were below several clusters of brush in the middle of a wide area, exposed from above. Only one man stood. He carried a rifle; the other four sat on the ground. They were over two hundred yards downhill on the ridgetop's greener, flatter, less rocky section.

Bruce Arnold was one of the four sitting on the ground. His face was clear.

"Mark, Bruce is on the left. He doesn't look good," Brent said.

"Who has the strongest binoculars?" Mark asked.

"I have a twelve-power pair," Tom handed them to Mark.

Mark raised the binoculars to his eyes. "He's taken a hit. His nose looks broken, and there are bruises below his eyes. Either he took a bad fall, or someone beat the shit out of him. I would bet the latter."

"Those assholes," Tom muttered.

Brett turned to the group. "Let's move into the rocks and the bushes in the middle of the ridge. Stay away from the left side. It would be like walking through an empty parking lot, but there is good cover down the middle."

"I agree," Mark said.

"The guy with the rifle seems to be focusing downhill," Brett said.

"I don't see anything below him," Tom replied.

"At least he's not looking our way," Mark said.

"Listen up!" Brett said. "When he turns his back to us, let's move downhill and into the cover. Stay low and keep quiet."

Brett called it right. The man with the rifle marched like he was on guard duty. He hardly glanced in their direction, even when he turned their way. The riders ran low, out of the rocks, downhill into the middle of the ridgetop. It didn't take long to make it to the thick cover. They glassed the ridge again.

"What do you guys think?" Brett asked.

Tom pulled down his binoculars. "They don't look like they expect company." And with a slight grin, he said, "We have the high ground."

"This isn't what I expected," Brett said. "Bruce and three of the young Ninety-niners are positioned like prisoners. They don't appear to be armed."

"I see what you mean. The guy carrying a rifle looks older," Mark added.

"Sage said there were four Ninety-niners. I only see three. Maybe that explains the gunshot," Brett said.

"I don't see a body," Tom added.

Mark jumped in, "I have a question. What are they doing? If that guy is holding Bruce and the Ninety-niners as prisoners—what is he waiting for?"

"Good question. Let's go find out. Keep your eyes open—we don't need any surprises." Brett said.

"Are we sticking with the plan?" Tom asked.

"Yes," Brett said, looking Tom in the eye.

Mark turned quickly toward Brett. "Are you sure?"

"Yeah, it's our best bet; I feel good about it. And they don't know we're here—let's keep it that way until we take charge."

Mark and Tom nodded.

"How about a line of code?" Mark asked.

Brett thought momentarily. "*Let's ride for the brand.*"

"Here we go!" Tom said.

CHAPTER FIFTY-SEVEN

The Rider's Club had ridden through the wind and rain, dangerous terrain, and had climbed thousands of feet. When they topped out on Lookout Ridge, the cloudless sky had turned a deep blue, and a light breeze brought crisp, cool air. They felt like raptors touching the sky.

The friends gathered behind a large cluster of mountain scrub brushes. They quietly hustled further downhill while the man guarding Bruce had his back turned to them. Their last scamper put them in a position to execute their plan's next step.

Forty yards below them, Bruce and the Ninety-niners sat together, back-to-back, while the armed man walked a slow, wide circle around them.

Brett removed his pistol from its holster, set it on the ground, and set his rifle beside it.

Mark hit Brett's shoulder. "Brett, what the hell are you doing? Don't leave your guns; take your pistol at least."

"It'll be all right. I'll be more credible, unarmed."

"Brett. Don't do that!" Tom whispered. His voice cracked. He started to rise. "Please...."

Brett faced Tom. "Stay down. Don't worry. I'll be okay."

Brett stepped into the open and marched forward. He planned on being an approachable negotiator. If the negotiations fell apart, Mark and Tom would back him up with their rifles. It came down to how well Brett could control the narrative. He stopped ten yards short of the Ninety-niners and straightened his back.

The captives' eyes widened.

The armed man hesitated, checked his watch, and glanced north, skyward.

After making eye contact with Brett, Bruce gave a subtle, appreciative nod.

Brett kept his eyes on the man in charge, who would react one way or another within the next few seconds.

The man turned and snapped his eyes toward Brett. Startled, he shouted, "What the hell!"

Brett raised his hands, palms forward, and spoke loud and clear. "I'm unarmed. Don't shoot."

"Are you alone?" He asked.

"No. There are three of us. I came solo so you and I could have a conversation. But before we talk, keep your rifle down, aimed at the dirt."

"Why should I?" the man asked, frowning.

"Because you're covered. Two sharpshooters have you in their sights. If you shoot, you're dead. Even an aggressive flinch could trigger them. They won't miss."

The man contemplated his situation. He scanned the hill behind Brett. "What do you want?"

"My friend Bruce Arnold is behind you. I'm concerned. He looks like he's been roughed up." Then Brett asked Bruce, "You okay, Bruce?"

"I'm okay. Fred's a liar. Don't trust him!" Bruce calmly responded.

"Shut up!" Fred shouted. He kept his eyes on Brett.

"Calm down. Listen. We're both in danger. I'm not a

policeman. I don't have the authority or the desire to arrest you. Like I said, I'm Bruce's friend. I want to take him with us and let you walk away. It's your best out. Honestly, it's your only out." Brett kept his hands up.

Fred's pupils were fully dilated. His brow furrowed, and his voice morphed into a high-pitched snarl. "You're full of shit! If you had two guns aimed at me, I'd be dead. I know who you are. You're the guys who turned and ran yesterday. I'm not backing down, and I'm not buying your bullshit."

"Calm down. My backup isn't bullshit, and I can prove it. We're going to give you a demonstration. Stay cool. We are not going to shoot you. We'll just show you. Do you understand?" Brett's voice was clear and steady.

"Bullshit!"

"Riders ready. Fire."

Two rifles fired. A bullet smashed into the dirt on Fred's left and another on his right. A second later, two more shots followed.

Fred threw his rifle to the ground, raised his hands, and fell backward toward his captives.

He was within reach of Bruce, which he took immediate advantage of when he wrapped his arm around Bruce's neck. Fred pulled Bruce to his feet and jammed his pistol into his ear.

"Anyone makes a wrong move—Arnold is dead!" he shouted.

Brett wasn't ready for that.

Fred pulled Bruce toward his chest while he tightened his arm around his neck and locked him into a human shield position. Bruce struggled to keep his feet under him. His eyes closed as he fought for breath.

"Easy, be careful, or you'll kill him," Brett yelled.

Fred loosened his grip without letting go.

Bruce opened his eyes and drew in several deep breaths.

"You started this, asshole. Be careful, or I'll end it. Back off now!" Fred shouted.

"Hold your fire," Brett yelled as he sidestepped uphill.

Fred glowered, then turned away and scanned the sky to his right. In his agitation, he tightened his grip around Bruce's neck.

Brett sidestepped uphill, keeping his eyes forward. Tom stepped behind him to his right. He whispered. "I'm right behind you. I have your rifle."

Brett held his hand behind his back and took the handoff.

Fred backed up until he and Bruce stood five yards behind the three Ninety-niners. The situation was turning into a standoff.

Brett didn't understand the logic of Fred's actions. He was slowly distancing himself from the Riders, but he was well within their rifle range. All he had behind him was a large, flat area without any cover.

Fred acted nervous, distracted, and maybe confused. He slipped back another ten feet behind Torch, Digit, and Bright while keeping his grip on Bruce. He then looked to the north again.

The Rider's Club knelt behind some decent cover and huddled. Brett looked at his friends, took a deep breath, and said, "That was my fault; I've been too idealistic. I think this Fred guy is waiting for something or someone. He's stalling. So, we need to take charge."

Mark and Tom looked at Brett with wide eyes and nodded.

"We need to move into a position of strength. Then we'll be ready to fight. We'll spread out, move forward, and close in on this asshole. There is good cover below us, and our radios are working well. Mark, take the right side. Tom, the left, and I'll take the middle. We'll need to work together, but when we're spread out, we may need to react individually. I am canceling our *rules of engagement.* If you have a clear shot, take it."

While keeping a tight grip on Bruce, Fred moved back again, slightly increasing the distance between himself, the Ninety-niners, and the Rider's Club. Once again, he looked toward the northern sky and moved toward the ridge's wide, flat surface.

Fred didn't keep his eyes on anyone or anything for very long. So, Brett focused on him. There was nowhere he could hide or make a stand. Was Fred waiting for someone to rescue him?

As if on cue, the sound of helicopter blades cut through the mountain air.

"Shit!" Brett said to himself.

Fred reset his grip on Bruce, pulling him away from the Ninety-niners and closer to the wide-open area behind him. He pulled his pistol away from Bruce's head, motioned uphill, and shouted at the Ninety-niners. "Get the hell out of here. Get up and run uphill, now!"

The Ninety-niners hurried to their feet and charged uphill. Digit turned around, put his hands at the side of his mouth, and yelled at Fred. "You are dead meat, asshole!"

Fred laughed.

Bruce took advantage of a less aggressive neck hold and shouted. "Brett, remember the code!"

Fred drove a knee into Bruce's back and doubled the pressure of the chokehold. A few seconds later, Bruce Arnold's legs buckled.

The helicopter was a distant flutter when the Riders caught sight of it. It was high in the sky behind them. It flew north, well past Lookout Ridge, and then circled back. It slowly dropped altitude as it came their way.

"Move forward ten yards and set up a firing line behind that brush," Brett said as he pointed downhill. They kept low and moved. Brett slipped behind the brush and dropped to his knee. The brush wouldn't stop a bullet, but it was decent camouflage. They'd be safer behind the rock formations uphill. But the riders preferred their offensive position and its closer proximity.

The helicopter dropped altitude and hovered two hundred

yards north of Lookout Ridge. Its roar removed all the quiet from their serene surroundings.

Brett shifted his eyes from Fred to Bruce and then to the helicopter. Fred was no longer paying attention to the Riders' movements. Instead, Fred's eyes were locked onto the helicopter.

The Riders moved in and set up their firing line.

Fred looked the other way.

"Hold this position and be prepared to fire," Brett said. "That's a small helicopter, not a vehicle I'd take into a fight. We might be able to blow them out of the sky. At least we'll scare the shit out of them."

The commercial helicopter had limited seating and was made to fly into tight spaces. The cockpit was glass, and its metal nose was painted red. It was great for tourism, hard to defend, and probably locally rented.

The nose of the helicopter dropped slightly as it moved forward and crossed over the flat area. It slowed its forward momentum and hovered for a moment. Then it slowly dropped and landed with the engine running and the blades churning.

The helicopter was positioned to pick up Fred and Bruce Arnold. A side door slid open, and a husky, broad-shouldered man jumped out. He held an assault rifle in his hands. He looked at Fred and Bruce, nodded, and waved toward the helicopter. Then he raised his assault rifle, stepped forward, and slowly panned the terrain in front and above him.

Brett spoke above the noisy copter. "Ready, fire!"

Three bullets hit the husky man's chest. His knees buckled, and he collapsed face-first.

Brett spoke louder, "Target two. Three volleys. Ready, fire!" The Riders stood, pulled their rifles tight against their shoulders, and aimed at the helicopter as if they were duck hunting over the Snake River.

Three bullets slammed into the nose and body of the

helicopter and then hit it again and again. The pilot's reaction was immediate. The helicopter's engine roared as it lifted off, swung to the north, and jumped higher into the sky. A cloud of smoke trailed behind it.

Brett watched Fred, wondering how he would react. He stared at the helicopter as it flew away. He kept his grip on Bruce while moving toward the ridge's south side. He never looked uphill. If he was trying to escape, he was moving too slowly. An uncooperative Bruce Arnold struggled against his grip.

Brett stepped out of his cover while keeping his rifle in his left hand and his pistol holstered. With his eyes locked on Fred, he walked downhill and stepped in front of him and Bruce. "It's all over, Fred. Time to surrender," Brett calmly said.

"No, I've decided to take your offer. I'll release Bruce and walk away," Fred said confidently.

"Too late." Brett stared at Fred.

Fred took several deep breaths, released his grip around Bruce's neck, and shoved him toward Brett. In the same motion, he raised his pistol.

Brett matched his move when he instantly reacted with his rifle.

As quick as the two men were, it didn't matter.

A bullet hit Fred right above his right ear. He was dead when he hit the ground.

Brett spun around and looked uphill.

Tom slowly lowered his rifle.

CHAPTER FIFTY-EIGHT

M ark rested on his right knee while he examined Bruce's ankle. "You have significant swelling, but until we get an x-ray, I won't be able to determine the extent of the damage you have done."

"Good thing I'm riding a horse out of here," Bruce chuckled.

"You plan on finishing the tour?" Mark asked, surprised.

"Yes, that's why I'm here."

"You've been hammered with a rifle stock, choked half to death, kicked in the back, and hiked up a mountain on a damaged ankle. You need to get to the hospital. I can get a Life Flight up here within an hour."

"I appreciate your professionalism and your concern, Doc, but I know my body, and I think I'll be all right. How about I stay off my feet and ride out of here today? Then, let's see how I'm doing tomorrow morning?"

Mark wrinkled his brow as he appraised Bruce. He was used to people not listening to his orders. "Okay, that sounds like a plan."

"Was my satellite phone in the saddlebags when you packed the horses?" Bruce asked.

"I think so," Mark said. He yelled at Tom. "Did you pack Bruce's satellite phone?"

"Yeah, you want me to grab it for you?"

"Yes, please," Bruce said.

———

Brett looked up when he heard another helicopter approaching. As it moved closer, he saw the markings of the US Forest Service. It landed, and he was surprised to see DeShawn Terry step out. DeShawn wore jeans and an outdoor coat, and his injured right shoulder and arm were immobilized and held tight against his chest by a sophisticated medical sling.

Brett walked downhill to meet him. The men fist-bumped, left-handed. "It's good to see you," Brett said. "How's your shoulder?"

"It's useless right now. I refused to have surgery until this situation was resolved."

"Well, you can take care of it now."

DeShawn shook his head and smiled. "Brett, I'm so proud of you guys. I'm sure it was an overwhelming challenge, but I knew the three of you would come out on top."

"We're all relieved it's over. Are you on the job?" Brett asked.

"Yes, I'm here to clean up a few things."

"I'd like to help, but first, let me bring you up to date."

After a lengthy debrief, the two men went to work. They had to move the three bodies to a more appropriate private location. As usual, Tom showed up and helped with the heavy lifting. The SNRA rangers were halfway up the horseback loop. They would take the bodies to the morgue in Ketchum.

DeShawn's next duty conflicted with his personal feelings. Fred had manipulated the Ninety-niners and used them for his agenda. He murdered Alex and Rage. He shot Randy and him.

However, the Ninety-niners would still have to face the consequences of their actions. Even though they didn't follow through on their threats, they were responsible for the attack at the Valley Airport and the kidnapping of Bruce Arnold. It would be hard to dispute the evidence they posted on social media.

DeShawn sat down with the Ninety-niners while Brett quietly watched. Bright glanced toward them and then solemnly dropped her eyes.

"I understand Fred manipulated you, and I'm sorry you have lost a close friend, but you have committed several crimes. You'll have to face the legal consequences," DeShawn said.

Bruce smiled while engaged in a lively conversation on his satellite phone. He was less than twenty feet from DeShawn and the Ninety-niners. Suddenly, his smile disappeared, and he walked toward the group. "I have to hang up," Bruce spoke into the satellite phone. "I need to deal with a problem. I'll see you soon." He hung up and then approached DeShawn. "Hold it." He boomed.

For the first time in a week, he took on the role of a powerful corporate CEO. "There will be no arrests. Not today. Not ever. No court will hear a criminal case against these kids if I oppose it. I was the victim at the Valley Airport, and I was the victim here. Without my support, you won't have a case. I will fight it with my entire legal team. These kids were manipulated well before they came to Idaho."

DeShawn raised his chin and replied, "You aren't entirely correct. You were the primary target but not the only victim at the airport or here. You know that, Bruce, and that is just the beginning. The world was shocked by the images the Ninety-niners posted everywhere. I need complete statements from the Ninety-niners. After which I can guarantee that they will be charged. There will be a cry for justice."

"They aren't making statements without legal representation, which can't happen on Lookout Ridge," Bruce confidently said. "I'll contact my legal team and follow up with you next week, agreed?"

DeShawn stared at Bruce for a moment. Then he smiled and said, "That is a good idea. Agreed."

As Brett and DeShawn walked away, DeShawn shook his head and said, "In a way, I'm too close to this one. I'll be happy to pass the case to another office."

Fifteen minutes later, another commercial helicopter approached, circled the ridge, and landed on the flat area.

Bruce smiled and said, "This helicopter belongs to me."

The pilot shut down the helicopter, and a young man wearing gray slacks and a navy sport coat stepped out and approached Bruce. "Anything else you need to tell me, sir?" he asked.

"Take care of them. Get them whatever they need and take them wherever they want to go. Get their contact information and set up a meeting with our attorney next week."

"Will do, sir."

Bruce walked back to where he had left the Ninety-niners. "Let's do our video."

"You still want to?" Torch asked.

"Now's as good a time as any. You have a ride waiting."

"You mean the helicopter is for us?" Digit asked.

"Yes. I also have a car at the airport to take you wherever you want." Bruce smiled.

Digit set up a high-resolution camera with a wind-protected shotgun microphone.

Since Digit had a part in the video, he asked Tom to operate the camera.

The spectacular backdrop of the mountainous territory north of Lookout Ridge stood prominently in the frame. The sun was low in the sky, providing warm light with deep shadows, capturing the texture and beauty of Idaho's wilderness. Bruce and

Bright walked in front of the camera and stood side by side. Digit took his place next to Bright, and Torch entered the frame from the other side and stood beside Bruce.

"Good evening," Bruce said in a deep, strong voice. "I am Bruce Arnold. I'm here with my good friends Bright, Digit, and Torch. We have formed an alliance committed to reducing income inequality." Bruce reached forward with his right hand. Bright reached out and put her hand on his. Digit and Torch reached out, and all their hands came together.

The four of them spoke as one.

"Together, we will change the world."

CHAPTER FIFTY-NINE

D awn arrived with cool air, warm sunlight, and one of nature's most beautiful sights. The natural light reflected off Christine Lake, illuminating the water, forest, and shoreline. Pockets of morning fog clung to the shore where springs entered the lake. Silver Mountain rose fifteen hundred feet above the waterline, a mountaineer's dream of vertical climbing. The lake could not capture its complete reflection.

Ruby sat next to Brett with her head resting on his shoulder. Sage sat with Michael, holding hands. Bruce and Luis were thankful they were able to finish their journey. Tom, Mark, and Randy sipped hot coffee, treasuring the experience.

"I do have a question," Luis said to Ruby. "When we visited Sara Lake, you discussed its history and explained why it was named Sara Lake. It was quite interesting. Can you give us the background on Christine Lake?"

"Yes, but first, I'll have to tell you a story."

"Sounds even better," Michael said.

"We love a good story," Sage said.

Ruby smiled and said, "Okay, here it goes. In the 1800s, this land was occupied by Indians, explorers, trappers, prospectors, and mountain men. A family of four settled in this area: Arlen and Glenda Anderson and their two children. They built a home in the shadow of a great mountain lake. Arlen was a prospector who found a rich vein of silver. He and his family worked the claim and stockpiled enough ore to build a new life. But that all ended one horrible evening. A gang of claim jumpers raided the Anderson home. Their cabin was burned to the ground. The gang destroyed most of their equipment, ran off their horses, and stole their valuable possessions, including their stockpile of silver. They killed Arlen, Glenda, and their son. The body of their young daughter was never found.

"Ten years later, one of the gang members confessed, stating before Arlen died, he ordered his twelve-year-old daughter to take her horse and run for her life. She wrapped a rope around her black stallion's neck, threw herself onto his bare back, and disappeared into the trees. Legend says she learned to live off the land. She rode through the forests and mountains of the wilderness and memorized landmarks, rivers, streams, and trails. She built high mountain shelters and made buckskin clothing and winter snowshoes. As the years passed, her curly brown hair turned straight and white. She was reclusive and wasn't seen again until she encountered a family with a young daughter, lost deep in the wilderness. They claimed that she led them to safety and then disappeared.

"Over the next ten years, people repeatedly reported seeing a woman with white hair leading lost adventurists away from danger. People called her *The Angel of the Sawtooths*. Her legend grew. She was never seen again until 1925. A work crew of eight men was lost, freezing, in a winter storm. They claimed a white-haired lady riding bareback on a black horse led them back to their camp. In 1942, a group of European mountain climbers were stranded after one of them had broken his leg. They claimed a white-haired lady riding bareback on a black horse led a rescue party to them. Four more similar rescues took place before the end of the century. Even as recent as 2002, a Boy Scout was separated from his troop and was lost during a fifty-mile hike. He said a white-haired lady riding bareback on a black horse led him back to his scout troop."

"Hold it," Bruce blurted. "If she is still out here, she'd have to be around 170 years old."

"Sounds about right," Ruby said.

"I like the story," Luis said. "But it doesn't answer my original question."

"Yes, it does. This is her wilderness, and this is her lake. Her name is Christine."

Tom, Brett, and Mark stared at each other. Tom laughed and raised his coffee mug. "To Christine."

Brett and Mark clanked their mugs together and repeated, "To Christine!"

END

ACKNOWLEDGMENTS

Thank you to my editor-book coach, Stacey Smekofske, for her excitement, skill, and polish. I couldn't have done this without you.

Thank you to my first readers for all of their valuable feedback.

Thank you to my friends for asking, "When will we see the next book."

Here it is. I hope you enjoy it.

ABOUT THE AUTHOR

Dennis Nagel was born and raised in Boise, Idaho. He is an alumnus of the University of Wyoming and has spent most of his business career managing his family's business.

Dennis has retired from his business career and is excited to have more time to write. He also enjoys spending more time with his family.

Dennis and his wife, Chris, live in Boise.

For updates, please check DennisNagelBooks.com.

AVAILABLE IN BOOKSTORES EVERYWHERE